To Dan,

Thank God for Montauk!
—
Enjoy

Richard + Linda

MONTAUK
THE BOWMAN

Richard Prince with Linda Prince

authorHOUSE®

AuthorHouse™
1663 Liberty Drive, Suite 200
Bloomington, IN 47403
www.authorhouse.com
Phone: 1-800-839-8640

First published by AuthorHouse 7/14/2009

ISBN: 978-1-4389-8896-2 (sc)

Printed in the United States of America
Bloomington, Indiana

This book is printed on acid-free paper.

other books by Richard Prince

Montauk The Disappearances

ACKNOWLEDGEMENTS

Our thanks and appreciation to those professionals who are so generous with their expertise and time: Eugenia Bartell our tremendously talented Editor, Robert E. Genna, Director of Suffolk County Crime Laboratory, Justin Cassar, Master Archer and Hunter, Anthony Bosco, East Hampton Police Department, Sergeant Manny Vilar, NY State Park Police, and Deputy Inspector Richard Di Roma, New York Police Department, Retired.

And special thanks to our excellent researchers, Corinne Capulet, Kenneth Prince, Steve Lubell, Bryan Midget and Nancy De Pietro.

We also wish to acknowledge the following people without whom Montauk the Bowman could not have been written: our parents, Gary and Judy Hall, Bob and Helen Amundsen, Reese and Lisette Jacobson, Mike and Odette Rooney, Steve Deal.

Prologue

DEATH BY ARROW

Storm: Good morning Sergeant Thompson. I am Dr. Storm, Suffolk County Chief Medical Examiner. Sorry we have to meet under these circumstances, but as you know, sergeant, whenever a violent homicide has been committed, our office has to respond to the scene.

Thompson: Morning Dr. Storm. Lieutenant Miller and myself found the victim; killed by a single arrow. It appears he was shot through the heart.

Storm: Sad, very sad. He must have suffered intense physical and mental pain. What disturbs me is the strange choice of murder weapon, Sergeant. In all my years with the office I've never heard of a bow and arrow scenario; barbaric, simply barbaric.

Thompson: I agree but why mental anguish Dr. Storm?

Storm: It was not instant death, sergeant; his life force held on for a number of seconds, possibly a minute before his heart stopped pumping due to massive hemorrhaging and severe trauma. I'm certain his mind struggled with tortured agony at how he perceived himself dying.

Thompson: Doctor, are you saying suggesting that he died two deaths; one physical and one mental?

Storm: As cruel as that sounds, Sergeant, that pretty much sums it up. I only hope this was some kind of grudge killing and not the beginning of a serial murderer game plan which could be just the tip of an ice berg with more gruesome murders to follow.

Thompson: You, of course, remember the Ferryman killings, doctor. As repulsive as that serial killer case was, I can't even conceive of what a deranged psychopath, running around with a bow and arrow, could cause.

Storm: Don't trouble yourself, Sergeant, this could be all conjecture. Right now we're dealing with a single murder.

Thompson: I agree and pray it remains so.

Storm: Time will tell us, Sergeant.

CHAPTER 1

The Bowman watched with an insatiable thirst of anticipation as Waldo quietly and slowly lumbered up the hill to his tree stand where he could either sit or stand to wait for his quarry. Knowing that Waldo's undisguised platform was twenty feet up along the tall oak tree, gave the Bowman the edge needed, for after all, wasn't camouflage the ticket? To be comfortable and confident in a bowman's presentation was as important as the weapon of choice one had in these wooded surroundings. Ultimately, hunting was the reflection of a man's or a woman's unique worthiness of the sport. It was considered a spiritual coupling of two souls; a hunter and his disguise, two souls with but a single thought - kill or be killed!

From splendid isolation, the Bowman observed Waldo climbing aloft on his tree pegs, placing his knapsack on a climbing notch and hanging up his bow. Scanning the area first with a pair of rusty binoculars, Waldo then settled into a somewhat relaxing demeanor and waited for his prey to appear.

Today, the day before the hunting season officially opened, was Waldo's time alone in the woods. For years his ritual was to set up and fantasize of what was to come. In the seaside paradise of Montauk one of its many best kept secrets was the vast deer population. In fact, Montauk's woodlands supported the largest and best eating deer in the state of New York. Waldo was among the several locals who on November 1st put down his pole and grabbed his bow.

Looking through the hand held range finder, the Bowman clicked at seventy five yards and took aim through the peep site. In slow motion, drawing back on the bow string to full bow draw at 75 pounds of pressure to the let-off position, and taking lethal aim through the site once again, the hunter squeezed the bow's black release trigger. The gray carbon arrow sliced silently through the air like a stealth fighter at 315 feet per second, slamming into the dead center of Waldo Maidstone's chest; the target, its thrust embedding Waldo to the tree.

The arrow's impact shot Waldo's coffee thermos out of his right hand twenty feet to the crinkly colorful carpet of leaves below. As Waldo was losing consciousness, he saw the bright frosty pink blood gush out of his chest, somehow knowing that the hit was a lung-heart shot. Lowering his head to his chest while his eyelids fluttered, he came to rest in the tree stand that had served him so well over the many years.

CHAPTER 2

Montauk Liquors' Todd Miller, the handsome, athletic, ace surfcaster, and a master bow hunter arrived as usual about 8:30 am after finishing up the household breakfast dishes and waving goodbye to his children Todd, Jr. and Nancy and his wife Jamie as the three left for the Montauk Elementary School. A proud father and good husband Todd thanked God for his blessings on a regular basis. The only time his and Jamie's marriage was almost on the rocks was during the terrifying disappearances case when Chief Becker deputized Todd as Lieutenant and appointed him lead investigator. Jamie's first reaction scared Todd to the bone.

After turning on the lights, the music and his VHF radio, he settled down at his desk to review orders and the ongoing bills, stopping every now and then to flick a long shock of blond hair falling across his forehead. Same old orders; he knew by heart what booze his customers drank. Glancing at his watch he was glad to see it was only 10:15 am and now with his bill paying chores all in good shape, he would relax until his customers wandered in a little later, on this nippy sunny morning.

Strange, he thought, where's Waldo? In fact, just where the hell is Waldo? Engine trouble again? Time to trade in that old Ford pickup, Waldo. I know how you guys get attached to your beach buggies but, shit, Waldo, it's a damn dinosaur pilfering your money!

At 11:00 am Todd started to wonder. In the three years he's been working for me he's never been more that say a half hour late; tops. Just as he was about to call the lodge, the rear door bells rang. Jumping up and all set to see Waldo's agitated face, Todd was almost annoyed and definitely disappointed to see Mrs. Whitehead instead. Bellowing out a "Top of the mornin' Todd, how's Jamie and the tots?" Betty Whitehead 's thunder just about caused the wine bottles to jiggle off the glass shelves. "Fine, Betty, and how's your Paddy doing?" "Keeping busy, my grand Paddy is; working like an Irish bull he is with all that's going on at the Fire Department and the Big Bucks Bonanza. He's such a good old tart."

"If you don't mind me saying so Betty, you're looking younger than ever, what're doing, working out, any movie offers yet?" "Oh Todd," a gushing Betty Whitehead replied, "You should go into politics!" Both laughed heartily as Todd slipped two bottles of Betty's favorite rum into a white bag.

As Betty counted her change she filled Todd's ears with the latest tidbits she had learned at Jack's that morning. Not only did she and many villagers know that Jack served the best coffee in town, and the tastiest fish and chips, they also

4

knew that Jack relished juicy morsels of gossip that he willingly shared. Like a true yenta he would ferret out the best from his customers. Todd's ears were burning with Betty's latest titter-tatter. How amused we all are with gossip, he thought, we love it; guess it's just part of our nature. Why, hell, the news industry thrives on it! Think about the newsmongers: they are like piranhas and grab hold of groundless rumors pieced together by senseless innuendos.

Checking his watch and shaking his head, he checked the wine cooler and added the necessary bottles. His hottest seller was the Duckwalk Wines, especially the Duckwalk Pinot Grigio, followed by Windmill Red, a light Beaujolais red wine, and a semi sweet Gatsby Red cherished by many of his lady customers. Now at 11:25am his apprehension turned up another notch. Damn, Waldo, where the hell are you?

Time to start looking he thought as he picked up his office phone and called Justin Winchester, Jr., the President of the Montauk Rod and Gun Club. Justin assured his pal he would get the word out. Next Todd phoned Jack. He knew Jack would spread the word in three shakes of a lamb's tail. Breaking into Todd's thoughts, Clive's cheerful voice called out, "Good Morning, buddy, it sure is a blue bird of a day!"

Clive's strength was exactly what Todd needed right now. The fact that Waldo was missing so to speak was becoming a worrisome burden. An extraordinary surfcaster but no longer a hunter due to his age, Clive, the tall, handsome, burly, blond Norwegian who had saved Todd's life during a frightening fishing mishap, had become not only Todd's idol but a true friend. "Morning, Clive, how's Helen, Waldo's hasn't showed up for work," Todd blurted out hurriedly. "His truck broke down again?" laughed Clive. "I hope that's it," a nervous Todd replied.

Todd poured Clive a mug of coffee as he sat down in Todd's white wicker chair. "Hey, have you heard the latest deer joke going around town?" "No, Clive, shoot." "Well, there was a large father buck and his son bedded down among the pine trees up in the county park. The father looked over at his son and said in an angry voice, I told you not to wash them! Now they look like two twigs hanging down around your neck. The son lowered his long reddened face and in a whimper managed to say, I only used mild soap on them, dad, and I followed the directions on the bottle. Son, it will take at least a week before your antlers rise again so best we hang here till they return to normal. Shit, dad, now I know how poor Rudolph felt. It's okay son, it's just that you're not going to be tree rubbing for awhile."

The two friends had a big chuckle. "Word has it that it's a Waldo joke, Todd, and that reminds me, I saw Waldo's truck parked up at the Recycling Center, near the walking trails." "Really Clive? You sure it was Waldo's?" "No doubt about it. With all those hunting stickers all over the back window and the bumper that truck would stand out in the crowded IGA parking lot. You didn't give him the day off to do opening day of bow season, did you?" "No, Clive, that's just the thing; he always goes the day before to set up and check out his range. He feels the first day is bad luck. You know hunters and fishermen and their superstitions, buddy." "Hey, maybe he decided this time to go for it and the hell with the wives' tales." "No way, not Waldo." "Did you try his cell?" "It's inoperative. What's new, that's my Waldo! He was going to pick up a new phone today."

The longer they talked the more red flags shot up in Todd's mind. "I don't like this scenario Clive, especially with his truck abandoned at the dump! I'm calling Roy, he and I can take a hike up to Waldo's stand and check it out." "Hold on, Todd, you're going to call Roy Thompson, Sergeant of the East Hampton Police Department? Don't you think you're over reacting?" "I hope so, Clive. I hope so." "Okay, I'll hold down the fort; go make the call."

Sergeant Thompson picked up on the third ring, "Hi, good buddy, what's up, fish breaking?" Reassured, hearing Roy's warm, friendly voice, Todd got right to the point. "Hey, buddy, how about you accompanying me up to Waldo's tree stand; I'm worried about him; never showed up for work and his truck is parked at the walking trails and........" "Got it Todd; no need to explain. Why don't you pick up eats at Jack's and I'll be there at noon" "Roger that, Roy."

"Clive, Roy will pick me up at twelve, I'm going to pick up lunches at Jack's, want anything?" "Helen's dropping stuff off. I'm fine. Good luck, buddy."

Jack, hunched over the counter, listened very carefully to Todd. Along with his other talents, Jack also had the reputation of being a philosopher and was known to have found solutions for many a customer's predicaments. With his steaming coffee pot held high and his ears at attention, the 6 foot, chiseled face Greek with the emerald green eyes and an emerging pouch made his way in and around the tables of his café where hungry, thirsty, tired fishermen and hunters ate, drank, relaxed and chatted, feeling right at home in Jack's welcoming oasis. In order to be even more of a part of his customers' interests, Jack kept two very detailed fishing and hunting logs that he updated daily.

Knowing Jack would spread the word helped ease the increasing troubled feeling Todd was experiencing. In the three years that had passed, since the diabolical killings in the village, that shattered so many lives, Todd remained ever vigilant and even a simple question of one's whereabouts ignited a sense of uncomfortable foreboding.

Jack handed two bulging brown paper lunch bags to Todd, squeezed him arm and said, "Not to worry Lieutenant."

Anxious to meet his good friend and police ally, Todd drove quickly back to his store, parked his truck in the rear just as Roy pulled in and jumped into the cruiser. The two buddies were a striking combination. Roy also an athletic 6'3" with dark curly hair and eyes as blue as the ocean had earned his Sergeant stripes the hard way, studying evening hours and working part time jobs. The two had worked tirelessly but well together investigating and eventually solving the monstrous disappearances ferryman case.

Now as Roy put the pressure to the gas pedal they talked the small talk and wolfed down Jack's humungous turkey sandwiches and fries. Pulling up next to Waldo's pickup, a quick exit found them at the edge of the path to begin their hike along the trail leading to Waldo's tree stand.

CHAPTER 3

Rambling along the pathway and chatting about Waldo, Todd also informed his partner that Waldo's coffee thermos was always filled with Red Beard. Acting surprised, Roy burst into laughter, slapping Todd on his back. "Why Todd, I never knew that Old Wild Turkey was also called Red Beard," as he stumbled over a log. "Don't you know it's a Montauk thing Roy?" "Oh, okay, whatever boss."

"Roy do you remember Waldo's DEC encounter when he was driving from the Lighthouse into town two years ago? It was near sundown when he got to the top of the overlook and he spotted what he thought was a ten point rack on a large buck on the edge of the road." "Hey Todd, please not that story again! You're gonna kill me!"

"Yeah, yeah Roy, he was so pumped up with Turkey that buck fever got the better of him, and he grabbed his trusty twelve gauge shotgun, hopped or maybe fell out of his truck, and started blasting away at the critter! And to boot Roy, Joe Blot, you know from NY State DEC, was hiding in the woods, full of camouflage, running the sting. He recorded all that lively Waldo action on DVD and all the while he could hardly control the remote 'cause he was laughing so hard. Remember Roy? Joe wasn't laughing at the slugs bouncing off the robotic metal buck; he was in stitches watching Waldo's truck careening down the hill, veering off the road into a ditch, and rolling over three times before smashing into a big tree. Poor Waldo's pick up was totaled; poacher payment in full Joe decided!"

Chuckling and howling, their tears splashing down their cheeks, Todd resumed some composure before he laughed quietly and said, "Do you recall Roy when Waldo shot the poor farmer's mule, mistaking it for a doe?" "Oh shit Todd, don't do this to me."

"Roy, he dragged the mule into the back of his truck, drove to the NY State Tag Station and unbeknown to him, Joe just happened to be working that day. So when Waldo pulls up a bit tipsy and goes inside and announces he shot a doe, Joe gets up and swaggers outside to have a look-see, and was almost knocked over by what he saw. Hey Roy, can you imagine what Joe thought when he saw a dead mule lying there with a bright yellow deer tag pinned to his right ear and his bushy brown tail sticking straight up from rigormortis?"

Holding their bellies, Todd continued, "From what I hear, Joe walked calmly back into the station, stood chest to chest with Waldo, and looking directly into Waldo's Turkey colored eyes, said in a loud, official voice, 'Nice mule you got there Waldo,' and proceeded to cuff him. Waldo's tortured face was red as a tomato."

"Talk about a scene right out of vaudeville," Roy laughed, shaking his head from side to side. "Well, our Waldo spent the night in jail and the next morning Judge Huckleberry revoked his hunting privileges for the entire year and fined him $120.00 and also made him pay the farmer $800.00 for the mule," Todd concluded. With that they dropped to their knees, pounded the ground, snorted and laughed like a pair of hyenas.

Sitting like an Indian and with a gleam in his eye, Roy glanced over at Todd resting against a log, ""But the best Todd was his fake antler ploy; he sure could fire up an imagination." "You bet buddy," Todd agreed. "So old Waldo goes about trying to shoot a deer, right? "He sure does Roy."

"Even though doe season had ended and buck season was to end in three days, he shoots a doe." "I remember," Todd grinned. "Okay, so then he takes a tan fishing line, a fifty pound test which is practically invisible to the naked eye, and very carefully places an eight point buck rack on the doe's head and ties it real tight. Then he tags the doe's ear so now it's recorded as a buck. Next he proceeds to the tag station and while he's filling out the paper work, Sergeant Jim Finder sees him and knowing Waldo's reputation gets suspicious, and goes outside to check the deer. He takes one look, walks back inside real fast and tells everyone to come out and look at the deer. All four inspectors plus Waldo surround the back of the pickup. Okay, got the picture,"

Ready to burst out loud but clamping his lips tight, his eyes bright as a newly decorated Christmas tree, Todd quickly nodded his head.

"What we got here?" Roy says, mimicking Sergeant Finder's deep voice, "what we got here folks is not a buck but rather a buck-doe!

If you gentlemen will observe, the specimen is the size of a two year old deer, approximately 150 pounds and it hosts an eight point rack of a five year old buck. Now pray tell, how could this be? Is there a new deer species breeding out there in them woods that we do not know about? Hell, I don't think so."

His arms crossed over his belly, and his hands holding tight to his sides, Todd listened as Roy summed up his scenario. "Hey, Waldo, what say you?" the Sergeant wanted to know, as Waldo froze, watching him cut through the fishing line and remove the buck's rack. Then turning to Waldo he barks, "You know the position," and cuffs him.

While sputtering, chortling and having a real good guffaw, Todd interrupted, "Listen Roy, let's cut the jokes and get a move on."

"Right Todd but we gotta give Waldo credit for putting his tree stand in the best location in Montauk at the edge of Green Apple Cove."

CHAPTER 4

As Todd and Roy approached Waldo's stand, they looked up and saw him in what looked like a sleep position. Roy commented, "Shit Todd, he's had too much Turkey and is sleeping it off!" "Sure looks like it, you're right! I'm gonna kick his ass all the way back to the store." "Hey Todd, suppose I cuff him for theft of services just for the fun of it till we get back?" "You know Roy that might be just the right medicine!" "Okay buddy, I guess I'll climb up the pegs and wake up young Rip Van Winkle." As Roy took a step he was stopped abruptly by Todd's vise like grip on his right shoulder. "Don't move, Roy," pointing down at the large patch of dry blood splattered in a four foot circle among the leaves.

Staring in disbelief, Roy managed a "What the hell Todd; is that what I think it is?" With an edge of tension in his voice, Todd answered, "Yeah Roy, its dried human blood." Their eyes riveted upon the bloody blob as the woods erupted with the sounds of nature taunting them while their drama unfolded. Todd broke the silence, "Look, Waldo's red thermos," waving his hand in its direction on the ground. Pointing to the oak tree, he explained, "What I thought was tree fungus is actually human blood that has trickled down its side." Roy's eyes followed the tree line to the leaves. "I better get up there Todd; he may have cut himself with his hunting knife." "Don't move," Todd said, once again, "we must treat this like a crime scene." "What the hell you say, Todd, a crime scene? He may have just cut himself, I'll go up and check him out." "Move back ten paces," Todd lashed out."

"Roger, Lt."

At a safe distance they both tried to regroup and sort things out. "Do you think he's…" "Yes Roy, no doubt about it. That's too much blood loss to be caused by a knife cut. Let's move back twenty yards to the right; that will put us directly in front of him."

Reaching Todd's desired location they stopped and looked back at Waldo's lifeless body. "Roy, hand me your binoculars." Adjusting the lenses, Todd announced, "There is a large blood patch in the center of his chest that's definitely the source of blood loss."

"Do you think it was a hunting accident?" "No way Roy, there's always a chance event that a ground level accident is possible but this one was intentional. Waldo was twenty feet up in his tree stand and someone had to aim up at him so in all likelihood this was premeditated."

Next to something happening to my family, the most horrible thing is to have a friend, a real good pal, down, Todd thought as his mind rushed back to over three years ago when he and Judy were staring at Craig's reel in the water. Closing his smoky gray eyes and thinking that something similar was in the works, he was jolted back to the present when Roy nudged his shoulder, and asked in an almost too loud voice, "Hey Lt, what should we do?" "Call forensics; get the whole team up here plus dogs."

"Am on it sir."

Roy reached for his shoulder mike but they were in a "dead zone."

Sickened by their surroundings and Waldo's lifeless body up in the tree, Roy walked slowly back to the cruiser with his head bowed forward. Lifting the mike from its cradle he put out the word and decided to sit in the cruiser and wait for help to arrive.

As Todd sat on the cool, leafy forest floor with his back against a black oak, his throbbing head between his hands, tears trickled down his cheeks. From about fifteen yards away he could hear a very quiet rustling of leaves. Could it be Waldo's killer returning to the crime scene, he wondered; they often do that. It's a psychological thing these homicidal nuts do, you know, he said to himself. If that creep spots me, I'm dead, too. Sure should have known better; my John Jay College professor pounded scenarios just like these into my head; fifteen percent of the killers return.

Out from behind a large pine tree, stopping in his tracks, with absence of any motion, he stood as still as a statue in all his regal, mysterious, powerful, and beautiful splendid sovereignty, even appearing to have a divine attitude. Every inch of him a king; he was the emperor of the forest. Peeking through his fingers, Todd was confounded at the sight of him. Here was a glorious white albino buck with a majestic large rack. The length of its main beam was huge; his handsome head full of mystical bones. To Todd's astonishment, he counted fourteen points! This mature warrior was a sight to behold; the Holy Grail of the white tail deer. Watching him move cautiously and wisely scenting the air, Todd attempted to hold in a cough but did clear his throat as quietly as possible hoping the sound would blend in with the noises of the woods. His highness froze again, glanced in Todd's direction, cocked his elegant head up to his left, smelling the wind for any scent of danger, moved forward as his dark brown piercing eyes burned down upon the crumpled bundle of nerves cuddled at the base of the black oak tree. Todd had no choice but to hold his breath and pray the liquid in his throat would not make him cough again.

His lordship in full battle readiness and Todd overwhelmed and scared, stared down one another for what seemed like an eternity, until sirens were heard in the distance. Miraculously, the beast; prince among deer, lowered its revered head and nibbled on some fresh fallen acorns, its tail wagging side to side, reassuring his family of does that all was well. Moving off to his right in the direction of the apple grove, he would every so often dip his head down to pick up a few more nuts. Speechless and elated, Todd's spirits were lifted; his saddened state of mind and mood changed to a sense of peace and purpose.

Lead investigator, Lieutentant Jim Minx of the East Hampton Police Department's forensic team, shook Todd's shoulder, "Hey Lt. are you okay?" "Fine Jim, glad to see you buddy." "Lt. my boys are working the crime scene; soon as I know what's cookin' I'll call you." "Thanks, Jim, please don't miss anything. Waldo was one of us." "Shit Lt. you don't have to tell me that. Besides, my guys are the best; my people are like bull dogs when it comes to gathering evidence." "Jim, I didn't mean..." Holding up his hand, Lieutenant Minx replied, "I know Lt, I know. Best you get back down to Roy; this up here is what we're trained for." "Thanks, Jim I'll wait for your call."

As Todd walked down the hill he noticed the Suffolk County Medical Examiner's large black truck parked alongside the cruiser.

The Assistant County Medical Examiner, Dr. Storm and Sergeant Thompson were chatting through their open front windows. With a quick nod to Storm, Todd stepped into Roy's cruiser, grabbed a bottle of water and gulped down half of it. "Where to Lt. headquarters?" No, Roy, go to Jack's; I need a good cup of coffee, how about you?"

"Roger Lt, you bet."

CHAPTER 5

When the doorbells jingled at Jack's Coffee Shop the regulars perked up as if to ask "any keepers" during the fishing season, and now that the hunting season had begun, all heads rose in anticipation for reports from the woods. Today as Todd and Roy walked briskly through the door, Jack suspected something was amiss and with his coffee pot held high in the air, he motioned them with his left hand to the front corner table.

"Hi guys, still have the hungries?" grinning broadly. "No Jack, just coffee," Todd answered curtly as his eyes hovered over the red, white and blue table cloth. "Find Waldo?" Jack inquired as he poured two mugs of coffee. "We did, Jack. Waldo's dead." Jack froze, stared into Todd's steel gray eyes, and loosing all sense of presence, starting pouring more coffee into Todd's already filled mug. Roy sopped up the brown river that flowed from the rim of the mug, on to the table and down the cloth to the floor. Jack jerked the pot upright, then set it down on the table, as he slowly lowered himself into a chair, and sat weak kneed between them.

"Sorry to drop that on you, Jack but it's the horrible truth; Waldo is dead," Todd said. "How's that possible, heart attack, hunting accident?" Todd critiqued his not so jolly old friend with what brutal facts he had at his disposal and informed him that Lieutenant Minx should be calling soon with forensic information.

Overhearing his boss' sorrowful conversation, Fred, Jack's loyal friend and chef was shaken. Shit, Waldo ordered blueberry pancakes with hot honey and maple syrup from the first day they met. In fact, that's how their friendship began Fred remembered.

In no time Fred was back in the kitchen, throwing pancake batter mix on the griddle, whipping them off with his special spatula and decorating the tops with Waldo's favorites. Seconds later he had written Waldo's name next to the blueberry pancakes on the wall breakfast menu.

Picking up his cell and in his "take charge" voice, Todd greeted Lieutenant Minx, "What have you got?" "Todd, Waldo was shot with a carbon arrow that pinned him to the tree. The killer used a Grim Reaper super razor-cut broadhead carbon arrow that has superior penetration allowing for massive hemorrhaging. Consequently, as you surveyed at the scene, Waldo incurred a major blood loss." The words Grim Reaper sent ice through Todd's veins and once again his thoughts raced back to the analysis chart he had developed for the disappearances case; the big bold red letters THE FERRYMAN at the top.

Grim Reaper - Ferryman........ Is this just a coincidence or the more burning question, is this an evil premonition, Todd wondered.

Lieutenant Minx continued and informed Todd that from the type of arrow used, the weapon of choice, was most likely a compound bow. "What brings you to that conclusion, Lieutenant?" Todd persisted. "Todd, that's why I like working with you; you always dig. By the way Bobby Anderson is here with me." "Great, I know Bobby; his reputation is right on the money."

"Right on, Todd, and as I was saying, Bobby being a certified expert in arrow technology, researched this particular carbon arrow to verify his theory. According to Bobby, the arrow has all the consistencies, field point weight and correct arrow length for compound bow use. Furthermore, Bobby stakes his reputation on the fact that this arrow was shot from a compound bow. He further states that a shooter can get plenty of draw with virtually any arrow length. Additionally, the small diameter of carbon arrows is preferred by compound bow users."

"Lieutenant, you make a strong case; I'm convinced. Okay, so we have the arrow of death and the determined weapon of choice; now all we have to do is track down the killer." "We're working on it pal; we conducted an angle projectile the arrow was fired from, and determined that the point of departure of the let-off release position was northeast by east, approximately 75 yards. Inspecting the site revealed the shooter was in heavy brush and most likely well camouflaged. Todd, this prick, knew exactly what he was doing. This is premeditated murder and one last thing Todd, according to his rigormor-

Montauk The Bowman

tis, Waldo was killed Sunday morning; we estimate about 11:00am. Whoever did this was wearing scentless spray on his boots and clothing; dogs couldn't pick up a trail." "Thanks Lieutenant; send your report to Roy."

"Roger Todd, out."

Gazing into his coffee mug, his fingers tapping his lip, it seemed like an eternity before he spoke, "An arrow, Roy, a fuckin' Grim Reaper carbon arrow killed Waldo!" Jack and Fred sensed the horror of Todd's words; their ashen faces revealed dread. "Trust me guys, we'll get the killer," Todd bristled. "In the meantime Jack, keep your eyes and ears open. You're still a team member buddy; just like before," Todd reassured Jack, patting him on his shoulder. "Let's go Roy."

It didn't take the town crier long to spread the word throughout the small hamlet. Waldo's murder was taken very seriously and sadly by the Montauk hunters and fishermen.

21

CHAPTER 6

Slamming the cruiser into drive, turning sharply west, pressing hard on the pedal and turning on the sirens and lights, the police car took off like a rocket. "Hey, Roy, what's with the speed?" "Shit Todd, I'm worn to the bones, this helps clear my head." "Okay buddy, let's see what she can really do!" "There you go, Todd, hang on buddy!"

A jubilant smile crossed Roy's face as he smashed the pedal down hard with the cruiser responding like a hell fire demon on all four wheels bolting forward, the RPM needle almost in the red zone. Their adrenalin rush rocketed as they flew at eagle speed flying on the wings of the wind. In short order they were at HQ's. Delightedly, Todd slapped Roy on the shoulder, "Boy Roy, I needed that." "Hey buddy," a very pleased Roy retorted, "I don't feel like a squeezed lemon anymore!"

Back to their serious composure, the two officers walked in unison into Chief Becker's outer office, stopped to greet Lindsey who waved warmly, and continued on down the hall to the chief's private office. No matter what the situation, they both admired the large room which included a long conference table surrounded by twelve leather chairs, two comfortable couches, a stuffed bookcase and a fireplace stacked with kindling and oak logs, ready to go. Numerous personal treasures adorned the walls: police portraits, a gun case, a rifle rack and a colorful collection of police badges from all over the world in a glass and rosewood case. On the wall behind the chief's desk was a trophy case of target shooting awards and standing on the floor were the American flag and an East Hampton Town flag.

Expecting them, Chief Becker looked up from a file he was reading at his mahogany desk, grinned, and welcomed his two pros. In his fifties, he was rather young for this position but with his silvery hair, broad shoulders and eyes like a hunter he exuded energy and experience. He was a man's man yet charmed the ladies with his humorous Irish brogue, polished winks, and wore his meticulous uniforms very well.

After the small talk was over, Todd sat in one of the two leather chairs facing the chief's desk while Roy strolled over to the corner of the office where a wooden buffet table displayed an appetizing assortment of donuts, juices and coffee. As Roy stuffed himself with chocolate and sugar donuts, washing them down with orange juice, Todd filled the chief in with as much detail as he had at his disposal. Listening intently, while placing his right hand over his mouth and tapping his cheek bone with his index finger, and squinting his wise eyes pensively, Chief Becker waited a moment after Todd was through before he spoke.

Lowering his hand and staring directly into Todd's eyes, "I don't like the sound of those words, Todd," the chief said. Measuring each word he continued, "Grim Reaper 'tis the angel of death, lad; surer than hell if it doesn't sound just like the 'FERRYMAN'." "Dittos, chief; my exact thinking, too!" "Lad, I hope this is just an isolated case such as someone had it in for Waldo. Todd, I'm depending on you to resolve this case ASAP! You have the department's full resources; anything you need lad, just call me, understand?"

"Roger that, sir."

Roy caught the word ferryman but soon went back for another soft round sugar donut. "Son, this is not some amateur out there. This 'Bowman' as you call him could be dangerous to our community. Remember, even though it's been about three years since we closed out the case of the disappearances, the folks of Montauk who steeled themselves to that predator, have his memory still fearfully locked in their minds. By all of the immortal banshees' asses in Ireland, I can't have some phantom Bowman running around our village shooting people with Grim Reaper carbon arrows."

Pounding both fists on the top of his desk, the chief once again stared deeply into Todd's eyes. Roy stopped chewing and stood at attention. Todd grasped the full, frightening reality of Chief Becker's point.

"To be sure lad," Chief Becker continued, "the way you coordinated the task force in the dreadful disappearances serial killer case was an outstanding piece of investigative work. I brag to my peers whenever I am at those high level conferences throughout the country about my experienced detective police complement. Indeed, son, you have that rarest of gifts that the

Lord gives out only once in a lifetime; you have the uncanny ability to go right to the core of the puzzle. There is an old Irish expression, Todd, that goes like this; 'To know a hawk from a handsaw; such an endowment must be nourished, not wasted.'" Swallowing down a gulp of coffee, the chief winked at Todd, "Get my meaning, son?"

Humbled and honored Todd stood and saluted the chief and with a lick of a grin said, "Like they say in the military sir, never volunteer but I'm your man," as he motioned Roy to join him, "We won't let you down, chief; together Sergeant Thompson and I will get this killer." Becker reached into his bottom desk drawer, took out a new set of silver lieutenant bars and walked around his desk, "Son, you're still under deputy status, in fact, I remember it like yesterday when I deputized you while Jamie was standing at your side. I have reasons to believe Jamie will be concerned about you being reassigned." "I see no problem, sir, since Jamie was the only family Waldo had; they're second cousins." "Yes, that will help I'm sure, but again what about your liquor store?" "Gary's back in town, he can handle it and Sly Stone is on a winter layoff; we're good." "Fine Lieutenant Miller, and by the laurels of St. Patrick all will work out." Both officers proudly saluted Chief Becker.

"To begin sir, Roy and I will conduct interviews at the lodge to establish alibis for Sunday morning." "As a working member of the Montauk Rod and Gun Lodge, I'll be the first to account for my whereabouts," Chief Becker laughed, "My missus and I were attending 11:00 mass at St. Therese, then we went home to Mrs. Becker's outstanding dish of corned beef and cabbage." "Wow," interjected Roy, "wish I had been there for lunch. I've heard about your wife's secret recipe from her mother." "No secret Roy, just cook it nice and slow with

25

three pints of Guiness and voila, corned beef and cabbage extraordinaire!" The three laughed; the chief knew how to take the tension out of a stressful situation.

CHAPTER 7

On the way back to the Liquor Store, Todd briefed Roy. Arrangements would be made with the lodge president to set up a 10:00 am meeting the next day with as many members as possible. "Pick you up at 9:30 Lt." "See you then, Roy."

Clive was just about to lock up when Todd returned. After reviewing all the details with him, the newly re-deputized, exhausted and disheartened Lieutenant Miller sat down and gazed through his large front window and tried to find some relief from the agonizing events of the day. Watching the clouds sail by on their journey across the Atlantic with the reddish-tangerine background of the glowing sky as the sun melted down on the horizon, Todd's thoughts were of a possible snow storm. A few locals passing his store in huddles were breathing out white puffs of vapor. A stiff wind chilled the village.

Returning him to the present, Clive said, "Todd, your face is drawn, you're tired buddy. Go home to the family; get a good night's rest." His good friend always knew what to say and spoke with resolve and strength. He gets his gift from the bible, Todd had known for years, and luckily this had rubbed off on him, too. "You're right my friend, let's call it a day."

Star shaped snowflakes danced to their own rhythm's slow beat as they brushed against the warm bay window. The soft white flakes were soon transformed into tiny raindrops; striking the window reflecting Jamie's somber mood. Occasionally she blew her nose with her pink Victoria Secret's handkerchief. She heard Todd enter the dimly lighted room, softly illuminated by the crackling, flickering warm fire and raised her face to greet him. He crossed the distance between them and gently held her trembling shoulders, looking into her damp green eyes and noticed her quivering lips.

"Jamie," he said softly, "we all loved Waldo but he's gone now. You have to accept this and be strong for the kids. We'll get the bastard, I promise you, Jamie." Looking deeply into her husband's devoted, sad eyes, she whispered, "I know sweetheart; you're a wonderful husband and father. It's just poor Waldo; he was so innocent, so naïve. He had the spark of a child, he was harmless and always here for me and our children." Almost choking she continued, "and… and he was a prankster; had us in stitches, he loved to joke. Oh Todd, this is so inhuman, so cold blooded." In a loud voice, she cried out, "Todd I want justice; get that son of a bitch who did this to Waldo!" Good, she's regrouping thought Todd. "Trust me Jamie, I'll get the bastard." A few tears dampened his neck and ran down his collar as he continued to hold her.

Nancy and Todd, Jr. announced that they knew why Mommy was feeling badly as they walked into the living room. "Cousin Waldo is dead," they both uttered in unison. "Yes, guys, it's true but Mommy was just telling me a little secret and it's going to be a surprise for you kids." "What Daddy, what?" they squealed together. "Mommy's taking all of us, our whole family, for a swim and dinner at the spa; now how do you like that?" In unison they yelled, "Mommy, Mommy," as they ran over to her with their arms outstretched. Peering over their heads, Jamie looked at Todd; her eyes said it all: this is just the ticket, damn that man. I love him so!

"Hope you have cash, Daddy," Nancy said. "Don't worry baby, we can always raid the cash register at the store."

Hell, aren't Daddies great when you have one, Todd thought.

CHAPTER 8

Close to 150 members already milling around the Montauk
Rod and Gun Club lobby greeted Todd and Roy with numerous questions and shock. To have one of their comrades killed
but even more horribly murdered was almost beyond their
understanding.

After hours of interviews, Lieutenant Miller and Sergeant
Thompson came up empty handed; no leads, no suspects, no
nothin' as Roy like to say. The evening session proved just as
negative. Turning to Roy, who was completing the interview
reports and shaking his head back and forth, Todd remarked,
"Well, that's it buddy; this is a wrap." "Yeah Lt., doesn't look
good." "Anything in Jim's forensic report Roy?" "No, Todd, it
was well written and all inclusive but again nothin'."

Standing up and closing his brief case, as he gazed over
the rustic dining room, Todd thought catastrophes blindside
us; life isn't fair but it's just the way the game is played. "Hey

Roy, the beers are on me." "Thanks Lt., man, could I use a nice cold brew!"

The bar was humming. Ten round tables with four chairs each in this redwood paneled room were all occupied, soft shoe dance music was playing on the intercom, the lighting was dim, a fire glowed in the huge stone fireplace; the atmosphere was cozy and friendly. Todd and Roy sat on the two empty stools at the end of the bar and nibbled the various snacks while waiting to give their order.

Noticing her sleek, smooth, rhythmic cat-like moves, Roy's motor raced. Her long straight black hair shined like silk. He estimated her height at 5'11" and breasts a B-cup. Her curves were solidly in the sexy range of damn eye catching. Now being a leg man, Roy observed her well defined leg muscles as well, but also admired her shoulders, arms, flat belly and tight ass. Perfect lips, he thought; a cute nose, high cheek bones and dark piercing eyes.

Finally, she stood in front of them, staring into Roy's bright blue eyes. "What'll it be guys?" Mesmerized by the sound of her voice and glancing at her rainbow colored blouse with a bunch of birds all over it, and her tight fitting jeans tucked into high tan rawhide boots, Roy was speechless. Looking from her face to Roy's, Todd sensed exactly what was going on. Clearing his throat and getting her attention, he ordered two Guinnesses. She wrote the order hurriedly and to Roy she sounded as if she was purring when she said, "Coming right up."

Leaning his elbows on the bar and resting his head between his hands, he watched her sway away. Amused by what had just transpired, Todd laughing, said, "Roy, you look like a wolf whose tongue fell on the floor!" "Damn she's hot Lt."

"Will you get a grip Roy, you don't even know her and besides someone that hot must be married." "I didn't see a ring on her finger Todd, did you?"

Carrying the two frosted beer mugs and setting Roy's down first, she said, "This one's on me Sergeant. I appreciate the work you do for this community." Stammering a thank you, Roy managed to continue and as he looked at her name tag pinned to the collar of her blouse said, "Hither...Hither..... that's your name, what's the rest of it?" "Hither Yellowtail Hightower, Roy." Delighted but confused Roy asked, "But how did you know my name?" Leaning over the bar but keeping at a respectful distance, and extending her right hand, she tapped the name plate on his uniform. "Oh yeah," a red-faced Roy replied. Talk about burning passion, this guy was hog-tied.

"Hither Yellowtail Hightower, that's very unusual, sounds like a North American Indian name." Cocking her head to one side, Hither laughed, "What's it to you, Roy?" "Nothing, Hither, nothing; it's just that I've never met an Indian before," Roy flushed and took a big swallow to wet down his parched throat.

Having not 'messed around with girls' as he put it, in a long while, Roy hoped that he wouldn't act foolish around this amazing new female he had discovered. After his one year long relationship with an Irish girl who had worked in Montauk for the summer a few years ago, and who had gone back to Ireland to medical school left him lovelorn and sad. Other experiences were with the summer city girls who when they got bored from too much sand and water looked to the hunky cop to amuse them. Now Roy laughed to himself whenever he thought of the logo; "Montauk, a little fishing hamlet with a big drinking problem" which all the tourists repeated fondly. Hell, those girls he played with could really put down more drinks than any locals he knew!

For over a year now his role as uncle for his sister's kids and his responsibilities to his aging Mom and Dad kept him busy, proud and out of trouble as he often reminded himself. Someday he would have kids of his own he liked to think. All in all Roy was a contented cop working for the village in which he had been born. Unsophisticated and not adventurous his only trip of any length was to NYC on a school bus and a ride in an elevator to the top of the Empire State Building. The composition he spent two long nights writing about that experience won him an award which he accepted nervously during an eighth grade assembly.

As Hither stood there, apparently studying his face, Roy said "I can identify each bird on your blouse." "Oh, so you're a birder, Roy?" "Yep, I love hiking in the woods; take my niece and nephew around the bays and the marshes and we watch the different birds and water fowl that come to Montauk. And, by the way, Hither I don't remember seeing you around the lodge; you a new member?'

"Kind of; Justin advertised for a barmaid, so here I am. Catch you later guys, not suppose to talk to the patrons too long and I see glasses that need to be refilled. By the way Roy, I'm a birder, too," she announced, winking.

Be social but brief with the customers was Hither's rule. Knowing that she was attractive, having the turkeys at the bar hit on her, was not unusual. Tending bar, with a bunch of guys staring at you, was the price one paid if the tips were good, to put up with that shit.

"I'm in Todd, did you see her wink at me?" "C'mon Roy, I bet she winks at all the guys; helps when she counts her tips." "No way, it was a special wink and beside she's a birder." "Okay buddy, just don't get you hopes up too high, it's a long fall to earth."

Hither caught sight of Roy's two fingers in the air; raised her thumb and in seconds put another two mugs in front of them. "How about walking the beach with me this weekend, Hither?" Roy asked. "Maybe," she answered, "depending on my schedule. I love puffins." "Good, give me your number, I'll call you Saturday morning." "I know where to reach you Roy; I'll call you Friday morning if I can make it." As she twirled around, heading for the tables, Roy grinning from cheek to cheek, said, "Well, what did I tell you pal?" "Good Luck buddy; birding wins the day, go figure!"

CHAPTER 9

For years for Todd, Roy and Justin, the idea of having a place in which all the fishermen and hunters could hang out finally took off when to their astonishment and gratitude, Marshall Held, a master surf caster and mentor, donated a large piece of land along East Lake Drive. His treasured gift ignited the spark for an onslaught of fund raisers held to raise enough money to build the lodge. Generous wealthy residents donated large sums of money, Architect Robert Heartstop drew the plans free of charge, Jack Wei, President of Montauk Construction, Inc. championed the endeavor contributing his men to build at no cost, Gary Half of the Ace Tile Company agreed to provide flooring as a gift and the list went on. Village electricians, plumbers, carpenters and painters joined forces and even several police gave of their free time. No doubt, this was Montauk's community interest and spirit at its finest!

Six months from the day the town building inspector, Jim O'Cleary, stamped the seal of approval to build, the doors of the Montauk Rod and Gun Club swung open to the cheers and tears of the villagers. Standing in all its two story splendid glory, the lodge had sweeping views of Gardiners Bay, Block Island, the Lighthouse, the Atlantic Ocean and Montauk Harbor. Rifle, pistol and archery ranges were housed in the sound proofed basement. On the first and main floor a trophy room, a kitchen and dining room (used also as the meeting room) shared the space with the Big Bucks Bar where a large fireplace surrounded by four massive deer heads was the focal point of the décor and actual portraits of animal and fishing scenes adorned the walls.

Offices for the president, vice president, treasurer and secretary were located on the second floor. Six guest rooms with two double beds in each and a combination game and TV room offered rest, relaxation and activities for members and visiting sportsmen.

By leaps and bounds the membership increased from fifty to 150 members the first year. A newsletter, first issued on November 1st 2004, was re-issued traditionally every year on the same date which coincided with the beginning of the new hunting season followed by three more issues during the year. President and Editor, Justin Winchester, was responsible for the contents and arranged to have the Montauk Print Shop graciously print it for free.

Smart, focused and a doer, Justin was also a ladies hunk with his thick black hair, eyes as green as a prairie cactus, the body of a quarterback, and a broad sunny smile. Dedicated to the lodge and respected by all the members, he was a master archer and rifleman who had collected a panoply of trophies and medals over the years.

This year the Montauk Rod and Gun Club Newsletter came out on the day Waldo's body was discovered. The following day, before and after the interviews, Justin did his best to keep the crew in an upbeat mood even though Waldo's murder hung like an ugly stinging thorn, ripping fear through them. For many his featured article only served to increase their anxieties. In large bold type it spelled: BLOOD IN MOTION - DEER FIGHT BACK and went on to say: *Monsters in the forests and deer attacks on hunters are more ferocious and numerous than ever before. To date throughout the country 275 sportsmen have fallen victim to buck assaults! Many trophy seeking hunters have been severely maimed by antlers. At this writing the death toll is at 24 across the US. Psychologists have been interviewed and cannot provide any answers for these horrific homicidal assaults on our hunter population. Hunting experts are dumbfounded and have no explanations for the deer's aggressive nature. All speculation on the causes and meanings of these alien attacks come up empty handed. Hysteria is taking its toll with the hunting community. The word going around is that it is not safe to be in the woods. Keep out of the forest until we come up with answers. In closing, keep safe and give the deer the respect they deserve. Solutions are in the works. Human beings do not belong in the woods with killer bucks!*

Gotcha didn't I, guys? This is just a fictional story. The point is: use common sense, use the buddy system and be safe in them there woods. THINK WOODS SAFETY!!

Justin continued with a brief sentence of advice: This is opening day of bow season and we're all a little rusty; use the practice ranges before going into the woods hunting out your trophy bucks.

The usual announcements filled the last two pages.

Jack's Coffee Shop has served us very well this past year. As a lodge member Jack is offering 10% off on all meals whether eaten at the lodge or at Jack's. Please note that chef John Ross is also on board for catered events.

The Big Bucks Tournament started November 1st and ends December 31st. Best of Luck guys!

First prize....................$20,000
Second "......................$15,000
Third " $12,500
4th, 5th, 6th.................$9,500
7th & 8th....................$7,500
9th-50th......................an assortment of bow and rifle equipment including lodge member Richard Prince's book, Montauk The Disappearances.

Let's have an action-packed thriller of a tournament. Last year first prize went to Sam Adams for his fourteen point buck. Sign up ASAP. Entrance fee is $500; check payable to the lodge.

Sign up for the Venison Donation Program. Remember there are people who love deer meat but can't get into the woods. Let's make this a banner year for them guys!

Mark your calendars for the National Sportsfishing Hunting and

Outdoor Exposition to be held at the Nassau Memorial Coliseum from January 18th -20th.

Montauk's Paulie's Tackle Shop is offering discounts to lodge members; 20% off on all equipment. Don't pass up on this winter sale, guys. Paul became a member this October. Welcome Brother Paul! If Paul is out in the woods, his trusted sidekick Susan will take good care of you.

Make sure to inform us when you get your buck or doe. We need date, time, bow, arrow and location of stand or ground shot. Deer sheets need to be filled out correctly.
Editor and President
Justin Winchester Jr.

Chapter 10

A bone chilling, stinging wind blew the storm clouds across the sky while the snowflakes continued to cover the village with a white blanket. From his truck to the front door at Headquarters, Todd felt the bitter cold and welcomed the building's heat as he hurried to Roy's office.

Settling himself opposite Roy he got right down to business. "Roy, assign two detectives to check out the local sport shops from Montauk to Patchogue and don't forget the ones on the north side up on Route 25A. Secondly, have them spot check the North Shore from Mattituck to Orient Point and thirdly have them research the mail order houses, you know, Cabellas, Bass Pro etc.. I want the names of any persons who purchased a Grim Reaper 500 grain carbon arrow who lives on Long Island and especially in Montauk. And Roy, I don't care if they sold one or fifty. Next have them inquire into those off-end mail order houses that sell sports equipment in bulk at discount prices. Research the internet and E-Bay. You know

Roy, there are a lot of hunters who build their own arrows so check to see who bought arrow kits. Tell the guys to go back ten years."

"Roger Lt."

"And finally, have them interview the taxidermist shops; they always make a plaque of some kind describing the kill plus the name of the bow and arrow or rifle and bullet that brought the animal down. Okay, that about covers it Sergeant. Now, I want this done ASAP; then we'll go to the lodge to interview the range control officer and Justin."

"Roger, Lt., I'm on it."

Later that afternoon they spoke to the range officer, James Springs and Justin; no new leads. Back at the office Todd called Lieutenant Steve Honeycut of the New York State Department of Environmental Concerns requesting that he review their data base for a similar case. Furthermore, Todd asked Steve to review all background checks on the East Enders who owned hand guns and rifles. DEC did not do background checks on any purchase of bows. Lieutenant Honeycut, happy to comply, would get back as soon as possible. Also calling Glen McCoy of the FBI and Manny Vilar of the NYS Parks Police, Todd knew the investigation was off to a thorough start.

"No leads in these reports Lt." Roy announced, finishing his last lodge readings." "I figured that," Todd replied. "Hey Roy, just for the hell of it, put an ad in the local papers - WANTED any types of old or new 500 grain Grim Reaper carbon arrows for my collection. Will pay good money." "Nice Lt." "And set up a phony PO Box and phony name in Wainscott; have one of the guys check in on it on a daily basis. You know Roy our killer may be hard up for money. Yeah, detective work is all trial and error, Roy; you can also crack a case by using pure common sense deception." "Damn Todd, that's good." "Whew, let's call it a day Sergeant."

"Roger that, Lt."

CHAPTER 11

Long line fishing, one of the toughest jobs in the fishing trade where one could find oneself in the open cold waters for two to six weeks doing what ever it takes to find the tuna, was how it was with the hardy crew of the Blue Star III. Fishing now for three weeks out in the Atlantic Canyon, three hundred miles off the coast of Montauk Point, they were returning to harbor with a boat load of tuna.

Mate Sam Adams watched as the boys unloaded the ice packed tuna crates for the truckers who lifted the boxes, filled their freezers with the precious cargo, paid the Captain and headed for the city. When Sam and his buddies signed the pay ledger, Captain Jonah Armstrong gave the men an added bonus, and a four day leave.

Planning to spend the next four days in the Montauk virgin timberland, Sam could not have been happier and drinking with his hunting pals at the lodge would be a welcomed respite.

Like a tiger, Sam was a skillful hunter and would rather be holding his long bow than a fishing pole. It was the shank of the afternoon; soon it would be dusk, he knew it was time to do something about his hunger pains. Free of the boat and with four free days ahead he drove off to Salivars ready to celebrate.

Sean greeted him with his usual 'Salivar smile', shook his hand and said, "Heard you made a killing out there buddy!" as he glanced over towards the Blue Star crew already on their second Turkey shots and shooting pool. "Yeah, yeah, we did pretty good out there Sean but my stomach is crying out for food; double my regular order!" "That'll be two six ounce burgers, extra fries and all the trimmings. How about your usual Montauk Slayer?" "Wild Turkey and a beer chaser sounds great to me, Sean."

Making his 220 pounds comfortable and swallowing the Turkey in one fast gulp, the tall handsome thirty four year old with auburn hair down to his shoulders, enjoyed the ice cold Guinness chaser and quickly ordered a refill. Locals, fishermen and hunters hung out at Salivars; it was a friendly place with big drinks and good food where the guys could embellish their yarn spinning and stretch the truths to knee slapping hilarity. After all, this was Salivars, not a confessional. You could unwind here, play pool cards or darts, and if it got a little rowdy, big Sean kept everyone in check, unless of course, you got his Irish up and found your ass outside on the parking lot.

It was 9:00 pm. Weary and full, Sam downed his fifth and last Slayer, put a hefty tip under his beer mug and waved to the guys.

He woke up at 4:00 am after a good sleep, chowed down on oatmeal and slipped into his jeans, blue woolen turtleneck, brown canvas work boots, red and black plaid woolen jacket, tan gloves and his favorite brown cowboy hat. No non-scented camouflage outfit for him and damn those face-makers; he hated them. Priding himself as a no frills man, he hunted the old fashioned time-honored way. Tree stands were not his style; he did his hunting on the ground. His weapon of choice was a long bow with a quiver of wooden arrows; talk about traditional, this guy was on the cutting edge! At home in the deepest of woods, he was well prepared and a mature warrior.

Contrary to hunting etiquette, rule one stating that one must be noiseless and scentless at all times, Sam a heavy smoker lit up his beloved camels in the woods any time he had a desire. In fact, as he liked to say, he had shot many a deer with a cigarette between his lips. His game plan was simple: he depended upon being noise free. His knowledge of topography, deer behavior and wind currents was extraordinary. Bow hunting for twenty years he held the Montauk record for the largest buck weighing in at 277 pounds with a royal fourteen point rack.

On this starlit early morning, Sam entered the woods like a commando. Moving with stealth and speed, his feet seemed to dance noiselessly over the twigs and leaves carpeting the forest floor. Stopping every so often, he slowly circled to check the downwind with his head held erect, ears at attention, his nose sniffing, his eyes darting. Suddenly the sun's bursting sheets of fire lighted up his theater; its warm rays drifting furtively through the forest like ghostly shadows among the trees. Nectar from the evergreens, pine needles and mosses filled Sam's nostrils as did the scents from the rotting tree stumps and the decaying crab apples.

These odors also wafted right to the nostrils of the heavily camouflaged Bowman crouched deep in the shadows of the apple orchard. Like a wolf on the prowl the Bowman damn well knew that chance always favors the well prepared. Armed with some knowledge of the Montauk hunter's prowess, the Bowman had to quickly execute a game plan to out wit this foe. Plotting to kill, smiling broadly and wickedly, the tormented soul waited and watched.

When Sam was within 150 yards of the Bowman, he reached into his backpack, retrieved his scent-drag and proceeded to round the trail, circling a thicket opposite the abandoned apple orchard. Now within 110 yards of the Bowman, he also read the signs that hunters refer to as the "Golden Triangle;" the intercrossing of deer trails, fresh deer scrapes and rubs. Observing his surrounding topography, Sam selected a spot to set up his shooting lane.

Sensitive to the hunter, the Bowman realized that too much foliage blocked any attempt at the target and a turkey decoy would have to be utilized for good measure.

Nearly finishing applying the scent-drag to his trail, Sam glanced to his left, catching sight of a large bird lying on its side, and walking quietly over to the bird, discovered it was a wild turkey. Figuring the turkey had to have been killed very recently, since the great horned owl or coyote hadn't torn it to shreds, he leaned down, turned the bird over, and could see the bird had been shot by a carbon arrow. Why would anyone shoot a male turkey out of season, he wondered, as he leaned against a black oak tree and lit up a camel? Inhaling deeply and closing his eyes to unravel the mystery, he thought if a carbon arrow costs between $32.00 and $35.00, what kind of hunter would leave an expensive arrow and prize bird behind, unless….hmmm……

In a flash of terror Sam knew without a single doubt that it was a decoy; a distraction. I'm being ambushed……..

The Bowman pulled the bow with lethal calm, the projectile was on its way; the carbon Grim Reaper arrow sliced silently through the air with smoking speed, shattering Sam's chest with such force and energy, ripped through his heart and exited his back. Like a deadly harpoon, the arrow impaled itself two inches into the oak. Death was instant. Sam hung motionless, mimicking a rag doll, his long bow and cigarette fell quickly to the ground.

The Bowman smiled; nice shot.

CHAPTER 12

High above an oblivious Captain Jonah Armstrong an orange colored sun shot its rays across the sky. Sitting and steaming at the helm of the Blue Star III, the captain knew they were two hours behind schedule, cutting down on productive fishing at the canyon.

Where the hell was Sam? They left the harbor late; Sam did not answer his cell or land phone, his front door was locked, and no truck in the driveway. Last time the crew saw him they told Armstrong was at Salivars the day they pulled in. His pissed off mood turned to pensive concern; he knew he had to make a decision and decided to call the police.

Busy with reports and phone calls, Todd and Roy were working Waldo's case when the phone rang again. Roy grabbed the receiver, "Sergeant Roy Thompson," an irked Roy answered. "Sergeant, this is Captain Armstrong of the Blue Star III, my first mate, Sam Adams has gone missing." "Well, hell captain, this is not the lost and found. What do you expect sir, me to do a check on every bar in Montauk?"

Overhearing Roy's curt comments, Todd picked up the extension. "What I'm trying to say Sergeant is that my first mate is not a lush; he's very responsible to his crew, his boat and particularly to me his captain! Do you get my meaning, son?" Before Roy could reply, Todd answered, "Excuse me, Captain Armstrong, this is Lieutenant Todd Miller. Has your first mate ever done this before?" In a loud, exasperated tone, "Never, Lieutenant, never!" Captain Armstrong replied. "I'm concerned; in fact I'm very worried about the lad. He planned to go hunting on his four day pass." The word hunting raised the hairs on Todd's neck. Looking at Roy, he gave a troubled glance. "The crew believes he was heading up to the old apple orchard, Lieutenant." Running his fingers through his thick blond hair, Todd continued, "Does he have a girlfriend or family?" "No, broke up with his girlfriend awhile ago; she didn't like him on the water so much, his parents live in Florida, you know, retired."

The two exchanged phone numbers and Todd promised to call as soon as possible with any news. Roy, already anticipating Todd's next move, was not surprised to see Todd dial Jim Minx's number. Filling Jim in on the situation they agreed to assemble the search teams up in the parking lot at the Recycling Center.

Montauk's weather patterns, unique to this remote end of the south fork, were right on the mark with predictions of snow during the week. Fortunately, the 40 mile an hour winds had subsided, yet enough snow covered the ground in the Hither Woods area to make tracking difficult. Nevertheless, the hearty residents' spirits shone brightly and many volunteers, fire and rescue workers, NYS, DEC, state troopers, park police and the EHPD packed the re-cycling site.

DEC's Lieutenant Steve Honeycut, in charge of the search effort, assigned the quadrants on the map grid to be searched by eight teams consisting of five men each plus dogs. The large map spread out over Honeycut's jeep hood was marked with multi-colored flags depicting the locations; each team had its color. After all teams set out, Todd, Roy and Steve waited for reports.

"Damn, if only he had set up in a permanent stand this would be easier," Steve complained. "What can I tell you Steve, ground hunters feel it's more challenging; they have more freedom of movement." "Yeah, well, according to the map our search area in Hither Woods is twenty miles - all inclusive, so I would think he should be found within the hour; that's if he's still in here, Todd."

"By the way Steve, we found Sam's pickup parked down in the parking lot by the old navy pier off Fort Pond Bay," explained Todd, "and all indications appear he entered the woods from the northwest, but what the hell, he could be anywhere." "Therein lies our problem, the forest is still thick with brush and foliage. He could be concealed in some heavy shrubbery or undergrowth," Steve noted grimly.

Stepping out of his cruiser, Roy walked over to the jeep, "Just talked to Justin Todd, our guy hunts in traditional clothing, does not use scentless spray and smokes in the woods to boot." "Go figure Roy, it takes all types, this guy must be a real turkey in the woods," chimed in Lieutenant Honeycut laughing. "Wrong Steve," an annoyed Todd retorted, "Sam Adams holds the lodge's Big Bucks record. And I know that he held a cigarette between his lips while he shot that trophy." "No way Todd, I don't believe that." "It's the truth Steve; he was downwind of the deer; it didn't matter whether he was smoking a cigarette or a cigar." "Are you shittin' me, Todd?" "No sir. Ask Marshall, he was leaving the woods when he saw Sam dragging his buck and he told Marshall he was glad he had a quick shot because his butt ash needed tipping!" Shaking his head, Steve grinned and said, "Some guys have all the luck!"

"Talking about hunting," Roy interjected, "it was right in that area at Bow Hill where I caught my forty pound bass; gotta hunt for them big guys, too." "That's a hell of a bass Roy, did you keep her?" "Couldn't Steve, she was a breeder; same thing with Todd, he picked a thirty pounder at Graveyard Point. Can't keep 'em."

"Great guys, DEC loves when you fishermen put the breeders back," Steve agreed. "It's funny," Roy added, "I remember the day I picked twenty- three, eighteen to twenty-four pounders, and as luck would have it, I was all alone."

Park Police Sergeant Roland Hawkins who had been monitoring the radio from his cruiser, interrupted the group, faced Steve and announced that so far, there had been no findings. Taking his red marker, Steve circled their flags, and summarized, "Well, that covers the west boundary of the orchard." Suddenly, Todd's cell rang, "Yes Jim, do you have anything?" As Todd heard the words on the other end of the line he closed his eyes. After what seemed like an unusually long time, in a quiet husky voice he said, "Yeah Jim, send the report," and pushed the off button. With his eyes still closed, Todd repeated what Jim had said as best he could: "Blue team found him; he was pinned to a tree by another Grim Reaper arrow. Not a pretty sight, he's covered with ticks and a coyote chewed most of his legs' flesh" "Shit Todd, right down to the bones?" Roy gasped. Todd didn't answer.

Speaking softly, Steve asked if Sam had a family. "Yeah, parents down in Florida," Roy confirmed. How about his captain, Todd thought, and dreaded the call. "Roy we're back to headquarters," Todd managed to say. "If they're any further developments Steve, call me." "Sure Todd, sure," Steve agreed and added, "Todd, think we have another cycle on our hands?"

"Looks that way buddy."

CHAPTER 13

The room was still; one could almost hear a pin drop. Three officers of the police department contemplating the abhorrent recent killings could not help but be reminded of the chilling events of not too long ago.

With his lips pressed tight on his weary face and his eyes staring down at his large interlocked fingers, Chief Becker, mulled over the latest events. One didn't get to his rank and position without thinking things through from every imaginable angle. Every so often Lieutenant Miller and Sergeant Thompson glanced up for a moment and caught what must be a sign of the enormous pressure their Chief was experiencing. Tension and silence hung heavily.

"By all the laurels of Mother Carey's chicken's, we're into the struggle of our lives lads. In all my police life, surer in hell, this is only the second time I've encountered such fiendish madness."

Both officers relieved that the lull was over were anxious for Becker's controlled, candid, opinion and direction. "Unlike the disappearances case where the bodies simply vanished, this monster is going about impaling his victims to trees," the chief continued. "This 'Bowman' as you call him, strikes with lightning speed, and fades away like a ghost, leaving no trace. It seems to me Todd, that we're heading into 'leach's storm-petrel' and we're all in you hands, son. It is you who must set a course to end this demon's run."

"Sir, storm-petrels?" Todd inquired.

"Forgive me lad, storm-petrels are birds shrouded in super-stition. Seamen regarded petrels gathering at the stern of a vessel as an ominous omen of the bad weather to come." "Sir, no matter the storm, Roy and I can handle it." "That's my Todd; you make me proud Lieutenant."

As Roy and Todd gathered their briefcases and put on their jackets, Chief Becker stood up, rested his hands on the edge of his desk, smiled at his two protégés saying, "As of today, I'm assigning you a control center; you know the drill. Good Luck, lads!"

CHAPTER 14

Entering police headquarters on another Montauk blue bird of a day, Todd was bathed in the streaming sunshine reflected through the large double paned windows of the control center. "Good morning Roy," Todd said as he walked to his desk. Roy jumped up while hanging up the phone, greeting Todd, "Do you know who that was?" "By the shit eatin' grin on your face, it must've been Hither!" "Yeah buddy, I'm in; told you that was a special wink." "Sure Roy, sure."

"She couldn't make it last week, but guess what, Hither and I have a bird date this Saturday morning," babbled Roy in excitement. "Okay buddy, I'm glad for you but just take it slow." "Right, I don't want to screw this up." "Good Roy, now are you finished with Jim's report; I need to read it?" "Give me fifteen more minutes Lt."

Ten minutes later the control room door swung open. "Hi Lt., hey Roy, hear you're working on a new hot gal." "Where the hell did you hear that?" Roy demanded. "Shit Roy, this is police HQ's; we're a regular rumor mill around here, good buddy." "Yeah Bob, and I think I know who the mill runner is," giving Todd a sideways glance.

Ignoring Roy's mumblings, the very thorough Forensic Crime Investigator Bob Anderson placed three bags of evidence on the large conference table, and was ready to get down to business. "As you requested Todd, these are the three arrows left at the primary crime scene; Exhibit A is a typical commercial arrow equipped with standard gateway top quality green feathers. Now, these arrows can be purchased at any sport shop. However, Exhibit B and C are custom-made; possibly by our killer. These arrows are identical to that one commercial arrow that took out Waldo. But, and this is important guys, there is one exception; these two arrows contain one new feature. Do you see the dark brown and white stripes? Okay, it just so happens they come from the wing of a wild turkey."

Bob paused a few moments noticing the perplexed expressions on their faces. Breaking the silence he continued, "These natural feathers are ninety five percent water proof compared to the commercial ones which are only water resistant and have to be treated with a powder to keep them that way." "But, why do they use wing feathers Bob?" wondered Roy. "Got me Roy; maybe it's because they're stronger, you know more durable; no doubt they can take a lot of punishment from an arrow." "Shit I'm a birder but never knew that, Bob."

"What's the possibility of having two killers?" Todd asked. "As you know anything is possible but I believe it is unlikely since all three arrows are similar except for the feathers. All three have a large cutting diameter (1 3/8 inch) combined with a high strength, replaceable cut on the contact top and their 500-grain model has a slightly larger ferrule to increase weight. Now all blades use Maxx-Edge technology which takes a tough .035 thickness blade and necks it down to .02 thickness for maximum sharpness. The killer had to know these razor-cut broadheads make the arrow screw through flesh, producing a spiral wound channel for massive hemorrhaging." Bob's detailed technical explanation raised chills and disgust for the two officers. "Nope," Bob went on, "I'm confident we're dealing with only one freak out there and not a copy cat.

"In summary, gentlemen, what we have here is one of the perfect high tech killing machines known to mankind in the hands of a deranged maniac. And this demented lunatic is a deadly shot on the sharp-shooting scale. His obsession with the Grim Reaper arrow scares the shit out of me. You have no idea, God forbid, what agony one feels being impaled by this arrow," Bob concluded.

All three sat with the absence of any sound; their thoughts fixed on the ghastly horror of the situation facing them.

"Please call me if I can do anything else guys," Bob offered on his way out the door.

"Hey Lt. this Reaper guy makes the Ferryman look like a pussy cat." "Not really Roy," Todd sighed thoughtfully, "they both appear to be of one mind and purpose and that Roy is to bring death and to hurt our fellow neighbors and loved ones. Like the chief said Roy, we're in for the fight of our lives."

Chapter 15

Like most all Montauk locals who cherished living in a village nestled between rolling hills, scenic pastures, thick forests, the Atlantic Ocean and the Block Island Sound, Sal Iacola had a dream; to bring his fresh, tasty, organic fed chickens to Montauk.

As luck would have it, everything came together for Sal when he found a way in which to purchase the four acre Shad Hill Farm. Of course, he and his wife Ellen and their son Andy continued to operate their renowned East Hampton farm while the newly hired help, Garrtett Baggage and Mario Pulumo ran the Montauk branch.

Naturally, the new chicken farm was a hit for who could resist fresh chickens and eggs that were laid daily. In fact, demand was so high that hundreds of chicks were slaughtered weekly. As a treat for his new Montauk customers, Sal offered goose and muscoly ducks (known by the locals as scobys) during the holidays.

Six out of seven days a week Garrett and Mario rose early and performed their routine like clock work. Feeding the chickens and gathering eggs was Mario's first task of the day followed by herding the pre-selected fowl into a narrow chamber room. Mario liked to think of this room as the parting room, as he pushed a six foot long by four feet high framed wooden fence on rollers, corralling them tightly together. Wearing gloves, he grabbed the animals one at a time, and placed each in a black carrying cage. Depending upon the size of the customer demand, he would fill anywhere from five to ten cages, and then drive the truck load to the three room building next to the farm's parking lot which housed the butchering room, the preparation area and the retail store.

Once the chickens were in the butchering room, Mario prepared to kill each one with the help of an eight foot long stainless steel table equipped with six steel funnels. Inserting the head of each chicken down into the funnel would cause its head and neck to pop out at the other end and explode. Garrett assisted by cutting each chicken's windpipe with his razor sharp three inch knife. Blood would flow from the chicken's warm body down the curved surface and into a pipe connected to a large blood collecting tank.

Next each was dropped into a scalding pot of 135 degrees of water; the intense heat loosening the feathers. After plucking was completed an ice water bath cooled body temperatures rapidly. Chickens not to be sold that very day would be placed in the freezer.

While dressing each chicken according to each customer's preference, Garrett enjoyed chatting and explaining how to roast a perfect bird and often shared his many delicious recipes. Mario manned the phones and cash register while he joked with the customers, often saying, "Don't ask me what I did so far today!"

The young lads were best of friends and grateful to have a year round job.

CHAPTER 16

Satisfied with the knowledge of the chicken farm's routine after two days of undetected scrutiny, the Bowman awakened at one hour before sunrise, dressed in full scentless camouflage and entered the small grain storage closet that was located within the chamber herding area at Shad Farm.

Waiting patiently with closed eyes, thoughts of animal killers continued to ravage; they were murderers who camouflaged suffering and death. Market hunting is killing domestic animals for that lousy commercial profit. At least out in the wild the animals had a chance to fight, thought the Bowman; here within this bob-wired compound there was no hope; ever. The most cruel act of all; the slashing of their throats was not to be tolerated.

A door slammed as the herdsman began to send the clucking chicks into the chamber. The Bowman's eyes snapped wide open, peered through the opened door, and watched as the chickens fluttered their wings and clucked raucously. To the Bowman it was the shrieking of the damned; their chorus of hell filled the room.

Clutching the instrument of death with such strength causing pain to ripple through the fingertips, the Bowman leaped out of the lair and ran silently behind the farmer. Suddenly Mario's head heaved back to his shoulder blades as a gloved hand held his chin like a vise. Trying to scream, there was silence, while the Bowman's razor sharp hunting knife sliced through Mario's windpipe. Blood shot out and splashed to the floor; its pungent sweet perfume of death filling the Bowman's nostrils. Ultimately the flow turned into a trickle. Snickering, the Bowman released the victim and dropped him to the bloody red floor.

Getting antsy, Garrett wondered what his side kick was doing.

Calls on his hand held radio were not answered. Guess I'd better check on him, he decided, and as he hopped into his red pick up, the Bowman from his vantage point, watched him kick up the dust as he made his way down the path to the barn. Blowing his horn to no avail, he hopped out and walked briskly into the dimly lighted chicken house. As he headed for the chamber room, yelling for his buddy and opened the door, he froze. The last thing he saw was Mario lying in a pool of blood.

CHAPTER 17

It was 9:30 am when Betty Whitefield pulled into the Shad Hill Chicken Farm parking lot and noticed her favorite gourmet shop truck already parked. As she entered the store, Jillian greeted her with her lilting Irish brogue, "Mornin' luv, my you're looking lovely and trim; been workin' out have you now, dear?" Whispering, Betty replied smiling, "Confidentially, I've lost eighteen pounds in the last two months." "Oh," her wide-eyed friend smiled, "it really shows."

Looking around the store, they were puzzled to find themselves alone. "Jillian," Betty asked, "is Mario working on your order?"

"Oh, no luv, I always call my order in the day before so I can make a quick pick-up and dash back to my shop. Odd that no one is here though." "I know," agreed Betty," I'm doing a big dinner tonight and have to get my chickens in the crock pot very soon.... oh here comes someone." Swinging the door wide and greeting the ladies with a loud "Hi ya girls and I might add sexy girls!" Bill, a big, burly local who lumbered in called out in his bellowing voice, "Hey Mario, Garrett, here for my birds." "They don't seem to be around, Bill," Jillian said. "We've been here for twenty minutes or so just waiting." "No way to run a business. Hell, you girls stay here and I'll have a look see."

Bill returned very shortly. The troubled look on his face alarmed both women. "They're not in this building. I even checked the frig; no chicken orders have been filled; something strange going on here, ladies." "Come to think of it Bill, there are no eggs on the egg table either," Betty remarked. "It's as if they never opened the store today," Bill added thinking, then abruptly took out his cell phone and punched in the Iacola East Hampton farm number.

"Iacola Chicken Farm," Ellen answered. "Ellen, is Sal there?"

"Sure is Bill, hang on." "Hi Bill, need an order?" Sal asked his old friend. "That's just it Sal, I'm down here in Montauk and no one is around." "What, no one there, you're saying?" "Right, no one Sal, just me and Betty and Jillian; we've been waiting for your guys. I checked the rooms in the back; no one, nothing." "Am on my way Bill, hang around." A bead of sweat formed on Sal's brow as he explained to Ellen what Bill had told him. "They're good boys Sal, something must have happened. Call the police."

Sal's 911 call was routed to Lieutenant Miller and after a brief conversation Sal hung up. "They're on their way," Sal announced.

"Tell Andy we're going to Montauk."

CHAPTER 18

The cruiser wailed across the Napeague stretch between Gansett and Montauk at 85mph. You know the scene; pulsating red bar on the roof, siren blaring. A peaceful morning interrupted by a frantic 911 call had put Todd and Roy on the road.

"Wha'da think Lt.; they just picked up and left?"

"No use speculating Roy. In fact, in a manner of speaking this very situation could be classified as Corpus Delecti."

"Corpus what?" "It's Latin Roy," "So what does it mean?"

"To be exact Roy, Corpus Delecti means the material evidence of the fact that a crime has been committed, such as at the primary crime scene, one discovers a corpse of a murder victim. Loosely put Roy, the victim's corpse is a murder case. Hence Roy, the golden rule of thumb: do not assume; stick to the divine medium of proof. Therefore Roy, extrinsic evidence and facts are paramount; they are the only course a criminal investigation must follow. Got it Roy?" "Yeah Lt. I got it."

"Remember good buddy, there could be a simple explanation to their whereabouts."

Flying past the overlook at Hither Woods, Todd asked," Roy did you ever consider Nascar racing?" "Sure did Lt., but this job is a lot safer. Can you imagine hitting one of those walls around the track at 140 mph; they don't give in Todd," he laughed, "the car does," Roy laughed even louder. "You get it Todd?"

That was the exactly what Todd "got" as they flew along side the trees at 90mph. "You know, I've been thinking," Roy said, interrupting Todd's thoughts, "this Bowman creep reminds me of a Northern Shrike. He's a fearsome predator that knocks his avian victims out of the air with some sharp blows from his beak and severs the vertebrae." "Hey Roy, tell me more." "Well, Lt., it's known that shrikes dispatch land animals in the same way. They're called butcher birds, Lt. and I might add with good reason."

Slowing the cruiser down to 50mph they entered the hamlet of Montauk while Roy continued explaining, "You see Lt. they characteristically hang their prey head up on a thorn or a barbed wire fence or even wedge it into the fork of a branch. Then they either down their catch immediately or allow it to hang like it was in an open air pantry, for a day or two - sometimes even a week or more before returning for a meal."

"Very, very interesting, Roy, damn interesting." Easing the cruiser into a right hand turn on Seaside then flooring it, the cruiser leaped forward. "The thing is Lt. the Bowman impaled both Waldo and Sam in the same manner, right? Now I'm not inferring he's coming back to eat them but it's pretty coincidental he uses the same technique, right?" "What an ironic twist, Roy; remind me to keep an eye out for a Northern Shrike!"

Roy hit the brake; the cruiser came to a screeching halt in the Shad Farm parking lot. Pacing anxiously and smoking a cigarette, Bill, relieved to see the police, tossed his butt and shook hands with the officers. Getting right to the point, Todd said, "Bill, the Iacolas are on their way; could you stay till they arrive?" "Sure Todd, no problem" "Great; Sal told me you checked out the building and it's clean; did you go over to the house?" "Yep, no answer." "We'll check it out; let's see who's home Roy."

After a thorough search of the little house they concluded it wasn't occupied last night or this morning. No beds made up, no dinner or breakfast dishes piled in the sink, no warm coffee pot on the stove. Checking the rear of the building where a clear view led down to the chicken barn they spotted two trucks parked side by side. "Those must be their vehicles Roy; get the cruiser."

Easing the cruiser beside the two empty trucks, "Shit Lt. this looks like a scene right out of 'Psycho'. No one was at that house either remember, and two empty trucks." Touching each hood, "They're cold," Todd announced. Looking inside, Roy saw keys hanging in both ignitions while Todd gazed into the dreary barn. "Let's go Roy, all the signs indicates they must be in here."

Unfamiliar with the turf, they walked carefully, observing as best they could every inch of the poorly lighted old barn. Screeching from hunger the chickens added to the unfolding drama. When they reached the chamber room Todd opened the door slowly. He moved forward one foot and suddenly stopped. Both drew their glock revolvers. Ever so slowly, Todd stuck his head through the opening and recoiled. Roy saw by the pain in his eyes and the look on his face that what Todd discovered was bad. A chill knifed through Roy body's as he started toward the opening. "Stop Roy, it's not a pretty sight. They're both inside lying in pools of blood; it appears their throats have been slashed."

Turning around Todd said quietly, "Let's wait in the cruiser. Call Jim, get the team down here."

"Roger Lt."

Walking back to their cruiser the sounds of eerie chicken chatter seemed to be telling them something.

CHAPTER 19

Sitting patiently in the cruiser waiting for the task force, Roy suddenly asked, "Lt. do you think there's a connection between these murders and the Bowman?" "Wait a minute Sergeant," snapped Todd, rubbing his closed eyelids as if to erase unwanted images.

"Don't you remember what we were talking about on the way here? Let's wait and see what Jim comes up with. He and his team, Sergeant, are trained forensic investigators. It's their assigned job to collect the hard and soft evidence at the primary crime scene and it's my duty to dissect, interpret and connect the pieces of their puzzle. Then I will set the priorities and ultimately mediate the direction of the overall investigation. I enjoy the challenge of the chase and to resolve problems, and hope to avoid the pitfalls, and to eventually close the case, but the order of events Sergeant is the protocol. Now, I'm sorry buddy if I sound abrasive and repetitive but the sight of those young men lying in their own blood was unsettling to say the least. It always rattles me to be the first at the scene."

Over at the retail store the Iacolas standing next to Bill, watching through the large front window and anticipating the worst, braced themselves as a sizeable police convoy arrived; six cruisers, a red and white forensic emergency truck and bringing up the rear two Montauk Fire Department ambulances. The group roared into the quiet little farm, barreling down the dry dirt road, leading to the chicken barn. Brown pillars of haze formed over the area; the ocean breezes trying to fan the angry clouds of dust.

Todd brought Jim up to speed and was assured by his Chief Forensic Investigator colleague that he would call immediately with any information. Deciding to keep as many vultures away, Todd posted a patrol car up on the parking field, since he knew that the news jockeys with their wireless mikes would soon be descending upon the farm. These twits had enormous appetites for any detail, no matter how irrelevant or trivial to the investigations. He also reckoned that when the news of the double homicide became public the entire hinterland would fall into a complete frenzy.

Facing Sal and Ellen Iacola was a part of police work Todd loathed. Knowing that there was no gentle way of breaking this sort of news, he bolstered himself to deliver the message as directly, professionally and briefly as possible. The obvious respect and confidence the polite, devastated couple displayed for the police delivered an even more challenging resolution to the unfolding nightmare.

Roy steered the cruiser on to Seaside, made a left and headed toward the village. "Where to, Lt.?" "How about Jack's?

I need some fuel like a caffeine light." " Damn Todd, that's exactly what I was thinking."

At their usual corner table up front by the counter which Jack reserved his VIP area for juicy scuttlebutt, Todd and Roy could tell that Jack's familiar smiling face was flat with fear as he placed two mugs of Mocha Java in front of them.

"What's going on boys? Rumors are flying all over town and what's with that police convoy that rolled through earlier?" asked Jack.

"Sit down buddy," Todd urged. "What we have here Jack is a double homicide. Both chicken farmers are dead."

Absorbing the news like a sponge, Jack probed for more, "What the hell you say Todd? Garrett and Mario dead? Why, who.....?"

"That's the million dollar question Jack; forensic is up at the farm working the case." Flabbergasted, Jack mumbled, "Two hunters and now this......."

Just then Bill O'Reilly walked in, spotted the three, approached their table and snapped out, "I sure as hell don't need mornings like this, Todd. Being chief of the Fire Department is hard enough but taking bodies to the County Medical Examiner is pushing it!" "Please Bill, don't be short with me; in this case I had no choice," explained Todd. "Time is of the essence; we have to establish a time line, Dr. Storm insisted they be brought ASAP. C'mon Bill, you know I've always cooperated." "Okay Todd, I'll let it go but my ambulance crew is not a happy group. It is one thing to take accident victims and patients to the hospital but hauling murder victims to the medical examiner is not in their training textbook. Both crews are pissed off at me Todd." "Bill, tell them I personally will handle any traffic violations they may incur, okay?"

"There you go, Todd, I knew we could work something out," a more relaxed, subdued chief retorted, doing a quick about-face and leaving. "You handled that well Lt." "Thanks Roy." "Sure did," praised Jack as he pressed for more information. "Do you think it's the same person who took out Waldo and Sam?" "That's speculation," Roy answered quickly, "we only deal in hard facts."

"Jack, I'll call you when we get something; in the meantime you have enough from what we just told you to double your business by this afternoon," Todd said. "Okay, see you Jack; we gotta go Roy; the chief will want an update."

CHAPTER 20

Todd slammed the door to the command center interrupting Roy who caught the steely look on the Lieutenant's face. "What's up boss, you in a whirlwind of thought? Your meeting went okay with the chief?" Ignoring Roy or perhaps not even hearing him, Todd scanned the bank of computers and telephones, then gazed briefly at the stacks of files on the conference table and at the maps and charts he had taped to the walls.

Roy knew it was the time to clam up. Todd continued wandering around the room, stopping to study crime scene photos. Turning to Roy, he declared decisively, "The Bowman killed the farmers. There is no doubt about it; he left his calling card." Surprised, Roy started to speak but was cut off as Todd said, "Yes, Jim's team located a Grim, Reaper carbon arrow with turkey feathers shot into the interior of the roof above the corpses." Roy's attentive demeanor took on a pained expression as Todd continued, "Two victims in one day. You know Roy, I once read a quote that sums things up; goes something like this, 'The feast of vultures and the waste of life.' I really fear we have reached the bellwether of things to come."

Settling down behind his desk and staring into space Todd added, "Killers are like addicts. To satisfy their increasing lust for violence, the regularity and evil of their acts escalate. Jim found no fingerprints, no footprints, and no tire tread marks near the point of entry to the barn or within the chicken house."

Rising and walking over to his large wall chart, he grabbed a red marker and titled the profile with the words GRIM REAPER. "Why Grim Reaper, Todd?" "Simple Roy, the Bowman has to date left four Grim Reaper arrows so I must assume that's what this psycho wants to be called. Listen Roy, sick minds perceive images we can never understand. You could have them on the couch for years and never figure them out. Their minds are like a black hole; they absorb everything but never relinquish a morsel or a glimpse of what's inside."

"Damn that's heavy stuff Todd." "No Roy, it's just ugly and deranged. By the way, did you know that serial killers are most active during holidays and hot, dry spells?" "That's news to me Lt. so may I conclude that people living in warm climates have more murders than people residing in cool areas?"

"No Roy, that's not how it works."

On a roll Todd pushed forward: "Think of it this way Roy. People kill people, agreed?" "Yeah, Lt." "Hence, some under duress snap. Why? Because stress pushes them over the edge and bingo! Now we have a new born killer lurking around in our friendly neighborhood. Throughout history killers have lived among us; they're like dark shadows in the forest. Each psycho has his own MO and there are an infinite number of reasons why these wackos take lives. Follow me Roy?"

Speechless, Roy nodded. "Okay, now with that said, from thousands of case studies over the years, it has been established that stress makes these nuts more prone to kill. For example Roy, a man sitting on a cool beach in Hawaii is much less likely to kill than a strap hanger in a subway. Following me Roy?" "Mmmmm...guess so."

"Okay, now Roy, picture this: the air conditioning is not working in the subway; it's a sweltering, slimy, humid, hot 99 degrees. Delays due to the switching problems have the people packed in like sardines, the lights are blinking around you, you could swear someone just touched your ass and the guy next to you is talking to himself. A kid starts crying for its mommy and just when you thought it couldn't get any worse than this, somebody cuts wind; the last straw, right Roy?"

"I get your point Todd; stress is a killer" "You got it buddy! Let's call it a day........ talk about stress!"

CHAPTER 21

Sitting in a brown cushioned Adirondack chair, Hither gazed through the large bay window, overlooking the Montauk Harbor shimmering in the early morning sunlight. Checking her watch, the large and small hands were perpendicular. She gulped the last of her coffee and placed the mug into the empty cereal bowl.

Her sharp eyes caught sight of Roy's black Pathfinder rolling up the driveway to the lodge. Good, she thought, I like punctuality; it says something about a person's character. People who showed up late she considered disorganized and unreliable. Lifting her optics tote she walked to the main entrance, held the door open with her shoulder, and welcomed the cold sting of the early day that brushed her face.

Pulling smartly to a stop, Roy waved, lowered the passenger window and called out a very cheerful, "Good Morning Hither, glad to see you! Isn't it a crystal clear morning, perfect for birding?" "You're right Roy! Is that Pavarotti you're listening to?" she asked, as she opened the rear door, placing her black nylon tote on the seat. "Sure is," a delighted Roy replied. "What a wonderful way to start the day," she said, closing the door and buckling up.

Roy felt a quiver run through his body, as he looked at Hither, sitting so close to him. "Where are we off to, Roy?" "To bird-land; the north side of the lighthouse. My friend Jake told me they're hundreds of migrating flocks resting and feeding on the water from North Bar to Jones Reef right under the state snack bar."

"I see you have fishing rods in your roof rack, Roy, expecting fish?" "Hither, anything's possible in Montauk; she's a charming unpredictable old lady, you know. A boil of fish could show up at anytime, the water's loaded with bait. My motto is always 'be prepared'." How clever, Hither laughed to herself; my exact thinking, too. "I don't want to be caught holding my ….uhmmmm, my car keys," a reddish faced Roy explained, catching himself before he let the word dick slip. "Roy, the expression is, 'I don't want to be caught holding my tool," a nonchalant Hither expounded. A tongue-tied Roy stared straight ahead while Hither after a dicey moment said softly, "It's okay Roy; I'm not a virgin. I am twenty four years old and know the ways of the world. Hey, the turkeys at the Big Bucks Bar use a lot of more colorful expressions than that. Goes with the turf, doesn't it?"

The girl's low, calm voice and her frank words put Roy at ease even though his heart beat much faster. Shit, he thought, this is great. I don't have to use the kid glove approach; they're no airs about her. Okay, I can be myself without the bullshit; she's not a priceless wax museum piece.

"You know Hither, Jake told me there's a variety of birds up there; Greater and Lesser Scaups, Common and King Eiders, Harlequin Durks along with Green Necked Mallards, Oldsquaw, Black and White Winged Surf Scoters, Common Goldeneye, Buffleheads, Ruddy Ducks, Common Merganser and Atlantic Puffins," rattled on Roy, proud of himself for last night's cram session.

"Well now Roy, did you know that puffins and penguins are similar; they both dive for their food. And they both use their wings for underwater propulsion and even repel the cold with their dense waterproof feathers," a savvy Hither responded knowing her expertise would outshine Roy's. "In fact these two birds look alike. Haven't you see them both sporting their black and white tuxedos, strolling comically with their endearing clumsiness, when they walk to the water's edge before they dive in, and knife through the sea like torpedoes?" she asked Roy demurely.

"Damn Hither, your good. You really know your birds." "I've been at it for sixteen years now Roy; it's all a part of my heritage.

In order to survive Roy, one should not take things for granted. So I've studied the wild life thatshare this planet with us. Knowledge is power Roy!" Fascinated by this unusual female, Roy could think of no words to utter and instead tried to concentrate on easing his beach buggy on to the pot holed filled dirt road leading to the beach.

The closer they got to the water the more birds they saw. Numerous groups swam together or pairs were feeding on the bait. "Look Hither, Northern Gannets!" "Oh, what show-birds! Look Roy, see how they move, rising and falling like a roller coaster on invisible rails?" Suddenly a number of gannets swooped down, folded their wings and plummeted into the water; a tower of spray marking the spot they found their breakfast. "Did you know Hither these birds dive from heights of more than one hundred feet and can reach that far down in the water?" "Pretty impressive, Roy."

Mesmerized, watching the roiling waters under a continued bombardment of birds while the bait lasted, Roy explained what he called a symbiotic relationship as the gannets pushed the bait deeper and the blues and bass pushed it back to the top. "Yes Roy, these animals know how and why to help each other. It's an awesome sight." A more confident Roy told himself that things were going just swell.

After awhile they set up their scopes and tripods, pointing, laughing and exchanging various tidbits of trivia. Time passed quickly as they enjoyed the magical feathery world. When Roy spotted a fish boil heading west with the terns and seagulls working them hard he said excitedly, "Hither let's top this day off with some fish!"

Stashing their equipment back in the Pathfinder and taking a ten foot rod out of the rack he handed it to Hither. She looked at the tin connected to the clip and asked what type of metal it was. "It's a two ounce homemade tornado," he answered, and, asked, "Can you handle the pole?" Turning toward the water she said, "Let's see." As Roy watched her move with clock work precision, she planted her feet firmly in the sand at the water's edge, unhooked the tornado and fired away. Perfect he thought; her cast went out forty yards to the inner rim of the boil, eliminating the possibility of cutting off her line. Okay, she knows what she's doing.

Together they fished; Roy spellbound by her abilities and wishing the day to never end. In all his life he never experienced a girl like this and he didn't want to lose this trophy. Each carried their one bass up the beach, placed it in the cooler and talked about their day as they drove slowly back to the lodge. Saying good bye to Hither reminded Roy of the lodge meeting at 8:00 that evening. "Keep two bar stools open at your end for Todd and me," he laughed, to which she winked, nodded and shook his hand. Hopping into his truck, he said out loud, "I'll never wash you off buddy," and drove off to HQs in a charmed-struck trance.

Chapter 22

Entering the command center control room, Roy immediately noticed Todd concentrating hard on his Grim Reaper chart. Not wanting to spook or disturb him, Roy shut the door quietly and tip toed to his desk. Glad for the silence and with the thoughts of Hither running through his head, he sat still holding the girl's image in his mind.

Todd's unblinking eyes were focused on the chart as if he were in a daze instead of probing the information and discerning its clues. To a criminal investigator this form of an art applied over and over again until something pops out from the obscurant maze was familiar to Todd and used often. When he tapped his chin with his right index finger, it appeared to the now focused Sergeant, that his tapping was keeping pace with his thought process. With his mouth shut tight and his breathing slow and measured, Roy continued to watch Todd, thinking he's like a pit bull; scanning the evidence, savoring each clue with relish, before he would attack with a vengeance.

When the finger tapping stopped, a surge of eager anticipation washed through Roy, and in a detached voice Todd commented, "We're like two auto mechanics Roy, we have some parts; now all we have to do is figure out how will they be useful to us?"

"So Lt., are you saying we must think outside of the evidence box?" "No Roy, not at all, what I'm saying is look deeper into the chart. Work with the intelligence we have; as the case expands so will the box grow with more ripe clues for us to ponder. Move on up here Roy, let's take a good look at what we have."

THE GRIM REAPER

CRIME SCENE ONE	CRIME SCENE TWO
Location	Location
.Hither Woods - Montauk.	.Hither Woods - Montauk
.Tree stand.	abandoned apple orchard
.Northeast Grid next	.Ground shot.
to apple orchard.	
Victim	Victim
.Waldo Maidstone.	.Samuel Adams.
.Male.	.Male.
.Age 28 years old.	.Age 34 years old.
Time of Attack	Time of Attack
.Between 10:00am -11:00am.	.Between 6:00am - 8:00am.
.Sunday, October 31.	.Wednesday, November 3.
Perpetrator:	Perpetrator:

MO
.Perp. shot victim in left
side of lung, middle of heart.
.Arrow impaled victim to tree
 in sitting position.

Evidence
.Blood type O positive.
.Grim Reaper carbon arrow.
.100 grain weight.
.Red thermos - half filled
with Wild Turkey Bourbon
belonging to victim.
.Vic. compound bow.
.Vic. knapsack containing
hunting items.
.No discernible traces.
.No finger prints, no shoe prints,
.No tread marks left by perp.

MO
.Perp shot vic. in upper
chest,
heart shot.
.Arrow impaled vic. to tree.

Evidence
.Blood type A positive.
.GRCA - 500 grain.
.Large wild turkey also shot
with GRC - 500.
.Possible decoy.
.Vic. Cigarette.
.Longbow.
.Vic. knapsack containing
hunting items.
.No discernible traces.
.No finger prints,
.No shoe prints, no tread
marks - left by perp.

CRIME SCENE THREE

Location:
.Hamlet of Montauk.
.Seaside Avenue.
.Shad Hill Farm Chicken Farm.
.Chamber room in chicken barn.

Victim
.Garrett Baggage.
.Male.
.Age 26 years old.
.Mario Puloma.
.Male.
.Age 28 years old.

INTERVIEWS WITH LODGE MEMBERS

Location:
.Hamlet of Montauk.
.East Lake Drive.
.Montauk Rod and Gun
Club.

Interview Results:
.No discernible leads.
.All had alibis.

Time of Attack
.Between 5:00am - 8:00am.
.Friday, November 12.

Perpetrator:
MO:
.The bowman AKA,
.The Grim Reaper.
.Perp. sliced vics. throats
with knife.

Evidence:
.Blood Type O positive for G.B.
.Blood type AB positive for M.P.
.No discernible traces,
.No finger prints,
.No foot prints,
.No tread marks left by perp.
.GRCA - 500 - grain shot into
interior roof above corpses.

Returning to their respective chairs after a lengthy re-examination of the charted information, Todd began to unfold a puzzling dilemma. "Point of issue Roy," he said, "I have this bothersome thought which has been nagging at me since the first homicide. Something is not right; something just doesn't fit." "What Todd, what doesn't fit?" "These are not high profile killings Roy. In fact like the 'Disappearances' case the targets are just average 'Joes' and I don't mean 'Joe' is average. I mean this in the literal sense; they're just the average run of the mill locals - Tom, Dick and, yes, Joes." "Keep going Todd, but I haven't the foggiest idea what you're talking about."

"Roy, something is gripping me; it's right here in my gut, gnawing away at me ever since Waldo." Rambling on, Todd tried to explain. "Let's assume for the moment the Bowman as we call him didn't know his victims personally." "Okay Todd, I'm assuming."

"Now, if this makes any sense to you Roy, the killings were not committed out of revenge or for some personal reason; follow my reasoning?" "As best I can," Roy offered. "Okay, let's go further. The Bowman is bringing the killings to the attention of as many people as he can possibly conjure up." "I'm following you Lt."

"Good Roy, so would you agree with Shakespeare who said 'all the world's a stage' and that our Bowman has made Montauk his stage?" "For what purpose Lt.? Is the reaper going to put on a performance?"

Rolling his eyes, Todd said, "Yeah Roy, you could say the Bowman has put on quite a few shows but Roy think, there's something ominous here. The killer is motivated by some self-seeking sense of self righteousness. His justification for his killings is his all-holy cause." "What cause Lt?" "Think about it Roy; he's murdering hunters, agreed? "Okay, agreed." Then bam we have a change of menu; he murders two chicken farmers and what do they have in common?" Blurting out, "Hunters kill in the woods while those farmers killed in the barn?" Roy answered. "Bingo Roy, you're on a roll." "Shit Todd, this is the stuff nightmares are made of." "Yeah buddy, you got that right!" "You know Lt., it's like he's carrying out a surgical strike; know what I mean? He conducts a lightning-quick assault on his prey and like magic he vanishes; reminds me of a gray kingbird. These birds, Lt. spring into the air so fast for the catch; called aerial hawking Lt." "You birders have some imagination but I do like your analogy, Roy, especially aerial hawking.

"Let's say we have the MO, now for the why. I believe that the evidence points most definitely to a wacko, animal-loving activist." "Damn, Lt. this is creepy. Do you mean we have a deranged ego-maniac sociopath among us?" "That sums it up Roy. Well done! Hey, buddy, be careful or you might wind up writing a mystery thriller one day," Todd laughed. Roy beamed with pride and asked, "Our next move, Lt.?"

"That's a great question Roy and my answer is: we proceed the same way we did in the 'Disappearances'; hard-nosed detective work. We gotta flush him out into the open so we're going to tighten the noose, right buddy?" "Right Lt." "Trust me Roy, we'll get this prick; we took the ferryman out and yes we'll take this reaper shit down, too!" "I'm with you Lt.; we gotta end this creep's activities." "Exactly Roy and that's what we're going do. He's motivated by a delusory struggle against a piece of humanity and I promise you buddy we're going to put an end to his madness. Roy, this is a sick animal and the faster we put him down the better for all concerned.

"Hey, by the way buddy, how'd it go this morning?" "Swell Lt., just damn swell," Roy said, grinning from cheek to cheek, his blue eyes shining.

CHAPTER 23

President Justin Winchester and Vice President Marshall Held were seated at a table in the front of the dining room. Above them a sign read, "THINK WOODS SAFETY." The overflow of members filled the outer hallway and the Big Bucks Bar where Todd and Roy were on their reserved stools at Hither's end of the bar. As per normal, at any large gathering at the lodge the noise level was high; the hot topic of conversation centered on yesterday's double homicide committed at Shad Hill Farm. Indeed, the quaint hamlet was in a whirl wind of fearsome frenzy.

Hitting the mallet down three times, gave Marshall the attention of all members. After reading the previous meeting's minutes, he opened the bible and began with Psalm 91:

> **He that dwelleth in the secret
> place of the most High shall**

abide under the shadow of the
Almighty.

I will say of the Lord, He is
my refuge and my fortress: my
God; in him will I trust.

Surely he shall deliver thee
from the snare of the fowler, and
from the noisome pestilence.

He shall cover thee with his
feathers, and under his wings
shalt thou trust: his truth shall be
thy shield and buckler.

Thou shalt not be afraid for
the terror of the night; nor the
arrow that flieth by day.

Nor for the pestilence that
walketh in darkness; nor for the
destruction that wasteth at noonday.

Other than a few barking coughs and a sneeze here and
there, the entire lodge was silent as Marshall continued in
his deep, resounding voice with Psalm 23.

The Lord is my shepherd;
He maketh me to lie down in
green pastures: he leadeth me
beside the still waters.

He restoreth my soul: he leadeth
me in the path of righteousness
for his name's sake.

Yea, though I walk through

the valley of the shadow of death,
I will fear no evil: for thou art
with me: thy rod and thy staff
they comfort me.

Thou preparest a table before
me in the presence of mine enemies:
thou anointest my head
with oil; my cup runneth over.

Surely goodness and mercy
shall follow me all the days of my
life: and I will dwell in the house
of the Lord forever.

Everyone chimed in with the amen.

Justin stood, surveyed his fellow brothers, felt their anguish and knew they were looking to him for guidance. If there was one word to describe their stone-faced discomfort, he thought, it must be the word painful. In a bullet-proof voice, Justin thanked them all for attending; then began his carefully planned address.

"Friends, we are all gathered here today to pay homage to two fallen members and two farmers. When I lost my kid sister two years ago, I thought my world would end, but, it didn't, of course; life isn't fair but we all know it goes on. The sun still comes up each morning, warming mother earth, the birds break the dawn's silence and the cold moon and stars still fill the dark night sky."

No one was moving; no one was coughing. "Yes, my friends, she was killed in a hunting accident," Justin explained, to the morose group. "We are all aware this happens throughout the country. We are all hunters and we know the thrill of the chase is the foremost lure of hunting. And in the broadest sense I guess I am trying to say that hunting is a life style. Yet, it is as much of a state of mind as it is an activity.

Stopping a moment, he scanned the anxious faces, cleared his throat, and spoke slowly, "We all need better safety management no matter what our degree of hunting knowledge. Training, my friends, is the key to a successful, safe hunt. The person who killed my sister by mistake, I might add, was drunk. He didn't know the difference between a buck and my sister." Fear rippled across the room.

Taking a sip of water, Justin glanced at the uneasy gathering and continued, "Life is precious; it is beyond measure. We all are bemoaning the fact we lost four Montauk residents. But it has to stop! Yes, we have all been vulnerable to this predator called "the bowman' or as he also has been dubbed "the grim reaper." The "ferryman" paid us a visit some few years ago; now we have a new psycho who poses a far more insidious threat. Starting right now guys, you must and I repeat must hunt in groups, and that, my brothers, is the order of the day. No exceptions, agreed?"

Loud applause from the bar, hallway and dining room lasted a full minute. "You must stay alert," Justin directed, "and recognize any, even the remotest signs, of danger. You must plan escape routes and you MUST have communications with you at all times," he almost roared. "No kidding around friends, do everything you need to do to survive out there in them woods. You must stick together and use the buddy system. If you keep a good watch on your brother he will do the same for you. We Montauketts are a strong and surviving people; we are at our best when we face the worst. And so, my fellow huntsmen think smart, hunt smart and live smart."

Another round of applause resounded in the lodge while Justin gathered up forms, holding one high for all to see. "From this point forward," he continued, "you will fill out this new "Quick Response document. It has been designed for your - for all our protection. So guys, prior to going out on your hunt, complete this form and drop it off with the range officer."

Waving the sheet in his outstretched hand while the group squinted from their seats, he announced there were ten items to be addressed; "Let's go over them. First there is the time the hunt will commence. Second the exact location of the hunt, third name or names of hunting partner or partners and number four specific position of your stand or ground spot and five the same for your partner. Okay, fifth fill in chart provides for locations, sixth give numbers of hours expected to stay in the woods. Number seven, cell numbers of all persons, in group, eight gives you the ranger's phone number 668-6868; it is mandatory you check in at least twice. Nine you must report anything suspicious to the range officer and lastly, number ten, the time your hunt terminates and please be specific. And another thing, if you are not signed in at the hour designated, you will be red flagged, and listen up, if communications are not established within ten minutes, EHPD, DEC and the park police will be notified."

Looking up and out over the members, Justin asked, "Any questions?" No one raised a hand. "In closing, please remember the Three-D Tournament begins officially Monday morning; all applicants must sign in by 9:00am. Good luck to all! Oh and by the by, last year's winner, Roy Thompson, took home $10,000! Let's see if he can repeat his effort or will someone among you take possession of his sought after trophy?"

Finally Justin sat down. No one moved until Marshall stood and began clapping. Roy leaned over to Todd and remarked, "Boy, Justin's good." "Think so buddy? Sure is to the point."

For most it was a time for a drink, for some a trip to the men's room, for others a rush to get home. Justin and Marshall joined Todd and Roy.

CHAPTER 24

"That was a hell of a speech," Roy commented, shaking Justin's hand. "Thanks Roy, let's hope you all heed the warning." "Hey, buddy how long is the Three-D course this year?" "We doubled it this year Roy," Justin replied, "to almost a mile long and we added a few new twists to test your skills. In fact, we increased it from ten animal stations to twenty. Yup, there will be an assortment of electronic sensitive animals, and once shot, the kill mark or arrow entrance point will automatically register on the range officer's computer. Everyone will be observed just to make sure the rules are followed. So Roy, you will be judged by quality of shot, speed of shot and time spent on the course. Hey, you guys are good so why not step it up?"

Anxious for more information, Roy pressed on, "What type of targets?" "When you sign in for the competition you'll get a printout describing the various targets, Roy, however, Marshall here can tell you what they are; he set up the range."

Smiling warmly, a self -confident Marshall chugged into gear, naming all the targets. "I can damn well tell you Roy, you're going to enjoy my course. Each target and its shooting value will peak your craft buddy. It's my 'coup de grace;' a thing of perfection, if I do say so myself; a thing of beauty!"

The captive last year's winner was all ears. Cheerfully Marshall expounded, "You must go on the attack Roy. My range will challenge your best fighting strategy, hunting tactics and your instincts. I pride myself in creating a conflict on this course which does not determine who is left but whose arrow determines the winner."

Slapping Roy's shoulder with his tough large palm, Marshall regaled in laughter while all three just stared and wondered at his fit of hilarity. Catching his breath and looking at Roy with his handsome face he snapped, "Roy, you have no idea what is waiting for you out there! I cannot tell you in what order they come at you pal but you'll encounter the following decoy three dimensional displays:

"There will be an assortment of fowls of the air and beasts of the field," Marshall pontificated. "White tail deer, the Holy Grail which as you know is a white albino will count for a lot of points, a black bear and a brown bear, a bora, a wild big tom turkey, and then a timber wolf, coyote, a woodchuck, raccoon, a Canada goose as well as the bald eagle and a red fox, the green faced mallard, a ring-neck pheasant, the barred owl as well as the great horned owl, the red-tailed hawk, a 'pandion haliaetu'; that's Latin for osprey. So how does that whet you appetite buddy?" "Wow," shot back Roy, thrilled by the diversified array of targets.

Coyly, Marshall fired back, "I hope you've been practicing, Mr. Markmans trophy holder of last year's competition?"

Glowing with pride, Roy retorted confidently, "Marshall, just make sure you spell my name correctly on the silver trophy. It's R O Y W; the W stands for winner, Thompson."

They all laughed including Hither who was listening along with Todd and Justin. Roy sure believes in himself, she thought; I like that trait in a man. "Can I get you guys anything?" she asked now that there was a bit of a lull. Marshall, never asleep at the switch, blurted out, "Four Guinessess and four deluxe burgers and put that on Mr. Winner's here tab."

Leaning over the bar, Hither asked anxiously, "Roy are you really that good of a shot; sounds like a hell of a demanding course?" "I'm not one to brag Hither, but three years ago in the target bow shooting competition, I split an arrow already dead center in the bull's eye to win the tournament; it's called a robin split." "Isn't that hard to do?" she asked dumfounded. "It's almost impossible. You could say it's like a golfer's hole in one or like casting a buck-tail into a bass' open mouth at 100 yards off the beach." Shaking her head up and down, then back and forth she looked directly into Roy's sparking blue eyes and said, "I'm impressed!" Tuning in Todd added, "I was also in that tournament Hither and let me tell you Roy's shot was the finest shot I ever saw a bowman make!"

After they finished their burgers and ordered another round of beer, they shifted stools, and made room for Hither to sit next to Roy at the end of the bar. "I watched you as you cast out this morning, Hither; you have a strong physique, you know. How about I teach you how to shoot a compound bow?

I know I'll have you shooting arrows into the targets bull's eye in no time!"

Chirping in, Marshall agreed, "That's a fact Hither; he's damn good. In fact, he's so good I bet on him to win the Three-D outright!" Both Justin and Todd nodded, "We did, too," Todd said.

Considering the proposition for a moment but knowing she was up to the challenge, she laughed and said, "You're on Mr. Bowman Extraordinaire!" They chortled at the word, 'extraordinaire' slapping each other on their backs.

CHAPTER 25

Stuie, a life-long local, born to fish and clam it appeared, often exchanged his scallops for Jamie Miller's "red-gold" tomato sauce which he, his brother and his mother loved. Known for digging the freshest clams in Montauk, Stuie's business boomed. On this early, cold, November day with the wind and rain easing up a bit from last night's blow, Stuie was ready to go clamming.

Sipping hot coffee and digging into a scallops and eggs breakfast, he knew that the clams would be pushed into what he dubbed his "critters hollow" which was a large cavity in the back of Lake Montauk. Between mouthfuls, he talked out loud to himself, "Yeah, them there critters will be filling my hollow by the hundreds. Shit, I found that pit by chance and it always pays off!"

As he put his mug and plate in the sink, he repeated his clamming mantra, "The God's of Crustaceans have never failed me."

Suiting up, he headed out the door and drove to the far end of the lake. "Harvest time boys," he announced, to all he planned to catch. Muscular legs pushed through the smoke-gray water with little difficulty. He loved his craft although he knew the life of a bayman wasn't easy.

The Bowman made a right turn off East Lake Drive onto 27 and drove west towards the village as the "urge" thundered through like shooting hungry spasms. Suddenly, making a hair-pin turn onto West Lake and a right onto Old West Lake, then spotting a truck parked on the side of the road, triggered an even more salivating lust to kill which could only be satisfied by blood. Pressing the brake down hard, the truck came to a quick stop.

While observing the target, clamming with a large rake and a basket floating nearby, it was only moments before the bayman turned to shore and trudged slowly through the gray angry waters. Waving at the bayman from the truck, the Bowman watched as the clammer lifted his basket and waved back with his rake. Approaching the pickup, Stuie greeted the stranger with a "Good Morning, you're up early." "Oh, I'm just hunting around," replied the Bowman, "you never know when you'll come upon something to shoot," feeling the itch; the ugly bolt of anticipation deep inside, but added, "by the look of what's in your basket, the clamming seems to be damn good." "You bet," Stuie laughed jovially, "this is my fourth load," as he lifted the full heavy basket into the back of his pickup.

Watching the bayman's powerful body leaping effortlessly into the rear of the tailgate and sliding his golden treasure into his ice cooler, the hunter listened as Stuie half muttered to himself.

"Damn, I estimate near three hundred clams," as he handled them cautiously, not to break their shells. "You know a cracked shell is a dead clam and a dead clam is worthless. These here clams are very cooperative," he laughed, "you see they have no tongues and aren't talkative; just make suckling, bubbling sounds." "Why the sounds?" the stranger asked. "'Cause they're just taking in air; the 'breath of life' as they say."

"Hey, I love Manhattan clam chowder; can't get that in the west. Can I buy two dozen?" "Sure thing; two dozen clams, coming right up, the freshest clams in Montauk!" "Make it three dozen; I'm also fond of baked clams." "You got it pal," the ever accommodating bayman answered. Vaulting out of his truck and handing the clams to the hunter, Stuie smiled his wide, toothy grin while adjusting his snug ski cap and said, "Since this is my first sale of the day, I'll give them to you wholesale; thirty-five cents per clam." The Bowman handed over the money and asked, "You going back in?" "Yep, you bettcha," he chuckled, "I'll clam until I net the last tongue-less critter." "You cold in the water?" "Nah, not in this waterproof dry suit." "Sure, go figure; the things you learn in Montauk," and walked away.

Heading back to his grid, wondering what the odd stranger was about, a burst of brilliant light shone through the dark gray clouds, which he took as a good omen, for his next catch. "Just me and them tongue-less ones," he murmured again as he turned up the volume of his headset to hear one of his favorite songs, 'Delilah,' singing, "Oh Delilah, what you do to me......" lowering his rake into the water, working it back and forth.

Stopping the truck at the stop sign before going any further, the Bowman decided it was the time to turn around and revisit the bayman, thinking, "all I need is five minutes." Slipping out of the truck and moving gracefully and quickly into the eight foot bamboo grass, the hunter took a reading with the hand held range finder, making a 65 yard adjustment to the bow sight.

Taking aim through the peep hole, sighting the bayman moving as if he were dancing, made the target a challenge but the shot to come sweeter. A quickening of the heart, the racing of the pulse, the euphoric breathless excitement, enhanced the moment when squeezing the release, the arrow sped along its fatal path.

The arrow penetrated Stuie's back with bone-chilling splitting power; a quick kill concluded the Bowman who watched as the arrow's kinetic energy pushed the bayman forward. His rake fell as he tumbled into the bloody wash. A pernicious grin appeased the executioner's shivering body. Talk about grim, this reaper was the Satan of Death.

CHAPTER 26

It was an outgoing tide and Captain Christopher Krauthammer had only one thing on his mind; delicious winter flounder. Well aware that the flounder season was between April
through the end of May, he was fed up with government rules
and regulations, and resented the lousy bureaucrats who cut
deep into his and Montauk's fishing fleet's pockets. He liked
to think of his plan as a kind of "Boston Tea Party" retaliation.
Using a secret technique to catch his beloved fish, it would appear to anyone nosey enough to wonder, that he was scratching
for clams.

Aboard his twenty eight foot Grady White named "The
Red Witch," he maneuvered out from Gone Fishin' Marina at
the north end of Lake Montauk, turned port into the channel marked by red and green buoys, and cruised to his pre-set
positioning location to the exact spot of a large flounder hole.
It was 7:00am, the conditions were perfect; a slight drizzle,

with winds at 10 mph, and no fog. After last night's blow, Captain Krauthammer monitored the radar scope for any logs, wooden planks or other debris which may have been washed up or blown off the nearby beaches.

Halfway along to the fishing area, the Captain's deflection modulation display sounded a hazard warning indicating the target image was two hundred yards off port side. Slowing down to two knots then peering through his binoculars, he was startled to see what appeared to be a large inflated rubber tube holding a clam basket. "Good God," he uttered, "could it be possible a bayman drowned?" Kicking up speed to twenty five knots and easing the Grady White portside towards the tube, he went into neutral, then reverse and back to neutral, gliding to an idle beside the body.

Rushing out of the cabin, he grabbed a boat pole and gently hooked the lifeless fellow. Almost immediately he saw an arrow sticking into the clammer's back; the unnaturalness and gruesomeness of such a sight causing him panic and horror. Trying to keep focus, he swallowed hard forcing back the churning bile in his throat, clutched the spring line, easing it over the victim's back, and with his boat hook secured the end. After tying a slip knot and fastening the body portside, he ran back to the cabin, grabbed a beer, drank it all in one gulp before he snatched his radio mike and turned to Channel 16.

"Coast Guard, Coast Guard, this is the boat Red Witch at waypoint ------ , he snapped, "please come back, over!" Coxman Waters, hearing the urgency in the caller's voice, answered calmly, "Red Witch, this is Montauk Coast Guard Station. Please advise us of your situation and location, over." The captain's voice crackled, "This is Captain Krauthammer of the Red Witch. I have a clammer tied to portside of my boat. Appears to be a victim of a bow and arrow shot; location north of Montauk Yacht Club, over." "Is victim deceased, Captain Krauthammer?" "Shit, yes, or at least appears to be. No movement, blood oozing out from arrow wound, over." "Sir, drag anchor, stay put, we'll be right there, over." "Copy that, over and out."

Ten minutes later the twenty eight foot Coast Guard cutter pulled along side. The captain relieved but sickened watched as the body and the clam basket were placed in the stern of the boat. The little he knew he repeated for the brief interview and as quickly as they had arrived they departed. Captain Krauthammer set his speed at twenty knots and with a second beer in hand headed for his berth at the marina. Thoughts of flounder had vanished.

CHAPTER 27

A relaxed and confident Lieutenant Todd Miller, with a grin on his face said, "How about heading up to Jack's, Roy? We need some breakfast eats; what say you?" "Count me in boss; I'm starved! You know Lt. starting work at 7:00am has thrown off my breakfast routine." "You'll get use to it buddy; most of our Bowman's activities seem to occur in the early morning so we have to be on the job, just in case there's another…. uh…. incident," he explained without actually saying the repulsive word 'killing'.

In no time they settled in the cruiser, Roy turned on the ignition, glanced at Todd and said, "Buckle up, Buttercup!" For a long second there was silence, then "Wait just a minute, WHAT did YOU just say to ME, Sergeant?" "Just reminding you sir; you know, safety first Lt. "Roy replied, with hardly a straight face. "Better forget that shit!" Todd growled, staring out the passenger window.

After a silent, speedy ride, a contrite Roy said, "Aw Lt. I was joking with you. Heard that on a commercial last night and been practicing, pretty good right?" "Yeah, real funny Roy."

Sitting in their usual spot at Jack's and in a few minutes looking up from his blueberry pancakes which he ordered in memory of Waldo, for after all, he sure would be missed for a long while to come, Todd noticed a puzzled look on Roy's face. "What Roy?" Barely controlling his excitement, Roy whispered, "Don't turn around Lt. I'm looking at smooth flat outsoles," his hand slipping to his pistol.

"There are two camouflaged hunters sitting up front at the counter; one of them has flat outsoles, Todd." "Are you sure Roy?" "No doubt about it; definitely flat soles." "Which one Roy?" "Guy on the right." "How about the other guy?" "No, he's got normal boot treads." "Okay Roy, go outside to the cruiser, call for back up; no sirens or lights. We'll make our move when they get here."

"Roger Lt."

The Montauk police sub-station arrived within minutes. As eight officers entered Jack's led by Sergeant Roy Thompson, a startled Jack barked, "What the hell......" Lieutenant Miller joined them as they all surrounded the two hunters; cutting off any escape route. "Good morning sir," Todd politely addressed the big guy on the right, "Been hunting in Montauk this morning; shot any turkeys?" "What's it to you?" the hunter lashed back. "I'm Lieutenant Todd Miller of the EHPD, answer the question!" Hearing nothing, Todd continued, "Look buddy, we can do this back at police headquarters; it's up to you."

Scowling, the hunter replied, "Saw shit out there this morning," taking another dose of coffee, "and they call Montauk a hunting paradise; some paradise," he laughed, nudging his friend's shoulder. "What's your name sir?" Todd asked. Muttering then looking up at Todd, "What's this about? Aint done nothin' wrong." "No one said you did mister; what's your name? And this is the last time I'm gonna ask!"

"Jake Longfellow." Todd and the rest of the officers shook their heads almost in disbelief. Redirecting his question, Todd asked to see his driver's license. "In my truck," answered Longfellow. Todd eyed Roy tilting his head toward the cruiser and gave him the go ahead signal. As Roy left to run Longfellow's name, the indignant clown yelled, "I've got my rights. What the hell is this about?" "We're conducting a murder investigation sir." "Murder, MURDER," he screamed, "Come to think of it, I heard some shit about some bowman; all over the news, right? Told you I aint done nothin' wrong," and wagging his finger, "I know my rights!" "Yes sir, I'm sure you do," Todd's calm voice retorted, "but I have a few more questions," then spotting Roy returning from the cruiser, he said, "just sit tight Mr. Longfellow; I'll be right back."

With the information from Roy, he resumed the conversation in a somber manner. "Now, I see you live in North Willport," he began. Jake shrugged his shoulders nonchalantly, "Yeah, so what? Is that a crime?" "No sir, but you've had run-ins with the law." "So, I've been clean three years; not even a parkin' ticket." " Sir, that's good, keep it that way. Now sir, is that your foot wear you have on?" With a blank stare, the dumbfounded Jake replied, "What the hell; you talkin' bout my bowling shoes?" A disappointed Todd glanced over at his partner's discouraged face.

"Sir, where are your hunting boots?" "My truck, I changed 'cause my feet sweat a lot and these here don't hurt my calluses."

Not the Bowman, not a killer, just a prick, Todd concluded. One more stab for good measure, he figured: "What type of arrow do you shoot?" Jake snapped back, "Crimson Talons XT, aluminum 500 grain weight. Them arrows shoot real good." "Thank you, sir. You and your friend here are free to leave, sorry for the inconvenience." "Not the last of it, copper, you'll be hearin' from my barrister!" The two hunters scurried out the door; the show was over.

"Well fellas, win some; lose some, as they say," Todd commented, while his cell phone rang. Answering before the last ring, he appeared dazed as he listened to the voice describing the discovery of another body. Snapping the phone closed, he announced, "Lieutenant Minx and his forensic team are on their way to view another vic. Let's roll boys." Jack walked quickly over to Todd and asked, "Who Todd?" "Some clammer up in Lake Montauk; can't be Stuie, everybody knows him."

CHAPTER 28

Agonizing over his evidence chart, Todd thought, what am I missing here; wringing his hands in frustration. Thoroughly scrutinizing every detail of his hand written notes on Crime Scene One, Two and Three he winced again; what am I not seeing? Applying his skills to the time-honored, hard nosed detective work was a system in which he expected results.

Once again he methodically reviewed Crime Scene One: location, victim, time of attack, perpetrator and evidence. The last three items in the evidence column were baffling; no discernable traces, no finger prints/shoe prints, no tread marks. His eyes narrowed even more so as they shifted to Crime Scene Two where the scenario was the same. Shooting over to Scene Three, he read the same facts. Then, like a bolt out of the blue, presto, it jumped at him! Glowing with triumph across his taut face and with an explosive laugh, "By God Roy, that's what I'm missing!"

Yawning and lifting his head slowly from the mounds of paperwork Roy remarked, "What Lt?" "No hard clues Roy, that's what's absent from my chart - no clues!" "Oh, oh, right Lt." Roy agreed, "no hard clues." "No prints or traces," Todd continued frowning, "because the Bowman is wearing gloves and a special camouflage suit and scentless lotion." On a roll now with Roy all eyes and ears, "No truck at crime scene; however no shoe prints implies special boots," he almost shouted, "and guess what, our creep is wearing smooth outsoles; no wedges, weaves, slip resistant traction pimples or angles in the heel design!"

"You figured all that out just from looking at your chart, Todd?"

"You bet buddy." "But Lt. wearing boots with smooth outsoles just doesn't make sense. You know that hunting in Montauk's rough ground, Todd, means you need all the gripping power and support you can get." "Shit Roy," Todd snapped, "You think our fiend is walking around barefoot, mocking us, saying ouch no shoes?" "Shit Todd, this crackpot must have elephant feet." "No Roy," Todd laughed, "this wacko is using a deception that is comfortable; this scum of the earth is wearing a special boot!" "Ahhh," Roy guessed , "flat soles, like uh, uh, like a moccasin?"

"Call Lieutenant Minx, have him check with all boot and shoe manufacturers who produce flat outsole foot wear; tell him to start up the island and work his way out here." "Am on it Lt." "And another thing Roy, check with FBI - Advance Name Identification System and have them feed in the names 'bowman' and 'grim reaper'." "Got it Lt." "It's a long shot, but what the hell; this is what the game is about." "Think we'll come up with something?" "We gotta try, okay buddy?" Todd said softly, with a hopeful smile.

CHAPTER 29

"Where to Lt.?"

"Old West Lake Drive; Coast Guard located the clammer's truck opposite the lake Roy, and Lieutenant Minx is on his way with his team. Coast Guard is securing the crime scene so here we go again buddy."

"All these killings Todd; do you think the perp is murdering for some kind of kinky pleasure thing?" "No Roy, our Bowman has a cause. I figure this bastard kills whenever it serves his interest. What's more frightening Roy is that it's difficult to anticipate his moves. If I'm right and I pray I'm wrong, if we don't stop him soon, we're going to have more corpses on our hands, and that means more families altered forever Roy. It's like throwing a pebble into the lake; the ripples spread out and affect so much, if you get what I mean."

"Lt. you're never wrong; I'm following you."

"Let me tell you something buddy, you're the best partner an investigator could ask for. Trust me Roy, we'll get this prick. He's not invincible; he's due for a slip up. The wheels of time are on our side and I got the feeling that his luck is running out."

A beaming Roy also blushed when Todd also commented, "I wouldn't work a murder case unless I knew you were there Sergeant Thompson, covering my back." Roy's heavy foot got them to the yellow taped crime scene in no time but Minx and one of the guys had already begun their investigating.

Walking around the back area of the lake, opposite from where the truck was parked, Lieutenant Minx enjoyed working the crime scene, getting a better feel for what may have ultimately occurred.

He knew that clam diggers would usually go into the water just up to their butts, particularly at high tide. Also Minx was aware of the habit of the clams to remain in deep water so that when the tide went out, they would still be protected under a foot or so of water, keeping their enemies, the seagulls, at bay.

Minx directed one of his team to go out to a distance where the water would be over his knees. Mentally calculating the height of the deceased which he had obtained from the coroner, he figured where Bob was standing to be the most likely spot where the clammer stood early that morning.

Now comes the tricky part, he thought. Knowing the arrow entered dead center in the victim's back and rejecting the notion that the Bowman would have stood at the thirty foot wide entrance to the lake where he was standing, since obviously there was no growth for cover, he surveyed the area to his right. This, too, he judged an unlikely area, for again, the coverage wasn't adequate. Glancing with his skillful, forensic eyes to the left, Minx reasoned that this spot seemed to be a perfect place to hide and take a shot. Oh yes, he said to himself, the eight foot high bamboo grass provided complete camouflage!

Getting to work and performing a grid search of the area with heightened suspense in the air, Minx was at top form, eager to start his hunt. Adorning a special lavender forensic suit so as not to contaminate the crime scene and wearing shoes that had been altered with detailed ridges in order to distinguish his tracks from those of the perpetrators, Lieutenant Minx was fired up, ready to enjoy the challenge.

From years of pacing grids, he moved like a lynx focusing on every inch of the ground below, gradually reaching the water's edge.

Pretending to be the shooter, he took 'aim' with his index finger at his team member, the 'target' standing in the water, off to his right. The angle, laterally incorrect, Minx shouted to Bob, motioning him to move left. Moving ten feet left, Minx raised his hand stopping Bob; that's better, mumbling to himself; walking nine paces to the right. Once again he aimed and took the shot. Bingo! Confident now of the angle, he turned around to observe the grass and noticed a subtle impression within the reeds. "Gotcha!" he just about yelled.

Remaining ever so focused, he walked six feet back to the edge of the vegetation impression. No doubt about it, this was the Bowman's exact shooting location. Making a careful inspection of the site, Minx observed how some of the grass was disturbed and pushed into the sand. As he leaned down taking samples of the broken bamboo with his wooden forceps, and placing the clues into his clear plastic evidence bag, he knew that in the world of forensic science, the word 'impossible' did not exist.

After recording the scene on his digital camera, Minx concentrated on his surroundings in order to establish the killer's means of escape. Tenaciously he examined the bamboo for any clues it might reveal. Determined to locate the wormhole the perp squirmed through, he had to envision the line of direction and the line of march, just as the forensic textbooks recommended. As he watched how the breeze whipped the reeds, he noticed they tilted towards the right. Then scrutinizing the impression once again, the forensic ace detected that some of the grass appeared to have been gently nudged to the left. I've outwitted the bastard, his foxy instinct told him! He knew that he had discovered the wormhole that the perp had followed as he headed away from his killing arena.

Walking gingerly through the maze, observing the high tide had not reached the shore line, he stopped all of a sudden, and stooped to focus on a slight impression. Yes! He knew this was a shoeprint!

Not wanting to disturb the ground, if there were more, he stood in his tracks and called to Bob for the print kit. Concentrating on the area immediately surrounding him, it was only moments before his eyes caught a tiny patch of camouflage cloth, measuring he judged roughly, one inch by one and a half inches. From the proximity to ground level, he concluded it must be a leg tear.

Suited up and standing next to Minx, holding the print kit, Bob quite agitated to be in a forensic suit, and feeling mighty claustrophobic like a squirrel in a cage, had to admit his excitement for the clues were what they both lived for. The two had an obsessive fascination to possess every crumb of physical evidence they could find. After molding the shoe impression, Bob bagged it and did the same with the tattered cloth clinging to the reed, before they ambled off deeper along the wormhole hunting for more evidence.

Lieutenant Minx announced jubilantly, "We have a shoe-print and what appears to be trace material from broken bamboo grass," holding up the two plastic evidence bags. "Excellent," Todd, exclaimed, "damn excellent!" Before Todd could say anything more, Lieutenant Minx fired back, "My report will be on Sergeant Thompson's desk early tomorrow morning," "Finally a break; you do good work, you two," commended Lieutenant Miller.

CHAPTER 30

Leafing through the latest issue of the outdoor hunting newspaper, Justin stopped when he heard foot steps approaching his office. Anxious to meet the girl he was planning to interview, he was delighted to see his personal secretary, Mrs. Malaprop entering his office followed by a very pretty girl who must be Meaghan O'Murphy. After reading the want ad in Dan's Papers for the RN position, she was just as eager to meet Justin Winchester.

All six foot three inches of him rose up like a tower and putting on his best smile he looked down at her, extended his hand, and enthusiastically welcomed Miss O'Murphy to the Montauk Rod and Gun Lodge. Sliding her hand firmly into his and beaming up at him she exclaimed excitedly, "What a beautiful lodge! I've been to hunting lodges before but nothing compares or even comes close to this place. It's so rustic and wooden," she continued wide-eyed, "the redwood, it's breath taking, Mr. Winchester!" "Thanks, it was a town effort and we are lucky to have some big benefactors who are members. The redwood is nice; imported from California. Umm...., we're not formal around here; please call me Justin." "Fine, Justin and I'm Meaghan."

Noticing the lightning between the two and smiling with her best stenographer grin, Mrs. Malaprop knew when it was time to leave and as she started to close the office door, which by the way she never did, she caught Justin's eye and gave him a wink, thinking, oh boy, to be young again!

He took a fancy to her right away; in fact he was totally infatuated. Their eyes met again; hers he thought were a peacock blue. Only after he stopped staring into them did he notice that her wide smile glowed and set off two perfect dimples near the corners of her lips. She looked strong and seemed to be alert to her surroundings.

Must be 5' 10" he decided and maybe 130 pounds and he liked the way she wore her sandy colored hair in a high ponytail with some strands trickling down the sides of her face. Free of make up she looked natural but who knows, maybe her pink cheeks wore blush, he thought. No rings but maybe she has a boyfriend or maybe, God forbid, a husband.

Bouncing these scenarios back and forth, he was unfortunately reminded of a girlfriend he had almost loved two years ago, and the time when he couldn't get a hold of her for six days. It disgusted him to remember that on the sixth night he parked near her house, and waited three hours for her to return from wherever she had been. When he spotted a truck pulling into her driveway, he drove up to the edge and got out. The driver put the truck in reverse, flew down the drive and turned left, peeling down the road. The driver was her ex boyfriend. Following right behind them, then parallel to them he eased them to the side, jumped out of his truck and started to pound his fists on the driver's window. Rocking his vehicle back and forth the guy managed to pull away, dragging a few bushes along with them. Yelling curses at out of shot ears, he rolled along home in a butt-horned mood.

Gazing up at him with a puzzled look, wondering why he was so silent after what seemed like a very long time, he finally said, "Sorry Meaghan, it's just that you are a treat to behold because, you see, most nurses I've interviewed this week fit the likes of a Nurse Kratchitt." Both laughed; her white teeth shining. "Why thank you Justin, I'll take that as a big compliment!" "Now let's make you comfortable; how about a cup of coffee?" "Love one," as she moved toward the leather couch, "just regular is fine."

"Back in five," he said, desperate to get out of his office for a moment and regain control, afraid she could tell how nervous and excited he felt.

Funny, she thought, I feel as if he was studying me and staring for so long, why? He sure has that tall, dark, handsome look but he's a serious guy with a kind of softness about him, I think. What a gentle voice for such a big hunk and no ring is a good omen, but I'm here for the job, not to go crazy over the boss, not now anyway.

Interrupting her thoughts with his "Here we go Meaghan," bringing her back to where she needed to be, she smiled and began sipping the extraordinary Mocha Java Justin had made. "Your perfume," he commented, "I like it, what is it?" I get it through Cabelas outdoor magazine; Wild Grape, I like a natural scent." Putting two and two together real fast, he asked, "You hunt?" "Absolutely, my Pa taught my brother Buck and me how to shoot a compound bow when we were kids."

Justin's heart and mind were racing faster than before, yet catching himself, he quickly brought them to the purpose of their meeting. "Let me explain what your duties will be here Meaghan." My duties, she thought, thank God I'm in; no more bed pans and Code Blues for me!

After Justin's detailed outline of her nursing responsibilities at the lodge he summed it up with, "Any questions, Meaghan?" She replied, "When do I start?" "Right now!" he answered emphatically, "Welcome Aboard!"

With a sigh and gently easing herself to the back of the couch, hoping Justin couldn't read her mind, she was pleased when he asked, "Hey, I've got a great idea Meaghan, let's shoot some arrows." Shrugging in a girlish gesture, "Sure thing, Justin, I'm game, but just one thing, how about a quarter an arrow?" "You're on!" Justin announced as they quickly stood up. "Do you know what the word arrow means, Justin?" Meaghan asked coyly. "No, I don't but clue me in." Very slowing and carefully Meaghan proudly said, "ALWAYS, READY, RE-MEMBER, ONE WINNER," with her peacock eye winking at him and before he could speak she said, "I hope you have a pocket full of quarters!" "Oh, I guess you've been practic-ing," he laughed. "You might say that; both my brother and father are out of quarters and my mom hid her change purse." "Hmmmm….. looks like I've met my match. Oh, and let me tell you that we have a lodge rule; it states WINNER BUYS LOSER DINNER!"

"No way," she fired back, "you just made that up!" "No, no," grabbing his rule book from the shelf closest to them, quickly thumbing to page fourteen and turning the book so she could see, he read Rule L118. Astonished, she looked at his very serious face, whispering so as to not break the spell, "and who pray tell wrote this book?" Bending down, almost nose to nose, his Brut cologne tingling, "I wrote the rules book; there are no losers in this lodge, at least not as long as I am president."

Experiencing a kind of heart stimulant she believed, and wondering if this was the parent of fate that had brought them together, she was encouraged by her warm feelings of well-being, great expectations and high hopes which she knew would lead her to shoot for the stars.

"Boy, you smell good," she said aloud. "Oops," her hands covering her smiling mouth. Chuckling and staring into her wide smiling eyes, Justin said, "Let's go sport," thinking, "I hope this chipmunk won't run off on me!"

CHAPTER 31

Maneuvering his SUV carefully as he backed out of his long driveway on to Navy Road, Todd glanced up into the turbulent smoky dark gray clouds out of the northeast moving quickly over Fort Pond Bay. The squall clouds were heavy with moisture and temperature on the down-swing. As soon as the mercury hit the right degree, these swollen billowing masses, caught by the teeth of the wind, would empty their white fury with a passion. Ominously, he estimated the ceiling low with winds at thirty five to forty knots.

Damn, he barked to himself, just what we don't need; the tension in town is bad enough. Shit, couldn't the weather cooperate? The hamlet was in fear; panic was the pace of the day. As he drove along his mind was fixed on the dire circumstances and he was anxious to chart the clues that Minx had gathered to date on the fifth crime scene.

Evidence, especially hard evidence such as a murderer's finger prints found at a crime scene, a license plate number, video tape of actual crime, a weapon with prints etc. would break the case wide open. Yet Todd was not optimistic about what Minx had found since it was categorized as soft evidence and included a partial print impression, a piece of cloth, dust-soiled particles and trace fibers. Although extremely important and would be utilized to its fullest as a beneficial aid that may help develop other leads, the evidence so far was not considered a case buster.

Todd knew only too well that just some of what they had could be used in sketching out a profile of the Bowman. By charting the evidence, categorizing and quantifying it you had an organized starting point where repeated studying might possibly give a lead to the identity of the killer. Talk about putting Humpty Dumpty back together again, Todd had 'slim pickins' from which to work.

With all the resources available to him, it was Lieutenant's Minx's role that was the most valuable in the ongoing investigation. From years of experience, Minx knew exactly what to look for, what to bag and break down. Dubbed the "Case Buster" his fellow officers fondly called him CB. In the past, as soon as Todd received the Lieutenant's forensic report, he began to analyze and plan the case direction, accompanied by what he termed "a time to think, think, think". Todd loved the maze; pouring carefully over the clues.

Finally, his mental ramblings ceased when he came to a full stop in between two white lines where the sign "Restricted Parking Lieutenant" welcomed him. Stepping out into the lashing cold wind, that quickly mummified his warm handsome face, he could hardly see the swirling white snow, as he plunged ahead to the door.

Sergeant Roy Thompson looked up from Minx's report as Todd entered the Control Center. "Wind got you Lt.?" a cheerful, smiling Roy asked. A disheveled Todd, flicking hair up off his face, grumbled a "Good Morning Sergeant," hung up his jacket and walked over to Roy's desk. "Guess what?" Roy said urgently. "What Roy, I pray Minx found something real hard from yesterday's evidence?" "Hey, Lt. I just got the report ten minutes ago, CB himself delivered it. I'm on page two of ten; don't be in such a hurry Lt." he laughed.

Walking toward his chart, shaking his head and chuckling, Todd asked, "Well then, by the devilish look on your face, and your mighty fine smile there buddy, something must be up with Miss Hither, right Sergeant?" "Damn Lt. you're good!" Taking a sip of his coffee while leaning back in his chair, then clearing his throat, Roy began: "Well Todd, I gave Hither her first compound bow lesson yesterday after work," the beaming Roy announced. "Yeah Todd, I started her at a forty five pound pull and showed her how to drop the bow naturally after each shot." "Good way to begin buddy." "Yeah, I think so and the target was set at twenty five yards, right, so she picked up on the proper breathing technique after I told her how to exhale, then how to release her arrow without jerking the bow, you know." Another swig of coffee and Roy continued, "After a lot of shots, I showed her how to adjust for yardage, you know, tuning up her bow sight for tighter arrow groupings." "Right on the mark, you are Roy." "You know Todd, for a beginner she's picking it up real fast; must be inherited from her Indian genes," then, holding up his hand, his fingers making a perfect circle, " boy she ripped one into the target with arrow number forty; no bulls eye but she connected!" a proud Roy explained. Talk about pride, he was grinning from cheek to cheek. And knowing Roy so well, Todd kept himself in check and just smiled approvingly at the right times, knowing there surely was more to come.

Puffed up with Todd's obvious interest in his tutorial accomplishments, Roy gabbed on. "I have her on a practice schedule of fifty arrows a day, working to one hundred; pretty good right?" "You bettcha buddy!" "Well, my goal is to build up her shooting muscles and then give her a seventy five pound pull."

"Sounds like a winning program to me!" Todd sang out. "Lt, I'll have Hither in the bulls' eye in two weeks!" "Hey, Roy, Mr. Best Shot in Montauk and trophy holder, my confidence is in you."

A delighted Todd hadn't seen his partner this happy in a long time. This girl, he thought, is bringing out the best in him. In fact, he further surmised, Hither was a whiff of fresh air in Roy's life. "Okay buddy it's down to business; you concentrate on Minx's crime scene report, I need some hard facts for the Grim Reaper chart."

"On it, I'm on it Lt."

As Todd shuffled papers at his desk he noticed the cover story in Dan's Papers, titled in black, bold letters: LOCAL CLAMER STUIE ARCBOGAST SLAIN BY FIENDISH BOWMAN'S

GRIM REAPER CARBON ARROW. Scanning the page, Todd picked out several gruesome words used to describe the fifth killing, got up and returned to his chart. Calmly surveying the clues once again and once more juggling the pieces of the puzzle in his head, the same question, 'what am I missing,' continued to gnaw at him. Who knows, maybe crime scene five's evidence will unlock some of the mystery, he hoped. But then again a curious scenario, flickering in and out of his mind, where he thought that perhaps the killer had wanted to kill for a long time but didn't act upon the urge until Montauk, could be leading to something.

As far as Todd knew there was not another known case like this in the nation or for that matter the world. So the burning question, what is there in Montauk that set this creep off?" It's as if someone or something gave this bastard permission to kill, Todd mused. I need to put my finger on what trauma or set of circumstances triggered this horrible, painful sequence of events. For what purpose does the Bowman revel in taking human life? Possibly there's an ego problem or a sexual dysfunction. Maybe this psychopath just enjoys killing for the thrill of it. For all I know the Grim Reaper is going for the Crown of Death; to be the best of the best.

Continuing to pace back and forth his ideas seemed to scatter in all directions but nothing clicked. His gray eyes, the color of a sea gull's wing, flipping over the chart found nothing new. Yet a pattern of a single victim followed by multiple victims, with the most recent a single killing, caused him to wonder if the Bowman would prey on a double target again. Beads of sweat dripped from his brow as he also wondered if he had hit on the behavioral pattern of this psycho. If I could figure out why certain locals were the marks maybe I could get ahead of this demon. Clearly this organized killer who is smart and slick has me baffled. But one thing is evident, at least in my book, another personality is assumed when the urge to kill becomes unavoidable.

"Got it Lt." Roy said, looking up from Minx's report. "Great Roy, I need all the help I can get," reaching out for the folder. "Just for your information, Todd, Lieutenant Minx did the best job he could manage with what little soft evidence he bagged." "Yeah, CB is truly a miracle worker up there in his crime lab. I remember when he told me how he busted a murder case wide open five years ago with just one human hair he vacuumed up at a crime scene."

Walking over to Roy's desk and deciding to get off his feet he sat down across from his partner. "You know Roy, our slippery eel perp leaves nothing to vacuum up and what makes it even more troublesome the freak works outdoors. "Sure does complicate the case ten fold, Lt." "And by the by Roy, this guy is a master bowman who uses deceptions and illusions. Follow me now Roy, yesterday our **B**owman slipped up because, Roy, the turf was different, right?" "Following you, boss." "Okay, now didn't the bamboo reeds rip a piece of cloth and didn't the sand show a shoe impression?" "Yeah, but what about the farm, Lt.?" "Good question buddy but what surrounds the farm?" "Oh yeah, woods," Roy blurted out. "Just maybe I'm fooling myself but I'm getting a better feel for this freak. In the game of chess Roy, your adversary expects you to exploit his weakness, okay, now I intend to prevail over our enemy by using the very same strength the Bowman has against him; if you follow me." "Jesus Lt., that's some strategy!"

"Let's see what we have here." With his discriminating eyes, Todd reviewed Roy's carefully chosen notes, selecting only the most relative information. Except for the sounds of the felt tip pen against the board and the crinkling of Roy's yellow paper notes, the room was silent. Every now and then Todd would stand back, studying each detail of the new evidence. Finally, breaking his train of thought Todd said earnestly, "Good job Roy. Even though it's not much, buddy, we're moving in the right direction." "Thanks Lt., looks like you did a pretty good job yourself," Roy replied as he moved over to the center of the chart. "Okay, here we go, Roy," Todd announced as he began to read the chart aloud.

CRIME SCENE FIVE

Location:
.Hamlet of Montauk
.Old West Lake Drive
.Lake Montauk

Victim:
.Stuart Arcbogast
.White Male
.age 29 years old

Time of Attack:
.Between 5:00am - 7:00am
.Friday, November19th.

Perpetrator:
.The Bowman AKA
.The Grim Reaper
.Victim killed by
 carbon arrow 500 grain

Evidence:

.Blood type O Positive
.One shoe impression on
sand - right foot
.Patch of camouflage cloth
measuring one inch by one
and a half inches; appears cloth
came from leg of perp.
.Camouflage is patented after Real
Gore-Tex hunting wear.
.No tell tail trace and fiber
clues on bamboo reeds; they
were destroyed by salt water.
.Dusty sand attributed to Mtk.
.Gray magnetite sand attributed
to Mid-Western territory.
.Soil and fibers indigenious to Mtk.
.Multiple and single victim pattern.

"You can see Roy that the time of attack in all five cases is pretty much the same." "Meaning our Bowman works the early shift?" asked Roy. "Right-0 buddy." In order to beef up the surveillance Todd asked Roy to make the necessary calls to Sergeant Manny Vila at the Parks Department, Lieutenant Luke Hall at State Troopers and Lt. Reese Goodfellow at the Sheriff's Department with the emphasis on morning patrols in the woods, the lake and the beaches. He knew it was time to tighten the noose.

Reviewing Lt. Minx's theories silently, Todd then laid it out for his partner. "Roy, Lt. Minx concluded from the eleven inch foot shoe size and depth of the impression that our boy's height is between 5'10" and 6'1" with a normal build wearing flat shoes. He also ran the camouflage cloth through the gas Chromolograph/Mass Spectrometer. This machine, Roy, isolated the cloth's elements into compounds and identified them and the results spike a bit of interest because he found dusty sand and that means the Bowman's been on our south and north beaches."

Nodding, Roy paid close attention, for it was during these kinds of investigative explanations he felt unsure. Nothing like this had happened in Montauk except, of course, the murders of three years ago. Watching Todd pouring coffee from his thermos, Roy could smell the Mocha Java, Todd's favorite that Jamie often fixed for him. "Curiously enough buddy, there were also traces of smooth gray magnetite sand from the mid-western territory; go figure that one." Roy shrugged his shoulders. "Maybe this suggests the psycho was out west on vacation and went hunting." "Could be," agreed Roy. "Let's hand that over to Justin; have him check with the airlines, see if anyone booked a flight from the East End." "Roger Lt." "However Roy, the soil traces are indigenous only to Montauk's forests. Wild grape and shad fibers were well imbedded into the cloth. Okay, Roy, I am sure that our boy lives here and no doubt has been active in the woods, right?" Walking over to the water cooler, Roy remarked, "Remember where the ferryman lived Todd?" "Good point Roy; assign a couple of detectives to check that out and one last thing buddy, this single and multiple pattern, if it's a behavioral pattern, it could mean the Bowman might be setting up for doubles again." "Jesus Todd, I pray you're wrong."

"We gotta think outside the box just like the creep. Tell Justin to increase all double hunting parties to triples." "Roger Lt." as he bent down for a slurp of water.

Todd answered the phone, listened for a moment and hung up. "Let's roll Roy." "What; not again?" "Relax buddy, the chief wants us up in his office for a briefing on the case." "Damn Lt, every time the phone rings I get spooked; it's out of hand."

CHAPTER 32

Lunch time at the Montauk School was from 11:30 am to twelve. From twelve to 1:00pm was recess; exercise and sports time. Today the sun was at high noon in the azure blue cloudless sky, its golden rays curving down, warming the cool soccer and baseball fields below that were surrounded by a barrier of woods which acted as a natural fence.

As twenty nine year old Father Flanigan walked on to the baseball field, he thought it was an ideal day for the children to be playing one of his favorite sports, especially at this time of year. The younger students sat in the bleachers with their teachers cheering on their fellow school mates. Father enjoyed watching the excited boys and girls and even the soccer teams were a pleasure for him. He taught bible class each day from 1:00pm to 1:30pm but always tried to be early to catch the recess events.

Finding a seat in the bleachers, located at third base, he sat with the others, watching as twelve year old Sean Kennedy, big and strong for his age, was up at bat. Christian Pitches was very talented but knew he was facing a difficult challenge with Sean at bat. Sean was hailed as the "Babe Ruth of the School." Staring Christian down, swinging his bat back and forth limbering up, always gave the pitcher the shakes; invisible ones he hoped. Sean figured Christian would throw him either a curve or a knuckle ball.

The stage was set. Little Timmy McClean, guarding the middle outfield decided to back up another twenty yards to the edge of the woods to compensate for Sean's ball striking ability. Christian wound up and fired a curve ball into his catcher's mitt. "Strike one," Coach Keath called out loudly. Breathing a sigh of relief, Christian wound up again and released. Sean eyed the knuckle ball flying at him, judging the ball's angle of flight perfectly and swung his powerful arms. The bat sliced quietly through the air like an arrow, the ball screamed off the bat arching high out to the middle of the outfield where little Timmy was positioned. His eyes were glued to the speeding, oncoming ball. Putting both hands up and holding his brown leather well worn out glove in the exact direction of the ball's flight path, as his father had taught him, he backed up slowly; then realized he was running out of room. Holy cow, this ball is going into the woods, he almost shouted. What a hit!

Watching the ball sail over his head, then disappearing into the tree line, he listening carefully and heard it careen off a few trees about ten yards into the woods. What Timmy should have done at this point was to return to his post on the outfield. Coach Keath's strict Rule Number One was never at any time to enter the woods alone under any circumstances. But

Timmy's father trained his son to be a ball hawk and pounded into his little head the fact that baseballs were expensive. "Go find the ball, Timmy," was in his little brain. Off like a golden lab retriever, jumping into the water to find the green neck mallard duck, little Timmy would bring back the ball for his father's approval. This dedication would prove to be his biggest mistake of his young little life.

Full of youthful enthusiasm he dashed off into the woods in the direction where he heard the ball ricochet off the tree. Dad always said, "If you can't see it, at least hear it." When he came to a small clearing, his bright blue eyes scanned the area for the ball. That's when he saw it. Fear gripped his young little nine year old mind.

Scared stiff, he squeezed his little frame so hard he became momentarily paralyzed. Suddenly, his body twisted to the right, arched and collapsed on to the leafy carpet of November's newly fallen crimson colored leaves. His body ever so often quivered; his life force fighting to keep him from losing the battle yet spiraling deeper into a vast darkness of sleep.

Umpiring from behind Scott, the catcher, Coach Keath saw little Timmy spin around and head for those forbidden woods. Keath screamed, "No Timmy, stop!" The Coach's voice never reached the boy in time before he vanished into the foliage like a sleek deer on the run.

Father Flanigan grasped the situation immediately, jumping from his seat, and racing almost full gallop on to the outfield, his black image fluttering across the grass. He appeared to assume the apparition of a large bird of prey swooping down over the browning field of autumn. Running at full trot, he reached the clearing and stopped stunned. Terror filled his eyes, his heart flooded with despair as he gazed upon what appeared to be young Timmy's lifeless body, sprawled out on the ground. What to do? Oh, what to do, he anguished. Sweet Lord, please no!

Coach Keath tore off his umpire mask and bulky body protection, flipped open his cell and called 911. A quick exchange of words and he, too, was off and running, calling and calling out their names with no replies.

Two police cruisers screeched to a halt, blaring sirens were turned off as were the flashing red and blue bars. The teachers with their horde of children gathered close, yelled to the officers and pointed to the woods where Keath had entered.

Coach Keath arriving at the clearing froze when he saw Father kneeling next to little Timmy. The priest raised his hand, signaling Keath to stay put. Thinking the worst, Keath thought that Father was either praying or possibly giving Timmy last rites. All at once four uniform officers burst through the clearing, stopping dead in their tracks, catching site of Father Flanigan hovering over the child.

Except for a crow's caw, there was dead silence. The Father looked up; a portrait of angst on his otherwise sweet face. Slowly he moved his arm to the right and with a shaky index finger pointed to a tree not more than eight yards away. The others followed his direction to the scrub oak. Six feet up from ground level, they, too, saw the arrow embedded into the tree; dead center. It almost seemed to quiver in the breeze coming off the ocean. Trepidation filled the air. Standing in place and drawing their glocks, the officers scanned the area as far as their eyes could see. Coack Keath felt a twinge of nausea in his abdominal cavity.

Father Flanigan, calmly and quietly, spoke in a soft voice, "The lad's fine! All is well; he just fainted. I assume he saw that arrow and thought the worst." No one moved or spoke. "You see, it happens to little children. You know they have seen their parents under stress these past few weeks; consequently they, too, take it on themselves, subconsciously, of course. So the site of that odious arrow was so frighteningly overwhelming for little Timmy, he didn't know how to handle it. As the good Lord would have it, his body shut down, just briefly - like the cooling of an engine as they say."

Amazed, relieved and dumbfounded, the officers and Keath remained in their positions. As he stood up, the good Father said, "Please officers, call the ambulance." Sergeant Danny Liason put the call through to the Montauk Fire Department Ambulance crew." "On their way, Father; five minutes should do it."

Coach Keath stepped over to where Timmy lay. As he started to kneel down, the little boy's eyes sprung wide open, searching into the two solemn faces above him. All at once, he began to cry, releasing an outpouring of warm, clear tadpole shaped tears. Father Flanigan whispered softly, "That's a good lad, let it flow," and then in a moment or two, "You see Timmy, it's your body's way of telling you that everything's alright." The others listened nodding and smiling, while the Father spoke soothing words and stroked Timmy's thick crop of blond wavy hair. Off in the distance the sirens wailed their approaching sounds. A more relaxed Coach Keath consoled his player, "You had quite a fright son; we were all concerned and by the way you almost caught that ball champ," gently wiping the warm tears off little Timmy's cheeks.

Sergeant Liason ordered his men to place yellow plastic tape around the tree in a five yard perimeter while he called HQ's reaching Sergeant Thompson. Roy directed Liason to hold on and quickly explained the situation to Todd who immediately told Roy to get Lieutenant Minx and his crew out there on the double. "Sergeant Liason, this is Lieutenant Miller, what's the status of the boy?" "He's doing well now sir. I secured the area but can't determine the character of the arrow or length of time it's been here." "That's okay Sergeant; it's Minx's job. Thanks for your help; keep the scene as clear as possible." "Roger Lt., out."

"Let's roll Roy."

Pulling up next to the two cruisers, Todd and Roy were greeted by Sergeant Liason who reported that Timmy was given a clean bill of health by Montauk's finest ambulance crew. Half an hour later Lieutenant Minx met the officers at the clearing. CB drew their attention as he held up the arrow that he had placed in his evidence bag, "It's not our bowman, guys. It's a wooden arrow that's been in that tree for some time. In fact, the tree actually grew around the broadhead; we had to drill it out." Again the group was dumbfounded but relieved and attentive as Minx offered, "My guess is some hunter lost it; lots of deer and turkeys in these woods. I call it a wrap Lt." "Thanks CB, I'll inform the principal; his staff will be real glad to hear the good news, all the way around."

Word spread, of course, but no one let their guard down. Next day in the Montauk Pioneer, the headlines read MTK SCHOOL PANIC - ARROW SCARE.

CHAPTER 33

It was another perfect bluebird of a day with a slight, crisp chill in the air when Roy arrived at the lodge promptly at 8:00 am. "The best of the best" as Roy was affectionately called knew he had to "do or die" to work his magic by testing his hard earned archery and hunting skills on the legendary and demanding THREE-D BIG BUCKS COURSE. Recalling Justin and Marshall's plans to up the challenges this year and to add an extra mile and more decoys he knew he would face a far more intricate challenge. Yet, not one to float in a sea of doubt, Roy considered his bowman-ship skills as pure woodland artistry.

Entering the dining room Roy spotted Hither sitting in the corner by the bay window evidently absorbed in a book. Funny, he thought, I didn't know she was a reader. As Roy made his way over to her through the busy dining room where the hunters chatted and were eating breakfast, he thought of the large crowds that would be in Montauk this day since this event like the shark tournaments for the fishermen was a big event and good for local businesses.

Greeting the guys who wished him good luck, and those who looked at him with envy while a couple gazed menacingly at their arch enemy, he managed to reach Hither, sat down beside her and gave her a kiss on her cheek. Shooting back a warm smile and moving close to him, she laughed, "Oh, Good Morning Roy, how did you sleep last night?" "Like a log, Hither, I slept just like a log after practicing like crazy for today. Good thing my Mom called to tell me she cooked my favorite stuffed cabbages; they're the best in the world, Hither!" "Aaah Roy, what's her secret?" "Well, she pots them on top of the stove, never bakes them, says they dry out. And after she rolls those little piggies, she pours her homemade tomato sauce in a pot and then she puts in sauerkraut, cabbage, onions and let's see, oh, you know, spices."

"Sounds like you could make them yourself Roy," Hither laughed. "Me? "Hell no, Hither! She's very careful especially when she makes her three layers and cooks them till they're done; about two hours, depending on the size of the batch. But I guess the real secret is the meat. Mom uses top sirloin, veal, and pork and mixes in rice, onions garlic, eggs and more spices. Talk about heaven, Hither, I had six for dinner and two for dessert!" Looking wide-eyed, Hither exclaimed, "Two for dessert?" "Yeah, you'll see what I mean at lunch; I brought a dozen. They're in my hot bag in the truck just waiting there for us!" "Got me hungry, Roy, I can't wait."

"Hey, Hither what's that you're reading?" "It's a book about North American birds; Justin loaned it to me." "Right, Justin's a good birder, too. You know Hither, those feathered creatures have an allure almost more than any other kind of wildlife. I think birds fire up a magical hold on our imagination; they're so vibrant and alive and they're everywhere to be seen and studied. Their beauty lightens up the world of nature."

Staring at Roy and sitting almost like a statue, Hither was dumbfounded as Roy continued to what seemed to her like an oration. "Just think, because birds are so enchanting, we even want them as pets. They're rich in color, sing like opera stars and their gift of flight is amazing. No matter how big or small they fly through the trees with such swiftness and fearlessness. And like all wild creatures they are only carrying out the role given to them by nature." Roy paused and after a moment or so Hither smiled and purred, "Roy, oh Roy, you put that all so well; I think there's a poet lurking somewhere within you."

Kelly inquired as to what they would like to order. Looking up they both asked in unison, "What's today's special?" Smiling, the young waitress announced quickly, "Jack's potato pancakes with a side of apple sauce; made the old-fashioned way, out of this world!" "We'll take two orders of "out of this world" and coffee Kelly, and by the way, how did Scott do on the course this morning?" "He's in fourth place, Roy but when you get out there he'll be pushed back to fifth. At least we'll still be in the $7,500 pool and boy with the new baby we sure can use the money. Roy, you know we're rooting for you. Scott bet a week's salary on you so Roy, please come through for our Erin."

CHAPTER 34

As they passed through the starting gate and began their walk along the trail, Roy remarked, "By the way Hither, did you know that the bow and arrow was adopted 500 A.D. by the first Indians who had landed in America?" "Really, where did you learn that?"

"Researching on google. See hunting with a bow and arrow is a very specialized craftsmanship so I like finding out about it as much as I can; gives me a better feel for the equipment and its purpose."

Roy talked as the two walked. Maybe these speeches he's giving helps to put the killings around here in the back of his mind, Hither thought.

"Did you know Hither that the throwing spear was the main weapon used by hunters way back then, before the bow and arrow? But the bow and arrow replaced the spear, that's for sure...." Suddenly Roy stopped; his training and reflexes took over as he scanned for a target, sure that he had heard a pounding somewhere along the path. Positioned at his left side Hither followed suit. Slowly and noiselessly she stepped back a foot to be out of his peripheral vision. Effortlessly Roy pulled back to the full draw let-off position, listening intently to the pounding hoof beats heading directly at them. A picture of grace, standing there in full bow draw, Roy tracked the dry brown dust as it rose furiously from the trail into the air.

Past experiences told him the animal he was about to encounter was indeed a wild boar. Like a speeding freight train it rounded the corner at full charge with its four tusks, shining brightly in the sun's rays, head held high in a threatening manner while grunting loudly in a tempestuous rage; his fierce black eyes not moving. A veteran of many a boar takedowns, Roy skillfully squeezed the firing trigger, releasing the precision missile at his target. The smart, well-considered heart shot caused the animal to stop. The projectile bounced off the three-dimensional display, falling to the ground in slow motion thirty six yards away.

Hither clapped her hands excitedly, "Nice shot Roy, damn nice shot!" "Thanks Hither, I hope the rest of this course will be as easy but knowing Marshal I doubt it." "It looked so real Roy; I actually froze!" "Yeah Hither you're right, even Marshal explained that there's no other course like this in the world! He's got new sound systems build into the 3-D displays that you would swear the critters are alive. Talk about target rich, hey these targets aint no sissy predators. These decoys are determined to challenge any archer's best bow skills."

Looking around the immediate area Roy finally spotted the infrared motion detectors, camouflaged to look like branches.

Pointing to them, he informed Hither, "We broke the beam two feet back. Damn clever how Marshal set this range up; you'll never know you've broken the beam until the 3-D target jumps out at you. Hither we've got to stay vigilant and become one with this course!"

As they passed the boar, Roy indicated the miniature train tracks on which the decoys move. Hither was speechless. "Leave it to Marshal to come up with this ingenious idea," Roy quipped. Noticing the arrow, Hither asked, "Aren't you going to take your arrow Roy?" "No Hither, the range officer collects them and returns them after we're done; can't reuse blunt headed target arrows. I'm allowed twenty 3-D displays and twenty arrows, no second shots is the rule."

Proceeding down the trail Roy continued his commentary on bow and arrow history. "The primary benefits include higher degrees of accuracy Hither. They provide rapid missile velocity and a hell of a lot of greater mobility. Think about it Hither, arrowheads also require less raw materials than spear heads. And for sure, arrows are much quieter than other weapons, right, allowing the hunter more chances to strike and not be noticed." "Oh my God, Roy," Hither exclaimed, pointing to a small shad tree. "Look, it's a Painted Bunting! But they only live in the south."

Roy replied laughing, "It's probably someone's pet Hither; must have escaped." "Go south," yelled Hither, "Go back to Texas!" She knew its Spanish name was mariposa which meant butterfly and in the south it was known as the rainbow for all its multi-colored beauty but decided not to do an up-man-ship on Roy. "Did you know Hither that because of its beautiful colors this bird is a very sought after pet?" "Really

Roy?" ""Yes siree! In fact capturing them is illegal." "If I had my way Roy I would cage anyone who takes them from the woods." "Ditto Hither."

The trail began to rise beneath their feet as they trudged along, both listening for any unfamiliar sounds. "You know Hither, bow strings, way back when, were made from animal backs or leg tendons. Yup; gut or rawhide or cord was made from the neck of a snapping turtle." "No kidding Roy?" "Nope, it's true and plant fibers such as the inner bark of basswood, slippery elm or cherry, even yucca and milkweed and dog bane were used for bow string, too. I read that plant fiber string is much better than animal fibers because it holds the most weight and doesn't stretch in damp conditions." "You sure know a lot Roy; ever think about writing a book?" "Me write?" he almost exploded, "no way Hither. My spelling sucks and I don't know an adjective from an adverb."

Reaching the 150 yard point, they came around a bend, putting them on the northeast side of the back end of Big Reed Pond. Roy stopped abruptly and raised his left hand; Hither stopped. With his finger up to his lip, they both stood in silence listening. Some fifty yards away Roy noticed a large patch of blueberry bushes shaking; must be some animal chewing and clawing in blueberry heaven, he figured. Wait a second here, bet that guy is a bear; soon he'll come out for a long, cool drink of water to wash those beauties down. Slipping an arrow into his bow, he glanced over at Hither, smiled and motioned her to get down low on the path. She nodded and quickly hit the dirt.

Roy's eyes danced from bush to bush following the movement till he finally spotted the big black tank. Talk about huge, Roy judged him to be close to 350 pounds. The bear walked nonchalantly on all four stout paws with considerable large under-pads to the edge of the pond. Rearing his head straight up, his sensitive amber eyes surveyed the surroundings; his snout quivered scenting the air for any type of danger. Satisfied he was not in harm's way he lowered his massive head and drank slowly from the pond's cool charcoal waters.

Hither watched intently while Roy aimed the shot. With lightning quick assault, Roy's arrow flew with deadly speed, like a spirited beast, right into the middle of the Red triangle - lung- heart- lung strike. The bear fifty five yards away didn't move. "Wow Hither, Marshal made these animated decoys so life-like; damn this is exciting - just like hunting out in the open wild!" Looking at Roy approvingly Hither grinned, "A damn good shot Mr. Best. You just earned yourself lots of points again." "Hope so Hither but we've got a ways to go."

Keeping up the pace they walked on as Roy explained more of the rules. "They score on yardage too, Hither, you know, how far out you shoot the target and also the accuracy of the shot, the degree of difficulty and of course the time of course completion." "You're doing just fine Roy," Hither cooed. ""By the way, how long is the course?" "5,280 feet divided by three gives you 173 yards or one mile," he replied with a grin. "Oh, so you're a mathematician now, too?" "No way, I read it in the rule book. Hey, if we keep up with this quick pace, we should complete the range in ninety minutes; how's that?" "Great Roy, as she started to run, yelling back to him, "C'mon, hurry up!"

Hiking up the steeper grade, Hither asked, "What do you think the next target will be?" "No idea, that's another trick!

You know Hither we've completed seven targets plus the boar and the bear so if I'm right we've eleven more to go." "You must be right Roy, let's see, so far a coyote, woodchuck, raccoon and boy was he real looking, the brown bear, a barrel owl, the Canada goose and the great horned owl. Okay, that's seven and the last two nine; correct you are!" "I have a hunch that the next just might be another bird; a hawk or an osprey, maybe an eagle, Hither. These surroundings are ideal for the birds of prey." "Now I know why else you are the best Roy; you don't miss a thing!" "Well, you gotta read the signs and try to figure out which critters would make a certain setting their home or set up an ambush to their advantage. See those tall trees; they're perfect for the warlords of the air." "You have eyes like a hawk Roy!" "So you think so, do you? Well, before long you will, too; we'll have you hunting and learning this treasured craft inside out!"

When they reached to the top of an overlook Roy stopped suddenly. With Hither right at his side, he gestured toward a red tail hawk, sitting about sixty feet high on a large black oak sixty five yards away. Securing his weapon he took lethal aim and watched curiously as the big bird took flight unlike the previous three decoys. Still Roy adjusted accordingly, leading the hawk, and sent an arrow zinging in a silky-smooth release. Cruising at electrifying speed it ripped directly into the hawk's breast. Screeching in its high-pitched tone - kee yee, kee yee, kee yeeeee..... it dropped straight down to the ground. Yelling in a fevor of excitement, "Roy was that hawk animated or real?" Hither asked. Instead of answering, Roy sprinted over to the carcass with Hither right behind him. "Look at that Hither, he's attached to the wire; my arrow is here," pointing to the ground. "Damn that Marshal, he wired this one up to pretend it was lifting off into flight, and if I'd missed, for sure lots of points would have been taken off." "What are you talking about Roy; you nailed him, I saw it." "Yeah, well maybe; remember Justin is a great shot-maker. I bet he wasn't fooled." "Forget Justin; you're down to ten targets so get real; you're going for the gold, remember?" "Right you are Hither."

Sure enough the next seven targets were a tribute to Roy's skillful marksmanship.

Coming upon a field of three foot high brown grass Roy stopped again. Observing the meadow, Roy commented, grinning, "This Miss Hightower is a perfect Big Tom habitat and knowing Marshal I shall say something's rotten here." "Why Roy, it doesn't look out of the ordinary to me?" "If I'm right there will be a Big Tom with a harem of hens lurking in there somewhere, so we'll stick to the trail and when we break the infrared beam I guarantee they will take flight." "Why Roy?" "Because Hither, he's probably gonna launch them from large mechanisms."

As they walked slowly Roy took out his only Flu Flu arrow with six large feathers at the end of each arrow's shaft. "These ought to do the job." Once they were 150 yards into the field, the turkeys started clucking excitedly and flew off to Roy's left. Moving in closer and with steel nerves, Roy began to lead one of the big Toms, aimed and pulled; the blunt broad-head slammed into the big turkey's breast. Both the Tom and the arrow arched downward, falling quickly back to the meadow from which they were launched. The arrow's blunt head drilled into the turf, marking the exact location of their landing.

A beaming Roy and Hither stood close together looking intently into each other's eyes. Lowering his bow his thoughts raced. He knew Hither was caught up in the passion of the course and probably liked him more for his hunting skills but what the hell. He moved his bow to his shoulder and without saying anything he took Hither's hands in his, drew her closer, and without realizing how it happened, he had his arms around her and her arms were holding him close as they both kissed each other intensely.

Their embrace did not go unnoticed by the figure who wrote the 3-D Rule Book standing a short distance away peering through a set of binoculars. It was a fact that Roy would be out of arrows after decoy number twenty was shot. Patience is a noble adversary; soon they would be here. A shot or two would be stunning!

CHAPTER 35

Hiking up the slope to the high ground, Hither and Roy paused to look down at the breathtaking view surrounding in all its glory, forty five yards out, Little Reed Pond. Her waters sparkled like diamonds bordered by the hearty ground covering of alfalfa and a peek of the fading emerald green clover.

"Did you know you can eat the raw clover flowers? They're very tasty and a good source for deer and other animals?" "Really?" answered Hither in her usual manner. "Sure thing and before they bloom their aromatic buds are used as spices." "That's interesting Roy. Go figure; the things you learn in Montauk! Roy did you ever think of becoming a weekend tourist guide?" "No way, I hate sharing Montauk with outsiders, except you of course," he grinned.

Quickly spotting movement off on a right angle, Roy turned to see the critter in his natural splendor. Directing Hither's gaze in the direction of the animal, they both watched curiously as it stood smartly on his two webbed hind feet, its tiny front paws gripping on to a good-sized sapling as the sun's rays reflected off the beaver's brownish yellow gray fur. His chiseled-like front teeth chewed rapidly through a branch while his paddle-like hairless tail balanced him as he crunched away. Suddenly he wrapped the limb in his mouth and ambled back toward the pond.

"Aren't you going to take a shot?" Hither asked. "Not yet, I'll wait till he gets into the water; the more difficult the shot, the more points, remember?" The miniature tracks that transported the beaver were probably only three to four inches beneath the water's surface, Roy assumed. As the animal entered the pond, exposing the upper half of his body, Roy sighted his target through the peep-hole, and launched the projectile. It reached peak velocity and slammed broadside above the shoulder of the decoy; a clean kill!

"Another crack shot Roy!" Hither said warmly, her face flush with a glowing smile. Lowering his bow and turning to Hither, he was grinning with the pride of a sharpshooter, "Thanks Hither, not bad, not bad at all, if I do say so myself. Well, that's decoy number eleven and I must admit that was really cool! Let's move, we're on the clock; "time and tide wait for no man", Roy proclaimed.

Like two gazelles they raced down the hemlock lined winding trail to target number twelve. After completing the next eight targets successfully, but where each became more intricately designed than the one before, Roy was anxious to meet and conquer his last objective with the same skill. He had to hand it to Marshal; so far this course was pure perfection!

"Nineteen down and one to go Sergeant Thompson, but I have to tell you when that humongous black panther sprang out from that tree I wasn't too sure if he was a decoy or a real panther especially when it stood on its hind legs growling and spreading its curved pointy claws. Gee Roy, he really looked as if he was going to attack us and I'd hate to wind up in his belly!"

Eager to get going yet giving in to his thoughts, and with his lips pressed together, he recalled what his father had told him at the young age of ten when he handed him his first compound bow, "Son, this is an instrument of death; never pull back your arrow unless you have acquired a target. Always remember son that the two things that separate the best of the best from the other hunters is: one, self control and two, 'having the patience of a gentle stream'; got that from the Bard son." Roy didn't know who the Bard was for many years but he never forgot that quote and lived his life by it. He kept his father's memory alive by fishing and hunting, always thankful that his Dad gave him these gifts. Guess I keep trying to repay him Roy thought over and over again. Now envisioning his last target, he again pictured a gentle stream, while at the same time his plan was as smart as a fox's as he focused on nature's signs. Hither's thoughts were interrupted when she heard Roy's deep voice command, "Let's move!"

Reaching the two hundred yard mark down the twisting trail, they came to a thicket which boarded an oak flat. Knowing exactly what the setting represented, Roy bowed his last arrow whispering, "This is a prime deer habitat and it would be just like Marshal to have our albino make its move as soon as we break the infrared beam. So Hither, let's walk slowly now; when I stop the deer will make its presence known off to my right." Hither nodded understandingly as they started cautiously toward the thicket.

After proceeding thirty five paces Roy detected motion to his right; he raised his hand slightly; they froze. In seconds, with extreme caution the wide-racked Albino buck was on the move behind the sparse foliage. Immediately Roy considered his four options: neck- spinal-cord, head, heart or broadside shot. He elected the neck shot. The buck walked slowly and was just about to pass a 3x2 foot opening in the thicket, sixty five yards out; there was little wiggle room for an arrow. However, this small clearing gave Roy the opportunity to try the neck shot card; risky at best. Knowing this shot could produce deadly results, dropping the deer at a split second, Roy decided to take the gamble; it was all or nothing! Yet he well knew this shot could fail miserably if he missed the small two inch area on the neck. From past neck shot experiences, he also was well aware of the exact location where his arrow had to penetrate in order to slice through the spinal cord; gutsy but doable.

Taking aim his dreaded concern was that his arrow could be deflected by an unseen little twig sticking out in the small opening preventing the hit in the sweet spot. Big points at stake here, he told himself. He did have the option to wait until the buck passed through the shrubs at which point he could take a clean broadside shot; much easier and safer but then again less tournament points. Oh well, let's go for it!

Pulling back to full let-off position, Roy's heart picked up a few beats, his adrenaline rising, his stomach muscles tensed as he watched the deer enter the opening. Looking through his peep-sight he adjusted for angle. His keen eye concentrated with steady patience on the albino's neck; zeroing in on the killing zone. Still as a statue and without a trickle of a lack of confidence, he readied his shot with nerves of steel. He squeezed the release trigger; the arrow exploded off the bow string speeding straight and true. It accelerated like a meat seeking missile smashing into the predetermined mark on the deer's neck.

Roy's shot resulted in an accurate, deadly precision hit. Talk about having the courage of one's convictions, that shot was a stalwart bold feat; Roy knew he pulled off a superb well-executed spinal shot. The deer's forward motion stopped him in his tracks upon the arrow's impact. Lingering for a minute, savoring his success, Roy was mesmerized for a few moments. His wide grin wore his feelings of jubilation and euphoria as his eyes drifted toward Hither.

Although watching every moment of Roy's expert shot, Hither didn't fully understand the complex significance of it. When a grinning Roy yelled, "I did it! Hither I did it!" she asked, "What Roy, what did you do?" "I took a big risk but it worked out just fine. I killed the albino before he came out into the clearing and I'll bet nobody, not even Justin, took that chance!" "Are you serious, do you mean if you had blown that shot you would have lost the tournament plus the prize money? Why didn't you wait for a broadside shot as is per normal Roy?" "Good question Hither. But, you see, what makes one a step above the others is when you're willing to take the gamble and go for the hard shot. Once you lose self-confidence you might as well resign yourself to second place. You see Hither, I had only one shot with four options and I chose to go for the neck shot. Hey if you don't believe in yourself who will?" Almost ready to bite the bait she said instead, "But the money Roy, $20,000, that's a big gamble you took." "It's not about the money Hither; it's about honor and the tradition of bowmanship, and it's also about the respect in which my fellow bowmen regard me.

Standing chest to chest, Hither hugged the ace hunter she was growing to like more and more saying, "You are the best of the best Roy and you don't brag about it. I like that in a man- my man!"

Shouldering his bow and holding it firmly with his right hand the two happily kept a fast pace on the last hundred yards of the course. Both had a sure feeling that the Big Bucks course belonged to Roy. Suddenly Roy's peripheral vision picked up movement off to his right about twenty five yards off the trail in a clump of rhododendron bushes. Stopping abruptly he grabbed Hither's right arm with his left hand. She was about to ask what he saw when all of a sudden she caught sight of something moving.

Trying to better focus on the apparition her mind struggled to interpret the ghostly figure she stared at. She squinted stupefied at the astonishing image. Roy, with lightning speed, twisted around to Hither grabbed her shoulders and thrust himself and her down on the trail. It was a second too late. The Albino, standing on its hind legs in full bow draw, released the arrow from its compound bow. The arrow ripped into Roy's upper right shoulder as the two fell to the ground.

"I'm hit," he uttered in a panic, "Run Hither, stay low to the ground, keep close to the foliage. Hurry Hither, please hurry before you're his target." "I'm not moving; I'm not leaving you Roy, no way!" she said defiantly. "Where are you hit?" looking directly into his eyes.

CHAPTER 36

"Something hit me, I'm sure of it," Roy said, stunned and confused, feeling his shoulder, "wait a minute, maybe the arrow ricocheted off …..no Hither, it had to have hit my bow and sheered off behind me." Looking over his shoulder, he spotted the rogue arrow two feet away, snatched it and with rage in his voice yelled, "What the hell is this?" As he examined the large Flu Flu rubber shaft with a rounded blunt-head Styrofoam broad-head top he was baffled until he saw the writing on the arrow shaft. Reading it aloud to Hither, it said, "Thank you for completing the BIG BUCKS MONSTER COURSE."

With their mouths opened wide in astonishment their silence was shattered by loud, good-spirited laughter. Turning their heads simultaneously in the direction of the supernatural figure they had seen, there standing erect was Marshal with his hands clasped around the sides of a buck head, raising it high over his head. "Got you, Mr. Best of the Best," he gleefully laughed. Placing the buck head beside him, he regaled in fits of laughter, slapping his thighs, and catching his breath in order to continue his merry-making.

Finally, a subdued, controlled and beaming Marshal yelled out, "I told you this was like no other course in the world!" "So you did Marshal, so you did," the pissed-off hunter replied and turning to Hither said, "he's lucky I'm out of arrows." Brushing themselves off, Roy and Hither watched as Marshal made his way toward them, carrying what they knew to be his most prized possession of the day.

"Well, if it isn't the Holy Grail himself!" Roy announced, as a smiling Marshal approached them. "C'mon guys, you gotta admit it was a heart-pounding ending, just as I promised," and grabbing Roy's hand, winked at him, then said earnestly, "Now, bowman to bowman Roy, wasn't that a stunning Montauk ending buddy?" "Sure Marshal, just stunning, but be on notice that I'll be planning a Montauk surprise just for you goog." Shrugging, Marshal continued smiling smugly and offered one of his favorite quotes: "Things must be as they may because what is decreed must be!"

"Oh so you know the Bard?" "Who?" exclaimed Marshal, "that's Shakespeare you goog!" Hither burst out laughing.

Slapping Roy affectionately on his back Marshal explained how he watched the arrow veer off the bow and said, "If it hit your back, buddy, it would have popped off you like a ping pong ball, besides I set a twenty five pound full draw pull and the rounded styrofoam broad-head would have felt like a big cotton ball; had it all under control Roy." Looking directly at Hither who was regarding him cooly, he winked and put up his hands as if she was going to attack him and proceeded to quote playfully, "I can express no kinder sign of love than this kind kiss," he said coyly, bringing his hand to his lips and then blew it to her. Shit thought Roy, Marshal could charm birds out of a tree. Gathering up his best heartfelt appeal in hopes to reduce the girl's icy stare, Marshal good-naturedly cooed, "C'mon Hither, humor me or kick me anywhere except in my family jewels!"

Knowing just how to relieve the tension, Marshal joined Hither as she laughed and laughed at the age-old joke, "Okay Marshal, you're off the hook but you are going to be the one to buy the drinks and dinners tonight!" "Deal; that's my girl," he prated and planted a real kiss on her available cheek.

While the three made their way back on the trail Marshal remarked to Roy that his shot was a real gutsy one and praised him for his exceptional skills. He also reminded himself about the bet he had placed on Roy and the money he could have lost. "I can't believe you shot sixty yards out through a three by two clearance hitting the decoy dead center in the golden triangle Roy!" You sure have the fastest time on that target; guess you know what that means, hey buddy?" Savoring the best for last and waiting for a reply, he was surprised when Hither asked, "So Marshal, Roy brings home the gold?" Hesitating a moment, he nodded and smiled and replied, "You bet and if you don't mind me saying so your Roy triumphed over the Big Bucks Range. Right now he's in first place and bumping his toughest competitor Justin back to second."

Marshal continued talking directly to Hither as if Roy wasn't there.

"You know, Justin's shot making was by all means excellent, don't get me wrong, but he like the others waited for the

Albino to clear the bushes before taking his shot. Not our boy, Hither, oh no! He went for it! Thank the Lord he hit the mark! You can just bet I held my breath, thinking of all that wampum I was about to lose, watching his arrow flying through the air. But when it popped off the decoy's neck and the deer stood dead still, Roy became my hero!

But hey guys, hold on, it's not over till it's over but I can't imagine anyone else doing what you have done Roy." Thanking Marshal humbly and without any rancor he also said, "Your course was magical Marshal; it sure did challenge every one of my skills and those I didn't even know I had. Your three-D targets were incredible buddy; how you did it is beyond my thinking. Yeah, Marshal you created a bowman's paradise. It sure was a lot of fun!"

As the two friends shook hands Hither blurted out, "Ditto."

"Just remember the bowman's old adage guys, "Keep them there arrows sharp and true to the target and so stand the hazard of the die which thee cast", Marshal continued. "Right Marshal and know that I am proud to shake thee hand," Roy shot back causing more good old fashioned laughter. "I got a big kick out of setting up a challenging range like this; one of a kind I'd say and the sound effects; how'd you like them noises Roy?" "Outstanding Marshal; especially that Red Tailed Hawk -kee-yee-kee-yee," Roy laughed.

Arriving at the range officers official check in table, Roy completed the necessary paperwork and signed the computer print-out card. Officer Orville handed him the blue receipt and shaking his hand said, "Fine shooting Roy; you've the lowest score recorded for the course, congratulations!"

Checking out the board Roy could see that Justin was in second place, Todd in third while Sean Brigsby, Justin's best friend, was in fourth, Gary Half clipped fifth and Michalis Limnios from the Greek Isles and related to the Salavae family by marriage was in sixth position. He was glad to see that Scott held on to seventh; good Kelly, he's in the money! Rounding out eighth place was Meahgan O'Murphy, Justin's nurse girl. Lt. Steve Honeycut from the DEC held ninth all by himself; not bad Steve, not bad at all. Reese Jacobson and Mike Rooney were tied for tenth; great Reese for just a novice and Paul Apostiledes was in the eleventh spot.

Back at the Lodge all was humming with the Big Bucks chatter. This was one course the guys would talk about forever. "Hey buddy," Todd greeted Roy with a slap on this back, "Real nice shootin' Lt.! How's about a nice cold Guinnness; I'm buying Mr. Best of the Best?" "Suits us just fine, right Hither, but then have lunch with us; brought Mom's stuffed cabbages." "No way I'd miss out on those fat piggies!" replied Todd.

CHAPTER 37

Another sober dawn arose on the last day of the Big Bucks Three-D Competition reflecting the solemn, weighty state of the social phobia fermenting among the villagers where anxiety was the rhythm of their souls. An aura of death prevailed, yet business went on as usual.

By noon the air was filled with vanishing autumn fragrances and the seemingly up-beat members of the lodge piled in the dining room in anticipation of the closing ceremonies. Although the tournament provided a diversion from the onslaught of the recent killings, no one was letting their guard down.

Sitting in the middle seat behind the podium, Justin was checking his notes while Marshal to his left was chatting with Range Officer Orville who sat next to him. After Marshal brought the event to order, Justin stood and read the names of the winning contestants in reverse order.

Clapping, whistling and the usual cheering evoked a feeling of the traditional norm, and when Justin finally announced that Todd Miller took third place, and himself second, the crowd hooted and hollered like a tribe of Indians! Settling down, after it what seemed like a ten minute raucous intermission, Justin held up the four foot silver trophy. Speaking in a loud, serious tone, he announced, "Roy Thompson is the all out winner of the three-D Bucks Tournament for the second time. Congratulations Roy; please step forward and take your silver trophy and your check for $20,000."

Again the crowded room sounded off in good-humored high spirits as Roy claimed his prizes and humbly thanked his fellow competitors for their participation but did not mention Marshal's costumed surprise.

Meanwhile Jack was overseeing the buzz of the kitchen activity as his chef Fred prepared one of Jack's favorite recipes. Hungarian Goulash would be served to all the members in honor of their Big Bucks middle of the day dinner. Jack knew the guys would devour the potato dumplings especially if Fred made the gravy just right.

With the view of the red ball of fire setting over Gardiner's Bay, the stuffed and content guys began to leave for home except for Justin, Meahgan, Roy, and Jamie and Todd who went into the bar and sat at a table in Hither's section. All were focused on Roy's big win. "Where's your trophy?" Jamie asked, surprised he didn't have it at the table. "Oh you know Jack, he talked me into letting him display it for a week at the coffee shop; said it would be good for business. And I'll get the left over goulash!" "You know how to drive a hard bargain Roy!" Jamie and Todd said in unison.

A playful Hither brought their drinks and even sat on Roy's lap for a moment, cooing just loud enough so all could hear, "My man, the best of the best!" Roy, watching her wiggle back to the bar, didn't notice that all eyes were on her.

Observing ten unfamiliar guys dressed all alike, sitting at two tables they had evidently moved together, Todd wondered who they were and better yet where they came from. Two, obviously drunk, were making cat-calls in Hither's direction and when the guy sitting closest to the bar got up, Todd read the gold letters on the back of his purple shirt; *Brooklyn Rod & Gun Club.* Turning to Justin, Todd remarked, "Another club buddy? You're doing some good business with that little hotel you're running upstairs." "Right Todd; it's good for the bar, too, as you can see. Would you believe that group is the sixteenth we've had this year?" "Hey buddy, with a charge of only $100 a night including breakfast or brunch, Montauk's sweet-smelling salt air wets their appetites which also makes them drink. You got a win-win situation here," Todd laughed.

After another round of drinks they all left including Roy who was meeting with Todd at the Command Center first thing in the morning. Hither waved, blew him two kisses, picked up a tray full of burgers and sauntered over to the visiting group.

"I don't think you guys are going to make it into the woods tomorrow," Hither said, shaking her head, picking up the empty collection of boiler maker glasses strewn all over the table. "Oh yeah, what makes you say that?" one of the more inebriated members of the group muttered. "Just look at you; you're as high as a kite. Think you'll just sleep it off and dance into the woods tomorrow morning, do you?" Hither sneered.

"Now wait just a minute, who d'ya think you are talk…" "No way Mr. Brooklyn Rod and Gun Club; not the way you're slammin' down drinks for that greedy big gut of yours," a disgusted Hither interrupted. The rest of the guys thought that was pretty funny especially with the barmaid giving them so much attention.

"And besides," Hither continued, "there's a killer bowman out there just waiting for the chance of sticking an arrow into a big belly like yours." Some of the guys laughed like hyenas at this but some frowned suspiciously. Trying to form a clear retort, the big mouth managed to blurt out, "Where we're from we got real killers on every block; we're not afraid of some wimple running around with a bow!"

"The word is wimp, not wimple Mr. Macho and if I were you I would wimple myself right up to bed," suggested Hither. Hoots, whoops and jeers filled the bar room; the guys slapped their knees, shook their heads from side to side and tried to catch their breath for the next jab. "Hey wimple, go to beddy-bye," someone yelled from across the room igniting the next wave of hilarity.

Amid all the jeering and cheering, Hither slipped off to the kitchen.

CHAPTER 38

As they drew near Eric and Whatley's tree stand, they stopped dead in their tracks. Almost paralyzed with terror Butch and Eldon stared down in shock at Eric's body sprawled out on his back. Almost surrounded by a clump of shrubbery, it appeared as if he had inched his way to the opening to find cover before the sickle of death took him. The arrow's broad head which pierced his neck left a jagged, gaping hole where his Adam's apple should have been. Dark red blood oozed from the opening down on to his camouflaged drenched hunting clothes.

"Oh my God, he's dead," Elton exclaimed, dropping to his knees. Crawling into the opening of the vegetation, he stretched his arm to feel the side of Eric's neck for any sign of a pulse. "No heartbeat," Eldon's voice trembled, reaching a stunned Butch's ears. Slouched and swaying from side to side, Butch could hardly contain the cold shivers of sweat flowing down his back. In a robotic tone, he asked, "What should we do?"

In his own cove of despair, Eldon never heard his partner speak. Leaning close to his cousin's face, Eldon's unsteady right hand closed Eric's bright blue eyes. His sense of loss, sorrow and wrath out-weighed Eric's jesting words earlier that morning before they split into two hunting parties. "I'm getting the first deer, Eldon, but don't worry cuz you can have its white tail to make a lucky bucktail lure." Shaking his head, Eric recalled himself saying, "Fifty dollars says I get the first deer; let's go Butch, we have our work cut out," and off we went. "Oh God," Eldon said again, "Why did I say what I said?"

Recalling how he took a compass reading and looked at the map the lodge ranger had provided which gave the markers for the apple cove, considered to be the primary deer habitat, he realized that what was done was done. And after marking his and Butch's position on the map which contained the exact coordinates for all areas, they decided to hunt the area which pinpointed their precise location at a mere glance. Well satisfied that the map was also designed to prevent visiting hunters from getting lost and also giving them distances, scale of area and cell numbers for trail and range officers, Eldon was confident he would win the bet.

Setting up their stand ninety five yards from Eric and Whatley's stand would keep the four within shouting distance. With great expectations the two hunters felt that they would be the ones to take down a large Montauk buck; the best eating deer in New York State, they reminded each other.

Encouraged by their lush surroundings where numerous green apples and acorns still lay on the forest floor as winter's chill kept them firm, the boys from Brooklyn awaited their buck. Shortly, a blood-curdling scream coming from the northeast where Eric and Whately were positioned shot through the quiet woods. Startled, then terrified, Eldon pulled his cell phone out of his upper vest pocket and pushed in Eric's phone number; machine picked up. He called Whatley; same result. "Let's go Butch," he said as they started to run before Eldon's words were spoken.

Now standing at the grizzly scene, Eldon watched Butch as his friend, hunched over, swiped at the flood of tears that were flooding down his cheeks and began to shake his head back and forth before he started to walk slowly away from the clump of vegetation. As he cleared the area, he took out his cell phone, punched in 911 and reported the situation and gave their location.

"Ten to 15 minutes," the operator said, "Please hurry," he replied, as he wondered where the hell Whatley was.

Walking nervously for about twenty yards to where their stand was perched high in the tree and stopping to scan the surrounding ground cover, Butch suddenly spotted Wadley fifteen feet off to his right lying on his back with an arrow firmly embedded into his chest. Diving for cover instantly in a thicket of evergreens, the panic-struck hunter shuddered in nauseous torture and shook as if he were having an epileptic fit. In a few minutes, the thoughts of his family prompted him to regain a bit of control; swearing to the Lord that if he escaped Whatley and Eric's fate he would never hunt again.

Bowing an arrow, Butch knelt motionless in the well camouflaged foliage. Taking note of his defensive position, his back was blocked by two large oak trees and to his right the tree containing the tree stand also provided protection. Preparing for a shot to come, he figured it would be a frontal or left side assault. Judging that he had a good firing lane in both directions, his eyes worked overtime staring intently at each leaf, twig and branch to determine if they were real or a disguised clothing pattern likeness. Listening attentively like a blind man, whose ears could detect the movement of a caterpillar walking its many legs over the leaves, he heard no movement, no unusual sounds other than the normal tranquil tune of the forest.

Estimating he was some forty feet from Eldon, he decided to call out in a hushed voice, "Stay put Eldon, don't move, we may have company." All at once the eerie silence sounded like the stillness one hears after a good old fashioned thunderstorm that did battle with the earth in the heat of the summer. Not responding to his call, Butch became gravely concerned, thinking the worst. Yet on the other hand, Eldon might not want to give away his position, he hoped. Grabbing his cell phone again, he flipped it open and punched in 911 once more. "I called twenty minutes ago," he said to the voice. "Two, possibly three hunters are down, hurry, please hurry, I think the killer is lurking somewhere in these woods for Christ sakes!" "Stay calm sir," the operator advised," You should be hearing the police helicopter any minute. Do you wish to stay on the line until their arrival?" "I'll manage but you better be right about that five minutes. I feel like shit; you getting my drift? I'm about to lose my place in the food chain," Butch sputtered back at the voice. Stay calm, easy for her to say that shit, he said to himself and closed the phone.

The sound came swiftly from the direction off to his left. A high-pitched whistling squeal pealed through the air. In it was a cadence of mortal terror. In a flash Butch ducked; the arrow sizzled over his head slamming into the oak tree off to his right. Dazed and trembling he felt weightless from the shock of the near miss just inches from his head. Groping for his canteen attached to its velcro holder, he managed to unscrew the lid and took a gulp.

Sweet sounds of the 'womp-womp-womp' from the copters' blades triggered the beat of his heart as he lay there on his back. Reaching for his knapsack, and fumbling with the zipper, he opened the bag and retrieved an emergency flare. He tossed it thirty feet in front of him. Spinning like a top as it landed, its red smoke curled upwards into a cloudless blue sky. In half a minute, the helicopter was directly over the smoke, pushing the swirling vapors back down to the ground. A loud speaker roared down to him, "Do not move; stay where you are. This is the EHPD Swat Task Force."

Inching his head upward, Butch's eyes caught sight of the blue and white copter hovering some ten yards over the tree line. In no time four ropes dropped from the chopper. Butch, approximately 20 yards away, anxiously followed the four dark figures maneuver down the ropes, hand over hand, as their feet squeezed their life lines. Once on the ground, they kneeled and formed a defensive circle; automatic weapons at the ready. As soon as one of them radioed to the copter, four new swat members appeared on the ropes, scrambled down to earth and joined the first group. An officer called out, "Butch stay put, don't move. Call out you name twice so I can pinpoint your location."

Two members of the team moved in Butch's direction; "Now give us another call." In a minute Butch heard, "Gotcha."

As soon as Officer James McCoy descended from the copter and was on the ground the swat team circle took up a new defensive position at McCoy's location. "Just relax," the officer said to Butch, "the rest of the taskforce is up there circling the terrain." "But, but my partner Eldon is over in the bushes where his cousin was shot dead in the neck. You gotta send one of these guys over there quick!" "No can do, Butch, my orders are firm; got to keep you safe till the rest of the guys arrive, then we'll check on the others in your party."

McCoy's shoulder radio jumped to life, "Sergeant McCoy, we're 175 yards from your position; keep your position secured. No contact with Bowman, keep heads up McCoy, the net may force the prick back to your area." "Roger Todd, sir, if he shows up here we'll try to subdue him or else we'll pepper his ass with enough lead to sink a ship." "Roger that McCoy, out."

A quick glance at Butch acknowledged the distraught hunter's visible shaking. "They're close pal," assured McCoy, and offered him a small plastic container, "here take a swig of this lad; it's good for the nerves. Good old Wild Turkey is a shake chaser; trust me, it works." Wincing at the burning sensation of the bourbon wash, sliding down his throat, Butch asked in hoarse voice, "You want a swig?" "Sorry lad, no can do, I'm on duty."

Watching the helicopter sway back and forth, hovering like a large hummingbird, while her engines roared out a tune to which the ropes danced over the leafy covered earth below,

Butch thought sadly of his two hunting buddies and their poor families.

CHAPTER 39

McCoy checked out the helicopter as it banked hard right behind its high-pitched turbulent blast of hot exhaust. The copter dipped its nose and hammered east, fast and high. Once
its tell tale sounds, faded into the distance, a hush of peace
settled over the forest.

At first, the snapping of twigs drew his attention off to the
right; then catching sight of movement, McCoy saw the search
party approach in their black swat team uniforms including
Lieutenant Todd Miller and Sergeant Roy Thompson. Todd
said, "Mr. Landale, I'm Lieutenant Miller," to which Butch
replied, "How's Eric, Lieutenant?" "What's his status Roy?"
Todd asked. "He hyperventilated and fainted but our medic
has him on oxygen; he'll be fine to walk out of here in ten
minutes." "A thankful but anxious Butch acknowledged, "I
was scared shitless till I heard the chopper; glad you're here
officers."

"Mr. Landale, how many were in your hunting party?" Todd asked. "Just the four of us sir; six stayed back at the lodge." "That checks out with what the Range Officer told me Todd," confirmed Roy, "and the other six are all accounted for at the lodge."

"Mr. Landale, did you see or hear your attacker?" "No sir, I never got a glimpse of him but I did hear something coming in my direction," as he pointed a shaky finger at the oak tree. "It missed my head by inches," he said as his voice trickled off flat with fear.

"Roy, inform Lieutenant Minx." "Roger Lt." "You guys seemed to have partied pretty good last night, did any of your group have an incident with any of the other lodge members?" "No sir, we stayed to ourselves." "Do you think Eric may have seen anything?" "No way, he was well hidden in that clump of bushes with his cousin. Please Lieutenant, why did he come after us?"

"I can only tell you that reason plays little part in an insane murderer's process. I know that's not going to satisfy you but that's what we're dealing with Mr. Landale," a solemn Todd Miller replied concluding the short interview.

DEC's Lieutenant Steve Honeycut, who'd been covering the western section, arrived shook hands with both old friends and asked, "How did we lose him?" "We're a loose net Steve; too few of us, too many cracks the prick could've escaped through," Todd explained. "Yeah, this high tech hunting shit puts us at a disadvantage," warned Honeycut. "That's right buddy, even the dogs didn't pick up a scent. Anyway, I diverted the chopper to survey the trails and roads for any abandoned trucks or cars in the area; might come up with something, who knows, meanwhile this is Lieutenant Minx's crime scene now," announced Todd, wrapping it all up. "Now let's get those two back to the lodge, Roy,"

"Roger Lt."

CHAPTER 40

Early the following morning Todd was back at East Hampton Police Headquarters adding the new victims' data to the list of five already on the Bowman Chart. When he finished he sat down at his desk, gazing over at the seven crime scenes, while he tapped his bottom lip with his fore finger, his blond shock of hair covering the two deepening lines between his fair eyebrows.

CRIME SCENE SIX

Location:
.Hamlet of Montauk
.North East Hither Woods
.Apple Cove

Victim:

Location:
.Hamlet of Montauk
.North East Hither Woods
.Apple Cove

Victim:

.Eric Ringwood
.White Male
Age 27 years old

Time of Attack:
.8:00am
.Monday, November 22

Perpetrator:
.The Bowman AKA
. The Grim Reaper
.Victim killed by
.carbon arrow, 500 grain

Evidence:
.Blood type O Positive
.No shoe or finger
impressions
No trace of fiber clues
.No tread marks

.Whatley Ashberry
.White Male
.Age 28 years old

Time of Attack:
.8:00am
.Monday November 22

Perpetrator:
.The Bowman AKA
.The Grim Reaper
.Victim killed by
.carbon arrow, 500 grain

Evidence:
.AB negative
.No shoe or finger
impression
.No trace of fiber clues
No tread marks

We're dealing with a clever, dangerous animal here whose reasoning I just can't figure out, he said to himself. Warped as the perp was, Todd knew there was definite logic to his irrational behavior. Hopefully the help he arranged for would pin point something.

Hunched over his desk, completing his Brooklyn Rod and Gun Club report, Roy reached for his coffee cup, took a swallow and peered into the almost empty container that was full of Brent's black special roast only a little while ago. Best make a new pot, he figured, knowing that coffee was the driving force in this department plus the donuts.

"You say something, Lt.?" "Yeah Roy, I asked you if you think the Bowman is a psychic?" Seeing the bewildered expression on Roy's face, Todd rephrased his question. "Roy do you think the Bowman has psychic powers, you know, like a clairvoyant?" "Damn Todd, how would I know, I'm not Freud! But first things first Lt., how 'bout I check to see if the donuts from One Stop Market have been delivered yet?" Roy suggested, as he walked quickly to the door.

"Be right back, Lt."

In moments Roy returned with a sugar donut in his mouth and carrying a tray of five others. "Couldn't wait, could ya?" Todd grinned.

Like the dog with the bone, Todd pressed on. "I'm not asking you a trick question Roy." Re-phrasing his thought, he said, "You know about ESP, right, okay, now do you think the Bowman has ESP powers?" "Frankly, Lt. I just don't know; anything is possible with this freak. He's bamboozled us right from the very beginning." "Ahh, and therein lies the enigma Roy, so is he a psychopath or a sociopath?" "Hell if I know! You're the John Jay graduate; out of my Bonaker league as the saying goes."

"Okay Roy. You know it's a good thing we're meeting Dr. Erin Young at Jack's today, Steve Honeycut's fishing buddy. He was head psychologist on the FBI serial killer task force for many years and we better hope that he'll give us some answers Roy." "Right, Lt. and you better ask him that question of yours; seems you're really hung up on the answer." "You messin' with me Sergeant?" "Who me? Not me, Lieutenant Miller."

After helping himself to another donut and starting a fresh pot of coffee, Roy returned to his desk and looked directly at Todd who was waiting to continue. "Back to the situation at hand Roy, how did the Bowman know the guys from Brooklyn were going out hunting yesterday morning and where exactly were they planning to set up their tree stands? That's the point of issue you and I must address before our meeting with Dr. Young."

Walking over to the coffee table, Roy motioned to Todd, "No more for me, thanks buddy," while he poured himself another cup. "Seems to me, it's got to be one of our lodge brothers," Roy pointed out. "The Bowman was more than likely sitting at the bar listening to their conversation, right, and that sure in hell was easy to do since you could hear them from across the room. You were there." "There you go Roy, good thinking, but, and I mean but, we can't assume it's one of our lodge members although I'll keep that possibility open. Think about it buddy, what other element enters into our realm of probabilities?"

Looking down into his half-filled coffee for a long minute, Roy looked up quickly and sputtered, "The lodge is opened to the public, Todd, the public, for dinner and drinks!" "Bingo Roy, when you're hot you're hot! So now we know the perp was there and now it's who; gotta reconstruct that night Roy, down to every human being at the bar and in the dining room."

On the edge of his chair as if he were ready to burst, Roy sputtered again, "Hither, it's Hither!" "What? Hither is the Bowman!" Todd sputtered back incredulously. "No," Roy exploded, "No, she's the bar maid, get it? She'd be the one to have noticed a stranger at the bar, ask her, ask Hither!"

"Glad we got that straightened out, buddy, okay, good idea Roy, and maybe the other bar tender, too, Tom or whatever his name is and Jack who was in the dining room, too, might give us some answers. I'll interview Jack today at lunch and Hither and Tom when they show up for work." "She's usually on from 3pm to midnight; I'll let her know." "Good, we'll be there at 3:00pm."

All of a sudden the motions of the two officers almost vibrated within the walls of their room as their pace quickened with an aura of purpose as they organized their data and articles that would be necessary to take to Jack's.

"Dot your i's on your report Roy: have to take it to the chief today, Todd reminded Roy with a wink, "and also Sergeant, have the task force guys interview all members that attended the Big Bucks dinner; you can get the list from Justin. You know we're gonna smear this bastard yet Roy!"

"Roger that Lt!"

Chapter 41

There was a good crowd of locals at Jack's Coffee House for this time of year what with the best coffee in town and mighty fine reasonably priced lunches. Even the tourists were treated to a small bowl of the day's soup along with their lunch orders, compliments of the house. Ever a good business man, Jack knew how to seduce his customers.

A New Orleans spicy seafood and sausage gumbo was a real rib-sticker for this bone-chilling late November day. To say the least, the atmosphere reflected gloom since the general chatter was about the Brooklyn hunters. Tempers were short and nerves were fried. Not even the sixties rock and roll coming through the in- house speakers helped to soften the mood.

Jack's yearly hunting log was a pitiful two pages of deer hunting exploits while his fishing journal burst at the seams of the binding.

The woods were taboo. Even the die-hard hunters were no longer willing to expose themselves to the recent lurking danger and risk their lives for a slab of venison. Trusting the police to bring a quick end to the dreadful situation, the guys bided their time, fished for a hit now and then in the sparsely filled late fall waters and otherwise lamented the circumstances.

As Todd and Roy walked towards the front counter, it was evident to them that a sense of low spirited gloom prevailed through the café. Noting the dejected expressions on the faces of his fellow hunters, Todd felt a sorrowful lump well in his throat, yet at the same time, he knew that the spirit of humanity hadn't dried up entirely in his community.

Jack, his elbows leaning on the rosewood counter, whispering busily to the newly-weds about the joys of marriage and giving his usual juicy tips, looked up when he saw his two tall police buddies gazing down at him. His wide, high-kilowatt smile greeted them with a hearty, "Hey strangers, you guys have been sorely missed, welcome home," stepping from behind the counter, shaking their hands, trying to make the best out of the current deadly conditions.

The unusually quiet group of locals slurped the piping hot soup slowly, chewed on various sandwiches, chomped crisp pickles and drank their ever filled cups of coffee.

Roy tapped Luke on the shoulder with a "Hi ya bubb, how's it going?" "It's going," Luke mumbled, staring into his soup. "Hey bubb, what's your problem: get up on the wrong side of the bed this morning?" Roy asked. Digging for another spoonful of soup, Luke turned his three day stubble and his blood shot eyes up at Roy and snapped bitterly, "My problem, Mr. Policeman, is my freezer - it's half full of bass and blue, but, can you believe, I aint got no venison? That's right and my family aint too happy 'bout that officer; can't make it through the winter without that deer meat." Taking a swig of coffee and clearing his throat, he barked, "That's my knot Mr. Policeman," and catching his hunting buddy Gabriel's eye asked, "What say you Gab?" "Pretty much sums it up for me Luke, too," Gab piped back.

The others, sitting along the counter, nodded their heads up and down as Todd watched. To say the guys weren't feeling very social would be to put it mildly thought Todd and Roy knew it was time to back off. That the ramifications of the killings went beyond the horrified and sad reactions of families, friends and the entire village with the threat still at large and not even a suspect to alleviate the dread, it was apparent that some of the locals who depend upon the hunting season to off set their cost of living were affected economically, too.

In his attempt to subdue the guys, Todd broke into the Beatle's singing something about a yellow submarine saying, "Guys, my office and many other agencies are working 24/7 on your and everyone's behalf to do everything we can to catch the killer that is continuing to sabotage our village. You gotta get rid of your sorehead attitudes, guys. We need your help - I need your help!"

Shifting around in their seats, the locals glanced at each other then faced Todd again. "Talk about half full freezers, my freezer doesn't contain an ounce of venison nor does Roy's," Todd said, driving the point home, while he turned around and grabbed a menu.

"Let's see here," reading from the menu: "venison and eggs -scratched off, hot venison sandwiches - crossed off. Hey, I'm starting to see a pattern here boys; let's go to the dinner section.

Guess what gents, no venison steaks, back ribs or London broil."

Looking up from the menu and glancing from right to left at the sheepish looking faces, he returned the worn menu to its holder.

"I don't want to stand here in judgment of Jack's freezer but all things considered, in my opinion, it's venison-free, too. So boys it does appear that we're all in the same knot; what'd ya think?" No one spoke; only Jack's footsteps pattering around the tables and the swoosh-like sound of coffee he poured from his high-held pot could be heard.

"Let me leave you my friends with this thought and hopefully good news: We know the Bowman was at the lodge the night of the Big Bucks celebration and there's a chance, a slim chance, but nevertheless a chance, that we may get an ID on the prick."

Expressions of relief shone and chatter echoed once again across the café. No wonder Todd is such a successful policeman, Jack thought, feeling uplifted by his obvious confidence. Scurrying round the counter, holding his pot up high and raising his left hand, he shouted, "Listen up everyone; dessert is on the house fellas! There's a choice of apple pie, strawberry rhubarb pie or Alaskan chocolate moose." Applause, hoots and whistles thanked Jack appreciatively. "And since Thanksgiving is next week, which I know we all almost forgot, it's time for a bounce; we're gonna have an early Big Tom Raffle!" Cheers and hollers accepted the treat as Jack bent down under the counter and brought up the red wooden raffle box.

Motioning to Luke to pull out the first ticket, everyone watched Luke shuffle up to Jack, grab a ticket, hand it to Jack and watch while Jack seemed puzzled but smiled and announced, "Luke, you just won yourself an organic turkey; compliments of Jack's Café!"

"Atta boy Luke," they all cheered and whistled. "Pick the next one, Luke," Jack urged. Holding it up high, he asked Luke to read the winner.

Turning toward Roy, Luke grinned, "Hey bubb, you just won a turkey!" A voice from the back yelled, "Wait a minute, this was fixed guys, don't you think?" "Yeah," they laughed and cheered and hooted and hollered some more. Finally after ten birds were won, everyone settled down in good spirits, chose their pies that Fred had arranged at the counter, went back to their places, smiling and with a sense of optimism.

CHAPTER 42

Jack walked over to the booth where Todd and Roy had settled, poured two cups of hot coffee and then on second thought poured another for him self and sat down. "Okay guys, it's quieted down, Fred can handle the counter. Now what did you want to talk to me about?" he asked smiling.

"You're still in the loop Jack, so I want you to sit in on the meeting we're having shortly with Dr. Eron Young who's a friend of Steve Honeycut's. Young's a retired FBI psychologist and I'm hoping he'll give us a profile on the Bowman." "Thanks Todd, glad to be invited." "It's important that you get a snap shot of our psycho, too, Jack. Who knows, he could be a regular of yours. You might just spot someone here but remember buddy, if you think he fits the profile, he's a killer so no heroics. Call me immediately!"

"Roger that Todd. I'm just a coffee refill guy not a Rocky Balboa," Jack laughed.

"As you already know Jack, Roy here and I believe that the killer was at the Big Bucks Dinner." "See anyone there that looked out of place?" Roy asked. "Shit Roy, I'm lucky if I can remember who I saw yesterday." "I know it's hard, Jack but try for the hell of it," Roy pressed on. "Sorry guys, I was pretty busy running from the kitchen to the dining room; nobody out of the ordinary I can think of." "Okay, but if you do get an idea, let us know; we still have to talk to Hither and Tom, too," Todd added.

"Bet this is the doctor," Roy announced, as the door bells jingled.

Todd waved Steve and Dr. Young to the table. After the round of introductions and the usual handshaking, Lt. Honeycut who told the group how hungry he was, ordered meatloaf on Jack's say-so and the rest followed suit.

Turning to Dr. Young, Todd asked, "Doctor, what do you think we're dealing with here and what motivates this psycho into action?" "Please Todd, call me Eron; I'm just a consultant these days. Now your question is a tall order for anyone in my field so let's do some background on previous known psychos."

There was something about the man Todd liked right away; maybe he reminds me of one of my John Jay professors he thought. Still has that high muck-a muck FBI image written all over his face but he's a regular guy with a take charge attitude and his plaid shirt and khakis are fine by me.

Speaking in a low pitched authoritative voice, Dr. Young began, "In all my years of hunting down these bastards' profiles, they seem, in general, not to be helpful and I do read them with a grain of salt."

Observing their quizzical looks, he said quickly, "Here, let me try this one on you," pausing a moment. "Okay, male Caucasian between twenty and forty, high school education and perhaps some college, above average IQ, could be a control freak who may have experienced childhood trauma such as mental or physical abuse, been raped or witnessed a killing at a very young age, possible dominant father or mother and is seeking revenge through a psychopathic fantasy. Finally he vents a floodgate of lifelong pent-up loathing toxic venom." Dr. Young waited to continue as the plates were placed in front of the team.

"Now these are some of the traits that are shared by a number of serial killers," he began. All eyes continued to focus on the eminent man whose strong forehead and electric blue eyes also captured their interest as well as his calm, serious demeanor. "Whatever is driving your boy is anybody's guess but I will say that what you're dealing with here is a standard, multiple, random, homicidal scenario. This case has the earmarks of a psychopath who is a purposeless repeater killer, and that, gentlemen, is the toughest kind of case to solve."

Digesting the words of Dr. Young was more important than the lunch; the plates were untouched but the coffee cups empty. While Jack left to fetch another pot, the group talked quietly. Taking a small silver flask out of his pocket, Young asked if anyone would like a splash of brandy in their next cup; no one did.

After a good swallow of his flavored coffee, Young returned to the subject. "Going around killing randomly, apparently without motive or relative relationship between killer and victim, one would assume the victims didn't know their killer." "As far as we know they didn't," interjected Todd.

"That's a good assumption Lieutenant," Young replied. "Let me give you my definition of a psychopath which I believe is a combination of mental illnesses that occurs in childhood as a result of heredity, trauma and the lack of emotional development. Now because of this lack of moral or emotional development a psychopath is not capable of understanding the feelings of others. Therefore, they do not feel any remorse when they harm someone.

"Let's think of a child. As a father Todd, you especially, will relate to what I'm about to tell you. Freud once commented, "A child would destroy the world if it had the power." In a sense the psychopath's mind can be compared to that of a child for the psychopath's mind has not had the chance to develop to that of a normal adult. Instead, because of their traumatic childhood, fantasy has taken the place of reality. If these children had been treated far better and were not surrounded by dysfunctional adults, we would have far less psychopaths today."

"Knowing Todd's kids and my own nieces and nephews Doctor, I sure relate to this," Roy commented, "and I see teenagers who obviously live with parents who need counseling more than their kids." "Very troubling Roy and I agree but then there is no concrete evidence that suggests what I have said to be true. We all know of children who have risen above the worst kind of treatment and surroundings who are model parents and citizens; go figure as they say. However, in all cases to date, most of the conclusions are based on the observations and interrogations of the suspected psychopaths."

"If I'm correct sir," Todd said, "then the psychopath suffers from a severe childhood mental disorder causing aggressive antisocial behavior." "You are dead on," Dr. Young assured him.

Todd glanced up from his notes and stared at Dr. Young as he rolled on. "Rarely do psychopaths kill for money; it's not their MO. Instead they kill for the thrill; perhaps because of an uncontrollable urge or because of rejection or because of just plain old life itself. Think of Jack the Ripper; you fellows know about him, and how revenge served him very well after he killed prostitutes because he believed one of them had infected him with a venereal disease." A ripple of agreement shot around the table.

"Let's take sexual lust, for example. We know it's rampant; every day we read or hear about rape victims. But not too often are the prey killed. A psychopath seeking the ultimate orgasm and who fails miserably in what we might think of as a normal relationship such as one with a wife, girlfriend or date, somehow experiences the realization of his own emptiness which often will drive his passion to commit a violent act and not always murder.

"So as you are beginning to see, in my field there are lots of theories, and then there are even more lots of theories, if you will, and who knows the answers and for that matter, will we ever discover the answer?" Moving closer to the table and leaning on his elbows, Young said slowly, "Psychopaths have a system of logic all their own gentlemen. What they do seems perfectly acceptable, justifiable and reasonable to them. It's not my logic or yours or any sane man's for that matter. To us it's obnoxious thinking but to them it makes sense."

Fred whisked up the cold lunch dishes, replaced each with a piping hot plate, wheeled his cart back to the kitchen as Jack signaled a high sign to his right hand pal, to which the doctor acknowledged saying, "Jack you run a fine operation here and I must apologize for usurping our meal time by talking to you all too long. Bon Appetite gentlemen!"

Hurriedly wielding their knives and forks the meal disappeared in no time, Jack even beating out Lieutenant Honeycut whose enzymes never had a chance to break down his food. Fred returned with more coffee and cleared the table, while Todd added to his notes.

"Let me see if I can put what you said in perspective," Jack said in a rather matter of fact way that visibly surprised everyone. Yet Dr. Young turned to him and smiled, "Yes Jack, go right ahead."

After Jack gave a fairly thorough review of what had transpired, his questioning gaze to Dr. Young in hopes of approval was rewarded when Young said, "You should hang a shingle on the front door; Jack; *Dr. Jack, Your Troubles End Here.*" The good laugh they all shared, Todd knew, was a nice break from the seriousness of this information, and to the killings to which it referred.

"I was a philosophy major doctor; we studied sociopath and psychopathic patterns." "Aaah, that explains your insight, Jack," noted Dr. Young. Speaking up enthusiastically, Roy asked, "Who of the two kills the most, doctor?" 'You go for it Jack; I'm interested in your answer."

"Not my area of expertise Roy, but in laymen terms and doc help me out, okay, I would say that psychologically the thrill-seeking motivated killer tends to be a sociopath. He's someone with a character disorder rather than a mind disorder. But like the psychopath he lacks a conscience, feels no remorse and cares about just himself." "But," interrupted Young, "interestingly, the Fox and Levin study in 1944 estimated that only 3% of all males could be considered sociopaths."

"Right you are, so Roy, and you guys, psychopaths outnumber and out kill sociopaths and I might add that their victims are more mutilated." "Hey Jack," Todd blurted out, "Looking for a job as consultant in the department?" Roy slapped his knee, joining the laughter. "Just kidding, sorry doctor; back to business, Todd mumbled.

"Many cases of random killings such as I mentioned, Jack the Ripper and others like Son of Sam, the Yorkshire Ripper, the Hillside Strangler, the Black Dahlia - well you know them all. Anyway, they were all male killer psychopaths. What I'm saying is that there were no apparent motives and by the way the killers were white," continued their guest.

"How about it Jack; want to take another turn?" "Doc, you're the expert, we don't get a chance like this to hear someone of your distinction, please lead on. I sprinkle enough of my philosophical seasonings every day around here. Please lead on."

"As I'm sure you know," resumed Young, "psychopaths operate in secrecy. Their cunning plans belie the notion that they act impulsively. A profile will clearly show how difficult it is for you to find your killer because a psychopath is usually articulate and even charming, maybe charismatic, too, and they are often educated, employed and trustworthy. Can't beat that, can we?"

Sober faces and obvious serious thoughts were evident every time Dr. Young paused. Knowing the complexities of the information he was reviewing for them could not immediately stop the flagrant killings, it was, nevertheless, a necessary overview.

"To address your question Roy, I would like to point out that a sociopath is usually someone in some sort of trouble or about to make trouble; a tough guy image, if you will. They appear to live and operate on the fringes of society; many have criminal records. I think we would agree that your killer is a psychopath."

"Without a doubt," Todd replied for the group, "so with no remorse and no feelings of guilt, does he know he kills?" "Think of it this way," Young explained, "when you swat a fly or mosquito, do you feel remorse or guilt? No, you did it in self defense. In fact, psychopaths feel a sense of heightened excitement before, during and after the murder. It has been said that the greater the risk the more intense their exhilaration. So what I suspect Todd is that it isn't a single cause you're dealing with here but rather a combination of many facets. Your psycho is driven by a chain of circumstances."

"A multi-motive nut; that's what we got," Todd grunted. "What you're describing doctor is like a match in a gun powder barrel."

"You've summed it up nicely," Dr. Young laughed. "But the burning question is what triggers the SOB?" "If we knew the answer to your question Todd, your bastard would be in custody and we wouldn't be having this little chat."

Stretching their arms indicated they knew conference was over. Dr. Young stood up, thanked Jack for the lunch and his knowledgeable contribution, shook hands with Todd and gave him his card. "A pleasure gentleman; keep me in the loop." "Before you leave, doc and everyone, Fred's got his homemade pies on the counter and a fresh pot of brew; help yourselves," announced Jack.

CHAPTER 43

The minute Todd and Roy walked out of Jack's they were surrounded by a herd of chattering, pompous news media holding their microphones close to their pugnacious faces and screeching their loudmouth questions in rapid fire. Pandemonium set in as they tried to out-shout each other in a whirling lynch like mode.

"NBX News, here, Lieutenant Miller, what progress have you made to date and when can we expect an arrest?" "CBX TV, Lieutenant, how many more people have to die before you capture the psycho?" The ACB newsman bellowed, "We hear you have finger prints; why isn't the Bowman in jail?"

Not to be out shouted, CNNZN cried out, "It has come to our attention the Bowman drinks the blood of his victims; true or false Lieutenant?" Screaming even louder, the BBP reporter shrieked at the top of her lungs, "Is the Bowman a vampire; the public demands an answer?"

"KKP World News, Lieutenant, we have information that the ghoul is a man-eater and lives in the woods. Have the victims been cannibalized and my follow up question, have they been drained of blood?" She, too, reached out with her mike, thrusting it forward to get Todd's response.

Taking a sweeping look around at the contorted faces and clicking cameras, Todd answered in a calm, authoritative tone "Ladies and gentlemen of the press, you must address your questions to our public affairs officer at headquarters. However, I will most emphatically state there is no cannibalism, no blood drinking, nor is there a deranged vampire living in our woods. We have a team of officers surveying the woods, beach areas etc. Thank you for your cooperation."

And with that said, Todd shouldered his way through the circle of clamoring reporters, marching quickly to the cruiser. Roy followed smartly like a healing lap dog.

Once locked safely in the car, Roy hit the siren. The media mob jumped back a few feet, their flabbergasted, wide, gaping mouths still yapping questions as the cruiser moved off smoothly.

"Damn Todd, talk about featherbrains, those boneheads should all be locked up! Where the hell are they getting all this shit about a vampire, blood draining, cannibalism and God knows what else?

Can't you just see tomorrow's headlines - VAMPIRE DE-SCENDS UPON MONTAUK - VICTIMS DRAINED OF BLOOD."

"That's the liberal press for you Roy, all theatrics; disingenuous and no substance. They're just a pack of spin doctors; they think the public are fools. Got a morbid sense and are obsessed with creating a frenzy Roy and all for what? To sell papers pal but don't they know that subscriptions are down all over the country?"

"Spin doctors, Todd? Now where the hell did you come with that one, Lt.?" "Don't you listen to NOX News buddy?" "Yeah sometimes but Mom likes to watch Turner Movie Classics." "Well Roy, when the host starts the show he reads his memo to his TV Audience. Then he says, "You are about to enter the no spin zone," and waving his pen around in circles at the camera, he says, "the spin stops here!"

"Hey, I like that Lt; the spin stops here. Maybe I can use that when I stop some one going through a red light or a stop sign or for that matter speeding. They all have some lame excuse, you know, and I'm not about to give everyone a pass. From now on I'll just say "the spin stops here buddy!" Elbowing Todd in his side, Roy laughed, "You get it Lt., 'the spin stops here'," he roared. They both had a real good long hearty chuckle as they approached the lodge.

Squeezing his eyes shut and placing his right hand over his forehead, Todd tried to mentally process the information that was gathered from Dr. Young. Roy asked, "What's bothering you Lt.?"

"Just thinking how extremely dangerous our killer is," Todd replied, lowering his hand and turning toward his buddy. "Only the Lord knows what he's planning next. And you know, what's strange Roy? Most serial killers have a weird desire for media recognition. They call or write to radio and

TV stations, the newspapers, even go on the internet. Not our perp as far as I know; not a peep out of the creep. And that Roy is what scares me. Must have suffered a ton of physical or mental abuse or a combination of both and is taking it out on our community. You know Roy we're hunting down a tormented mind who keeps the dark side real secret while acting normal until it's time to kill again. Like Dr. Young said we have our hands filled with this one."

"Damn Lt., I always wanted to be a cop, fight crime, put the bad guys away and keep peace but lately I'm feeling like we're walking down into the pits of hell with the monster always just one step ahead of us."

"Don't be so pessimistic Roy, this killer will eventually lose control and leave more clues. Got a gut feeling the Bowman wants to be caught." "What the hell you say Lt.; wants to be caught?"

"Think about it Roy. This is a person who feels completely isolated and just might not want to kill anymore but lacks self control to stop. But then there is the choice of weapon which is also very troubling. It seems to bring a kind of comfort to this dysfunctional bastard."

"Shit Lt. how does killing satisfy the Bowman's needs?" "Good question and I don't have an answer. All I know is our psycho is unemotional when it comes to guilt and remorse. We are being taunted Roy. It's a catch me-catch me if you can game."

"Your instincts are always are on mark Lt." Roy offered as he pulled up into the lodge parking spot reserved for police vehicles.

CHAPTER 44

Walking through the main entrance Todd and Roy were unexpectedly surprised when Meaghan jumped in between them.

"Hi guys," she said, grabbing on to Roy's left arm with both of hers and giving him a kiss on the cheek. "How's the 'best of the best' doing?" she asked with a seductive smile as they entered the Big Bucks Bar where Hither from her position behind the bar eyed them. That bitch, she thought to herself, a real flirt; how does Justin stand it?

Only when they arrived at the redwood bar counter did Meaghan release her grip on Roy's arm and join them on a stool. "So guys, what brings you here so early; I know it's not drinks since you're both on duty," Meaghan laughed coyly. "We're here to ask Hither and Tom a few questions, Meaghan," Roy replied, smiling at Hither. "What kind of questions," the two bartenders asked in unison. "It's Todd's show guys."

Todd, pressed his lips together for a moment and with a quizzical gaze said, "this is going to be tough but do either of you remember seeing a stranger, someone out of the ordinary, some character that didn't fit in with the group the night of the Three-D celebration? We're working on a theory that the Bowman may have been among the patrons and overheard where the Brooklyn Club was going to hunt the following morning."

Tom appeared startled at the thought that he may have served the killer but said, "I pretty much served my regular customers, Todd, no oddballs on my side of the bar. I'm positive about that, I think." "Thanks Tom but if anything should spike call me buddy." "Sure will Todd."

As Todd spoke, Hither filled a glass with ginger ale, placed it on the bar in front of Roy, and filled a second glass with ice cold water for Todd, ignoring Meaghan as if she were a bug on the wall to be swatted. Sensing Hither's vibes like women so often do but in order to neutralize the feline snub, Meaghan said playfully, "Nothing for me hon I only drink organic." "Oh really Meaghan, it may behoove you to know that all of nature's creatures also eat and drink only organic but they, too, perish." Ouch! Talk about the unkindest cut of all; Hither held her ground letting it be known that without a doubt Roy was her man.

In a matter of moments it dawned on Todd what was going on between the women and like an intuitive mediator changed the strained atmosphere with a direct question to Hither. "Anybody strike you as being unusual; think hard Hither." With her elbow on the bar, her chin resting in the palm of her hand and her eyes shut tight she contemplated for a brief moment. Suddenly, looking up at Todd, she said slowly, "I remember a deadbeat at my end of the bar; he wound up on my DD list of deadpans; never to be served again."

"A DD list?" questioned Todd. "Yes, it's a drink and dash list I keep in my head; it's for the ones who drink a few drinks and head for the hills while I'm busy with other customers." "Hmmm, surprising in a place like this," Todd remarked. "Well every now and then Todd, especially when we're crowded a deadbeat or two wanders in. This guy, I recall, had three beers and was working on his fourth, and before I knew it, he vanished. He could have gone to the men's room you know since his glass was three quarters full and returned to finish it; most do, but he took off."

"Never figured the lodge a place for hit and run Hither, but if you say so, guess it does happen. Now how would describe him?" "Kind of grubby looking; his clothes were messy, at least a four day growth on his face and his red hair was real long and tangled; probably lives in his truck on the beach." "Was there anything suspicious about him?" Todd probed. "Like I said, Todd, I was busy with a lot of customers. When I realized he had left I knew he played a DD on me." "Hither do you think you'd recognize him?" quizzed Todd. "Guess I could say he reminded me of that knife-wielding killer in Psycho," Hither giggled. "That would be Anthony Perkins," Roy honed in, "however, he was innocent; the mother was the real killer." Like a movie critic, Roy continued as he addressed Hither, "You see, the mother won out; she assumed his personality and his mind." "That's cool Roy," acknowledged Hither smiling sweetly, "but I rarely watch horror movies. They're too upsetting and give me bad dreams but who doesn't know about that knife scene, and the shower curtain and the blood flowing down the drain? In my opinion, it's the perfect murder."

Guess I'd better get my two cents in, Meaghan decided, annoyed with the attention focused on Hither. Looking directly at Roy she asked, "What did you think of Hitchcock's, The Birds, Roy?" Immediately Hither interrupted, "What a silly film; put a little pork fat here, a little there, and bird seed in the right spots, and you can train birds to hop through hoops for you." "So you do watch horror movies," Meaghan grinned devilishly. Gazing fully into Meaghan's eyes Hither spoke slowly, "As I mentioned dear Meaghan, I rarely watch violent movies. This film, however, shows what happens when people push too hard."

No one commented but Tom sliced through the tension when he said brightly, "Sometimes the mates I serve push me too hard; bam I just want to pound them like a nail into their bar stools!"

Noting Hither's odd, penetrating stare and evident animosity toward Meaghan, Todd returned to the job at hand and told Roy to have the Park Police check out all trucks on the beaches from the Lighthouse to East Hampton and then in a lighter mood, "Thanks for your patience guys, and you never know, Hither, we might get your beer money back."

With a quick wave to Hither, Roy followed Todd across the room.

A smirk curled on Hither's lips. Meaghan shot up to her office, Tom resumed cutting lemons and limes while Hither leaned against the bar in what appeared to be deep thought.

CHAPTER 45

He woke up hungry; hungry to kill. The wind at almost a nonexistent wisp was a definite plus and his battle-worn tan fatigues would keep him in concert with his surroundings. Checking his weapon (nicknamed the dragon slayer) meticulously for any dust, sand or grit that would produce an inaccurate shot was the ritual he followed to prevent being caught with faulty gear.

A final coat of lubrication on every moving part of his weapon assured him of his soon-to-be-success.

He was pumped up; he felt omnipotent. From inside his rickety camper, the roar of the pounding waves could be heard, the taste of the salt air cracked his chapped lips and reddened his weather-beaten cheeks. Although a relic of the past, his camper looked pretty spiffy in its new coat of green paint with brown and white trim.

Securing the back door with an old rusty combination lock and adjusting his gear, he stood still for a moment, leaning on his old rust bucket, thinking he was the perfect killer. I love the brine of Neptune's salt wash, I also love the scent of sweet smelling blood oozing from my prey, he mused to himself. In a whisper he said, "Tallyho, time to get on with the chase."

He headed toward Driftwood Cove or as the locals called it Deadwood Cove. As he zigzagged down the bluff, listening carefully for any inappropriate sounds, he stopped abruptly when an echo of fishing boot cleats resounded off the hard-packed rocky path. Swiftly fading into the thick foliage, he watched two fishermen trudge by, and resumed his trek as soon as they had disappeared from view.

Perfect water conditions, shimmering blue skies, spears of golden morning sunlight and temperatures in the low sixties; doesn't get better than this he knew as he hurried toward his oasis.

When he reached Deadwood Cove his first act was to shoot his yellow darter high into the air at exactly one o'clock, watch it arch, fall sharply into the water and vanish into the greenish-gray cold sea. A state of euphoric bliss enveloped the six foot tall, powerfully built Mike Dooney; affectionately called the "Metal Man." A sheet metal worker who fished with home-made metal lip plugs, Mike was a charismatic character who above all else loved to fish.

A hit on this first cast in the fifteen to eighteen pound range was mighty welcomed especially since it put up a good fight while the monster fisherman played him like a noble. All of a sudden Mike caught sight of movement from the corner of his right eye. A sleek brown phantom at full throttle headed straight for his fish. Like a thief in the night, he would show up every now and then without warning, making a quick and easy meal out of your expected catch.

"Not my catch, you don't," Mike roared across the fifty yard attack path. Completely ignoring the fisherman, the seal snatched the bass in its powerful jaws, slicing it in half. The sea turned a crimson red while the seal chowed down on his half of Mike's fish. Reeling in as quickly as he could to save the other half, the experienced local fisherman felt helplessly inadequate when at forty yards out, the seal grabbed the remaining part of the fish and swam off.

Cutting his line was the only remedy at this point but before his thoughts were complete, suddenly, like a bolt out of the blue, all movement stopped dead. On top of the hushed waters about thirty yards out Mike spied the brown seal with an arrow sticking in its neck.

Mike's neck hairs sizzled; the realization of seeing a brown and white red feather-tipped arrow in the neck of a seal was a fearsome sight. Visualizing himself as a second target was even more terrifying.

From a vantage point high on the bluff the Bowman watched the fisherman run across the beach. Estimating the time it would take for both to reach the lone camper parked along the dirt road will work perfectly the hunter figured.

Another fifty yards before I reach my truck Mike thought as he raced as fast as he could along the sand. His two pack-a- day lungs were holding up but each breath was nevertheless painful and his throat felt as dry as hot desert air.

At ten yards from his camper he gasped in stinging shallow breaths. Reaching the vehicle he grabbed on and edged to the trunk, took hold of the lock, turned the tumble and hit all three numbers. Barely able to swing the door open, he reached inside with a shaking hand, turned the doorknob and did his best to jump up on the tailgate and lunge inside. As he turned to close the door, an arrow sliced through the small opening between the door and the side of the camper.

The arrow's kinetic energy forced Mike forward; it was a perfect back shot. His body twisted and lurched to the right. In a few short seconds Mike reposed on the floor of his beloved old camper.

CHAPTER 46

Montauk's ace surfer drove slowly down the narrow, rugged road leading to Turtle Cove, the first large cove that dotted the beaches on the south side where the mighty Atlantic slammed against the pristine shore. Travis and his buddies knew this crusty, parched dirt road was like a washboard, having been jolted by its many pot holes for many a year. Yet it was a small price to pay to reach prime surfing waters.

Travis pulled into the empty parking lot at 7:30am; dawn was on the rise. As usual the surfers stood in awe and watched an ever-changing sunrise. Today a burning crimson-orange hued sun rose in a grayish sky streaked with eerie golden slashes over the ocean. The ground swells were perfect, Travis thought, as he judged the waves heights and speed. Clean, glassy waves pushed to the shore as a result of the east south east air currents. With a spacing of twelve seconds between each wave the action would be grand!

"We'll be able to cut left or right on our logs," Travis announced to the guys, "and maintain a speed of twenty miles and hour!"

Anxious to start the action, the four suited up quickly in their neoprene wetsuits. Within moments they appeared like four black phantoms pumping down the line, racing the waves and cutting back and forth.

A pair of beastly eyes followed the ballerinas dancing on the breakers. Knowing their energy levels would eventually run low, the Bowman waited for them to refuel.

Shortly before noon, Sergeant Roland Hawkins pulled into the lower parking lot, stopping his cruiser directly opposite the ocean. He relished these short breaks and reached into the bag Jack's had prepared for his egg sandwich and coffee breakfast. Spotting four surfers, he grabbed his binoculars for a closer look. "Jeeze," he whispered, "these guys are wave champs!" One of the surfers, only two hundred and fifty yards out, rode a beach bound wave like a first-rate ripper.

From the top of the bluff, the Bowman gazed at the inbound surfer and calculated that when he reached one hundred and twenty five yards, a Grim Reaper arrow, released from his position, would be a bull's eye. After all, yesterday's seal shot was trickier since the animal was in the water and not riding the waves. Lost in maniacal thought, the Bowman never heard Hawkins' patrol car pull into the parking lot.

As Travis neared the "kill zone" the Bowman stood and pulled back the seventy-five pound bow string to let off position. "Come on, come on," cheering the arrow along as a feeling of euphoria embraced the executioner.

While snatching the other half of his sandwich, lifting his head to drink a gulp of coffee and reaching around for his laptop on the back seat, Hawkins caught a fleeting glimpse of something glistening high on the bluff; over one hundred yards away, he figured. Raising his binoculars, his pulse began hammering as he focused on a figure holding a compound bow.

Sergeant Hawkins turned on his flashers and sirens as he pounded the hell out of the horn, getting the attention of the Bowman and the surfer, pushed the cruiser door open, using it as a shield. Just then he caught sight of an arrow speeding down in his direction. Fortunately it hit the rig's hood with a furious crunch and pierced through the thin bonnet, slamming into the engine with a thunderous explosion.

Kneeling down quickly, he unholstered his glock, switched off its safety, aimed and fired all sixteen rounds at the bluff-top creature.

A divergent tactic at best, he knew, since the glock's range was only accurate up to seventy-five or eighty yards, but, hopefully giving the surfer a chance to get away. Yet in seconds Hawkins caught sight of another arrow heading down in his direction.

Crouching behind the door, a second crashing of metal on metal further alarmed him. "Holy shit," a terrified Roland Hawkins, stammered. "Time for police cover," he mumbled as he grabbed his shoulder mike, entered the 910 emergency code; his clipped short message announced: "officer under fire, need immediate assistance, location parking lot 9, Turtle Cove." "Roger that Hawkins, we're on our way," Lieutenant Honeycut's voice roared back.

"What's your situation Roland?" "Being fired at; hunter up on the bluff, west of parking lot." "Stay under cover," directed Lieutenant Honeycut.

Another slam against the vehicle indicated the severity of his situation. "Never been through something like this," he muttered to himself. "Better stay safe behind this door for God's sake." Still he knew he had to react.

Pressing against the door and beyond it, he squatted into the best shooting stance he could manage. "Don't be a hero; that's not what your job's all about," rang clearly in his mind, somehow urging his return to the protection of the door which indeed saved his life when in a matter of seconds a fourth arrow cut through the door and landed in the ground next to the rear tire.

Time for Option B; get the hell out of here, Roland decided, and standing up in a half hunched position, turned and took two steps toward the back of the cruiser. A second too late; he felt the burning sensation of the arrow ripping through his left calf. Falling to his knees, he thought, it missed my leg bone, I think, and managed to roll to the side of the vehicle.

"Need medical assistance," he half shouted into his mike. "We're on our way Roland," Honeycut shouted. "How bad is it?" "I'll live Lieutenant."

At one hundred yards from shore, Travis heard the firing of bullets and saw the streaks of arrows. What the hell is happening, he wondered, as he moved quickly to the back of his board and dug down hard on the tail which forced the front high up over the water to become a buffer between an arrow and him self. Sliding off the tail and gripping the end of his board with both hands he looked toward the shore. Seeing what looked like a wounded police officer with an arrow sticking out of his leg crawling to the side of his cruiser painted a terrifying scene.

Through the splashing water the blurred view of a figure standing high on the bluff indicated to the young surfer that he was looking at the enemy who would release another arrow in a matter of seconds.

With a demonic smile of his face and a fifth lethal missile in release position, the Bowman aimed, discharged and watched the arrow speed toward the target.

Holding his long board over his head in his position under the water, Travis felt a vibration sizzle through his fingers, heard the sound of the arrow slam the board - dead center; its broad head glittering. Quickly, lowering his board and turning on his back, he kicked his powerful legs and began swimming backwards as fast as he could. Just then he felt the thud of another arrow careening into the front of the board. His lungs burned from the lack of air. Pushing himself to the limit, he thrashed on another ten yards before he knew he had to surface.

Another arrow sliced into his board a second before he raised his face behind it allowing just his nose and mouth to break the water line. Exhaling the deadly carbon monoxide from deep within his lungs, his body trembled in relief. A good blast of fresh air renewed the strength he needed to reposition himself in front of the board but just when he hoped he was safer an arrow burst into the tail forcing him under again. Sixty seconds - that's all I can do now, he knew, as he tried to think of his next move.

Reversing his post to the end of the tail and planting his finger tips on the stern of the board, he kicked his legs like racing pistons, moving his shield forward. Thirty seconds more would take him as far as he could manage before the life-saving need for air would impel him to surface. In five seconds the board slammed into something.

A hand gripped his arm yanking him up top side. Through bleary red eyes Travis could just about make out the face next to him.

The shaken surfer, sitting high on his board, screamed down, "You're safe Travis, you're safe," as the red and blue pulsating lights oscillated from the roof of a police truck and a siren wailed its shrill, soulful song.

The four surfers reunited at the edge of the beach and walked through the blazing stream of lights toward Sergeant Hawkins' vehicle. Holding his self-made leg tourniquet, Hawkins instructed the guys to take cover behind his truck even though two cruisers could be seen making their way through clouds of dust.

CHAPTER 47

Lieutenant Steve Honeycut and five of his DEC staff, working together with two state park police processing the paper work for a number of hunters, stopped immediately. There was no mistaking the anxiety in Rawlins urgent call. A fellow brother in serious danger signaled their response; get to him as fast as possible.

Grabbing their smoky bear hats, the eight officers rushed to their cruisers, leaving a stunned group of hunters at the check-in station.

The cruisers squealed out of the parking lot, made a right on to Old Montauk Highway, and headed east. Lieutenant Honeycut's cruiser led the way at a speed of up to 70 mph. Sirens and lights wailed and streamed as the cars sped along this road known to the locals as Old Flying Death due to its roller coaster bumps, hills and dips. A speed of 50 mph was pushing it; traveling at 70mph was pure insanity.

At various points along the jolting, rolling road the rescue party's adrenalin meter registered almost over the top as their vehicles actually became airborne before returning to the old black pavement, the tires screaming like a bunch of banshees loose in Montauk.

Passing the famous international spa and restaurant, Honeycut took hold of the cruiser's mike and speaking with extraordinary calmness, quickly explained to Detective Danny Swan of the East Hampton Police Sub-Station, the current situation to which he retorted "Roger that, we're rolling." In his next breath Swan instructed Officer Armstrong to call Lieutenant Miller at HQ who then placed a call to get an ambulance up to Turtle Cove pronto. Miller and Thompson along with four duty officers, raced to their patrol cars.

As their four vehicles raced into town, a pumped up Lieutenant Honeycut commented, "I want to nail this mother's ass to a tree and let him rot there for all eternity. This psycho is going down today, and I mean today!" Delaney, making a hard right on to Rte. 27, floored the gas pedal while Honeycut trying to visualize the situation at the cove felt that the grid search was the right move.

Speeding passed the IGA Honeycut spotted the two East Hampton cruisers making a left on to 27 from South Embassy. Calling Swan again, Honeycut told him of the change in plans. "We're heading to West Gate off Camp Hero to conduct a grid search east to Turtle Cove, Danny; you guys continue to the cove." "Roger Lt."

As the convoy of police cars cruised passed Jack's Coffee Shop and the Corner Store, the inquisitive and concerned locals watched anxiously. The first thing that entered their minds was another Bowman killing. To some it brought the fear of an Armageddon in Montauk. The brown tree sparrows, picking at the fresh bread crumbs, scattered around the front of the Montauk Bake Shop, took flight in a flurry of wing-beats, chirping frantic warnings to each other as the cruisers roared by the circle.

Barreling passed Martell's, Lieutenant Honeycut decided to place a quick call to Todd to review the plan of action he intended to initiate at West Gate. "Have your Swat team set up a perimeter line up on the dunes west of Turtle Cove. With a little bit of luck we may be able to flush the bastard back to Swat's position." Good plan, Steve; watch your ass!" "Roger that Todd. I aim to be home with Genie for dinner tonight; over and out." Todd knew that Steve was working on every detail of the search and to burden him with questions at this point would only confuse the dragnet. First things first, Todd reminded himself; if the trap works, these brutal killings will come to an end.

When they were opposite Rough Riders County Park, Honeycut ordered his team to close down their sirens. Four silent cruisers whizzed by Montauk Point East Overlook at 90 mph. In a few moments, Honeycut ordered his men to vest-up, arm themselves with twelve gauge shot guns with safeties off, and to bring extra ammo.

"Above all, keep it quiet," Honeycut instructed, "no talking, no slamming doors or trunks. Let's not give away our position."

Approaching Camp Hero Road, Troy made a right, passed Madison Hill Drive, and drove slowly to Camp Woods Trail. No cars were parked at the trails start-off point which indicated there were no hikers in the woods. As noiselessly as possible, the cruisers came to a halt at the West Gate fence, where in less than five minutes the team was ready and armed. Forming a football huddle around Lt. Honeycut, they listened to his low, soft voice, "I want you four on my left, you three on my right with a twenty yard spread between each one of you. The eight of us figure roughly to a 160 yard dragnet sweep, give or take a few yards. We'll work our way east to Turtle Cove bluffs, Swat will be positioned there backing us up. If we ferret him out into the open, and he tries to make a break for it and heads back to the cove, Swat will take him out. Everybody with me so far?" Honeycut's piercing blue eyes made contact with each one of the officers as they shook their heads in agreement. "Remember he's in full camouflage, we're in brown, and forest green but we'll be just fine. And guys keep in mind the Bowman is a formidable adversary and a damn good marksman. I don't have to tell you to keep a sharp outlook but keep a sharp outlook anyway!"

They all smiled; a good leader knows how to break the tension in a stressful situation. "Any questions?" he asked, looking around quickly. "Okay, let's move out."

After setting up the fence and spacing themselves approximately 20 yards apart, each raised one hand as Honeycut watched. Satisfied, he gave the go-ahead motion to advance into the forest. Enough sunlight was filtered through the trees to allow for good visibility.

The chase was on.

CHAPTER 48

Running in stealthy silence at a comfortable pace through the deep woods, the sunlight flickering between sparse layers of somewhat colorful leaves still clinging to the myriad branches of the oak trees, the Bowman considered how chancy and fraught with danger the chase had become. A wolfish grin mimicked the demonic memory of the recent exhilarating high-flying act when bullets and arrows pierced through the air. Yet replaying it was like watching a dark, disturbing dream. A feeling of vertigo washed through the Bowman's body; the dream seemed to spin out of control. It all happened too bow- gun quick.

Damn, that park policeman was an oversight. Winning the skirmish was one thing but I've got to be more alert. No more surprises.

Pushing the chase to the limits seemed to have quelled the cruel, unremorseful, murderous urges raging inside the killer's ravaged mind, at least until the next encounter. Now, quite familiar with the escape route, having completed a dry run the day before, the distance from the bluff to the truck was only a fast twenty minute run. Like a gray hound running west of Bunker Hill, crossing over Camp Hero's eastern road and stopping between two mountain laurel shrubs, the Bowman knelt down to retrieve the hidden camouflage canteen. Drinking the cool liquid slowly helped to quench a cotton-dry mouth and throat.

Excitement rippled through the Bowman's body figuring to reach Trail Woods within two minutes with no idea that the location would be right in the middle of the oncoming human dragnet.

Suddenly, with no warning sign, the Bowman was startled by rapid running strides heading toward the seemingly secure location. The hunter froze and in astonishment watched a twelve point buck appear out of a cluster of holly bushes in full hammering trot not more than twenty feet away. Reading the fear in the buck's body language was evident he was running from man.

Peering through range finders, the Bowman studied the woods for any signs of movement. In seconds, a brown uniform clutching a twelve gauge shot gun, came into view about 100 yards out. He was not alone. No way can I outflank that wide chain, the Bowman knew. To find refuge or die fighting these unrelenting bastards were the only options.

Rejecting retreat, yet realizing not knowing what lurked about especially with thinning foliage at this time of year, looking for an escape route from this escape route was daunting. The unnatural sounds of twigs snapping and crispy cold leaves crunching as the human fence moved forward spelled real danger. Spying a make-shift shelter, like a weasel, the Bowman vanished.

As the line neared the killer's refuge, it stopped. Sergeant Aaron Clancey walked five paces over to the large fallen decomposing oak stump. Grabbing a long branch, Aaron hoisted him self up to the top of the five foot stump and gazed over to where Lt. Honeycut stood, talking on his cell phone. Aaron whipped a camel into his mouth and lighted up. From his position, he scanned the woods, muttering quietly between drags, "Where are you, you crazy bastard?" Thinking about Roland was like having his insides kicked out of him, Aaron felt, as he shuddered with the thoughts of being wounded by an arrow.

Without an inkling of fear, the Bowman, lying beneath the rotting stump and covered with leaves, grinned and listened to the cop mumble to himself.

When Honeycut gave the forward signal once again, Aaron threw his cigarette butt on the ground, jumped down, and with his left foot twisted the butt back and forth.

Could take this bastard out right now with my knife, the Bowman thought, but then I might be caught, the rest are too close.

Aaron, out ten yards behind the line, decided to make sure his butt was out. Looking at the stump closely now, he wondered how the leaves and branches could climb up the old rotten trunk. Taking another look then raising his shot gun, his eyes squinted as he made out the outline of the phantom killer. A scream of outrage almost forced its way out of Aaron's throat. The arrow that cut through his wind pipe and spinal cord took care of that. Collapsing to the ground, he knew he soon would be wearing the pine overcoat.

Quickly dropping to sprint position, the Bowman raced off reaching Point Woods Trail, sped down the path, crossed over Rte. 27 to Seal Haulout Trail and wound down to the lower bluffs bordering Gardners Sound.

Like a careening deer, the Bowman raced, darted and cut across Money Pond Trail at Fox Den, headed north at full speed to North Road, then made a right back on Seal Haulout Trail to the Seals Observation Blind, just above where the truck was parked on the lower beach.

A rush of renewed energy shot through the demon's body as the truck headed west around Split Rock, passed by Carraries and rounded Shagwong Point. Firm sand at this time of year allowed the 40mph speed, and after making a left at the County Park cut, it was on to the deserted county check-in station. Making a left on to East Lake Drive, the Bowman maintained a safe 30mph speed.

When the dragnet arrived at the Bluffs Steve Honeycut's team merged with the Swat Team. Disappointment rang out in Steve's voice as he sputtered to no one in particular, "We missed him; how is it possible this beast just disappears at will?" Lowering his head, Steve clasped his large round face with both his hands. In the core of his stomach he felt a shudder of dismay and failure, thinking we were so close, yet nothing. And when suddenly Ryan yelled, "Where's Aaron?" Steve's heart crash-dived. "What do you mean, where's Aaron? He was posted on your left side; shit he was on your watch, son."

Panic gripped Steve as he raced back to the woods' edge yelling Aaron's name out repeatedly at the top of his lungs.

CHAPTER 49

When Todd and Roy arrived at Turtle Cove, the sadly familiar and reprehensible scene surrounded by the pulsating red and blue lights from the ambulance and the police cars, illuminated the beach grass up to the white walls of the Montauk Lighthouse. The figures in view, bathed in the flood of lights, appeared surreal as they went about their business. The surfers were still huddled behind Rawlins' truck, while he, lying on a gurney, was attended to by Mercedes, an advanced medical tech from the Montauk Fire Department.

Detective Danny Swan reporting to Todd and Roy informed them that the surfers claimed they had seen a camouflaged hunter high on the bluffs shooting arrows at Travis. "I'm going to chat with Rawlins now, Todd." "That's okay Danny; I'll take it from here," Todd replied.

Approaching the gurney, they heard Mercedes say, "Okay Sergeant we're ready to roll." Rawlins mustering up a laugh chuckled, "Hey doc, I don't know what you shot me up with but I feel real good." "Just a little thing we call a Montauk highball, Sergeant; it's designed to keep you comfy till you get to the ER."

"I have just a few questions for Rawlins," Todd explained to Mercedes, "alright with you?" "Sure Todd, he'll be fine; mostly a flesh wound. I cut the arrow down to his skin line; ER will extract the broadhead," she explained and handed the plastic bag containing the arrow to Todd.

Placing his hand on his buddies shoulder, Todd asked, "How you doing pal?" "Like she said Lieutenant I feel like I've had a few highballs."

A quick grin lighted Todd's somber face. "Try to recall Sergeant, anything unusual you noticed about the prick?" "Sorry Lieutenant, he was in full camouflage, 100 yards at least, up on the bluff. But you know, I took cover between reloading clips, and that bastard never ducked or flinched when I fired up at him. Wouldn't that mean, now that I think of it, that he knew my glock's range? Seems to me he knows his fire arms. Shit Lieutenant, maybe he has a police background, ex-military or a member of our gun club at the lodge."

For a moment the two officers locked eyes; Rawlins wiped a few beads of sweat off his brow. "He's good Todd. The way his arrows hit the surf board, let me tell you, was with dead accuracy. He was on a mission and he kept probing the board trying to flush the kid from underneath it. That kid has guts Todd, most surfers would have panicked. Yes-sir-ree Lieutenant. your prick is a marksman on Roy's level, no doubt about it."

"One more thing Sergeant, could you judge his height?" "Don't really know; nothing up there to measure him against. Regular height, I would say, whatever that is." "Give me a guess," prompted Todd. "Say between 5'10" and 6', slim build." "Thanks pal! Good luck and thanks Mercedes!" "Not to worry Lieutenant, this hero will be getting red carpet treatment," Mercedes replied winking.

As the ambulance rolled up the washboard road followed by the surfers in Rawlins' truck, Lt. Minx and his crew finished packing the several arrows and Travis' surfboard. Just when Todd began to fill Minx in on Rawlins' condition a roar of rapid repetitious gun fire startled the group.

CHAPTER 50

At a pace which would astonish the officer himself, Lieutenant Honeycut raced back into the woods for a quarter of a mile. Stopping momentarily to scan his position and catch his breath, he spotted a brown and white grouping of feather fins attached to an arrow in the not too far distance. Fearing the worst as he made his way closer, the sight of Aaron lying on the ground, with his face a whitish blue, his lips a dark purple and his eyes a dull wash of milk, terrified him. Kneeling beside his officer, Steve felt his neck for any sign of a pulse, yet knowing there would be none, reinforced the brutal situation.

Arriving moments later, Honeycut's fellow officers stopped five yards from the scene, stood silently and gave their agonized leader a few moments as he wept beside his fallen friend and officer.

Without any warning, as the Lieutenant rose to his feet, he bellowed a long curdling scream, followed by ear-piercing booming blasts as he pumped his twelve gauge shot gun discharging shot after shot After expelling all six shots, he hurled the gun, grabbed his glock, and squeezed out the sixteen shots the clip held.

No one spoke until Honeycut announced calmly, "That was for Aaron."

"Sir, speaking for all of us, we're feeling your pain; he was our brother too. Jesus Steve, don't punish your self. All of our lives are on the line. In this job we're between the hammer and the anvil." "You're right Troy. I just lost it there for a minute but......."

The ringing of Steve's cell phone helped to diffuse the charged situation and when Todd asked, "Hey Steve what's going on, we heard a number of gun shots?" Steve quipped, "It's okay Todd, you might say I just short circuited; let off some steam. Aaron's dead; the Bowman took him out and escaped."

"Secure the area Steve," Todd instructed. "Rawlins is on his way to the hospital; he's okay, Roy and I are on our way, Lt. Minx will follow. Meet me at West Gate; tell the Swat Team to meet us there for further deployment." "Roger Todd."

As Roy and Todd drove to West Gate much of what Roy had to say echoed Steve's feelings when he first found Aaron. "Don't you realize Roy that we're all feeling the same thing? We're a team buddy; all of us are a team and we'll get the monster."

CHAPTER 51

Roy made a violent left turn on to Camp Hero Road. Comfortable with his driving skills, yet strained, he blazed down the rugged lane at high speed coming to a fishtail, tire-smoking stop just outside West Gate. "Damn it Sergeant, this is not a Nascar race way." "Sorry Lt., but I feel like scrambled eggs after hearing about Aaron and Roland; hard driving eases my nerves." "Okay Roy, how about we not try to shatter any more track records today?"

"Roger that Lt."

Lieutenant Steve Honeycut and his partner accompanied by the Swat Team were making their way down the hillside to the gate as Todd and Roy arrived. An extra pang of sorrow welled up in the pit of Todd's stomach when he greeted Steve who was sweating profusely in the cool dry air and his body language saying it all as he moved in a rhythm of rage. Why, what had gone so wrong so terribly fast? What happened to

Aaron would linger forever with Steve. Todd knew the worst part of the job was to lose a fellow officer for whom you were responsible; a haunting burden which would not be easy to live with.

Gathering together the group chatted briefly with each other. When Todd asked Steve how he was holding up, Steve said, "I'll be alright, Todd, it was my initial shock of finding Aaron that caused my explosive behavior. The walk back here helped clear my head." "Good Steve," replied Todd, "I want you and Troy to take our rig back to Jack's and tell him you'd like the house special coffee. We'll take your jeep to do a sweep of the north side; won't be long so wait for us, Steve."

To Ryan, Todd directed, "Take your team to Seal Haulout Path, fan out no more than ten feet; follow the trail down to the Seal Observation Blind. Roy and I will be waiting down at Stepping Stones. If you flush the prick out, we'll get him!" And to Minx, "CB, if you find anything call me." "You got it Todd." "Let's go Roy; we have a Bowman to catch."

Gingerly approaching Senior Citizen speed on the way to Rte. 27, Roy glanced like a little puppy at Todd. Trying to control himself from bursting out laughing and knowing how hard it was for Roy to control his Nascar urges, Todd yelled, "Hit it Sergeant!"

With a broad grin and a heavy foot, Roy pounded the pedal down as if he were squashing a rodent and accelerated at devilish speed to the north side truck trail. Shifting into 4-wheel drive to navigate the pot-holed, crunchy, hard, bumpy road he kept a speed of 15mph.

At Clarks Cove they headed west to Stepping Stones. Todd laughed, when out of the blue, Roy asked, "Hey Lt. how come we never order the house special at Jack's?" "Because little buddy it's spiked with brandy; just what Steve needs.

Rolling at 30mph on the hard packed sand they made it to the blind in five minutes, armed themselves with 12 gauge shotguns and climbed up the dunes to the observation hut. Taking defensive positions in front of the blind, they first looked to the northeast scanning the spectacular maritime oak-holly forest for any sign of the Swat Team or the beast. An anxious fifteen minutes passed when suddenly two pheasants took flight in a westerly direction from the beach grass area. In unison Todd and Roy switched off their safeties; their eyes and ears straining.

Momentarily the Swat Team emerged from the tall grasses. Todd gave the "nothing wave" sending Ryan and his boys back to HQ'S.

"Now what?" Roy quizzed. Before Todd could respond a burgundy pick-up and a red truck rounded Rusty Waters Point some 75 yards up and stopped at the edge of the shore.

After a long squint, Roy said excitedly, "Hey Todd, that's Jack Yee and Paulie!" "Pull up to them," Todd said quickly.

Delighted at their chance meeting the four surfcasters greeted each other warmly. "What's happenin'?" asked Paulie, the renowned owner of Paulie's Tackle Shop, the hangout haven for the locals.

"Sneakin' in a little on duty fishin'?" teased Jack, the beloved Montauk fishing legend. "Usin' your glock sidearms for rods guys?" kidded Paulie.

"Nay, guys, you know that's against the law so we do one better, we use ESP and just think them in," Roy said with a straight face, tapping the side of his head with his index finger.

"Yeah, they just flop on the beach and bingo there's dinner!" "Shit Roy, don't let that get around; you'll put me out of business," Paulie laughed.

"No kidding guys, how's fishin'? Todd asked. Jack lighting his cigarette and in his soft voice said, "Quiet, Todd, that's why we call it fishing not catching." "I guess it's that time of year again Jack but how about bait; any around?" "Tons of it, all up and down the north side," Jack replied. "Just no fish," chimed in Paulie.

"Well, you know," added Jack, "yesterday the fish showed up at Jones Reef about one o'clock so today it'll be about two, hopefully," he continued as he exhaled a long stream of smoke. "Hell guys, you know these fishing grounds as well as we do; it could bust wide open anytime - anywhere. This is Montauk guys, an angler's dream come true!" Paulie said.

"By the by," asked Todd, "either of you notice any other truck going west bound on East Lake Drive on your way up here?"

"Only truck we saw," Jack stated, "was Joe the Plumber, trailing his boat back." "He had a shit load of flounder," Paulie pointed out. "What a sharpie good old Joe is!" Jack said.

"Thanks guys and good luck! Catch 'em up!" Todd said as he and Roy turned to walk back to the jeep.

Just as they approached East Lake Drive, Todd raised his hand and quickly said, "Take a right Roy." "To Gin Beach?" "Yeah, I want to check it out." Passing Gin Beach Metaphysical Market, Roy yelled, "That's Hither's truck, parked right there at the shop Todd!"

"Pipe down buddy, make a swing around the beach, then we'll stop at Susan's shop."

Gin Beach parking lot was deserted except for Susan's Gin Beach Café, locked and boarded up for the approaching winter. There were times Todd and Roy joined the hungry beach goers for tasty hotdogs that Susan, affectionately called "the hot dog lady," sold by the hundreds during the glorious summer beach days.

CHAPTER 52

Like an old-fashioned general store that provides something for everyone, Susan focused on necessary supplies for campers, fishermen and picnikers and believed in shopping locally. Homegrown vegetables from gardens as near as East Lake Drive and Thunder Island Coffee from the Shinnecock Reservation were top sellers along with the metaphysical tools including incense, candles, healing arts, affirmative tinctures and aroma therapies. With many customers who relished such an unusual, community spirited shop, its creative and adventurous owner fascinated everyone.

Susan's hands held the sides of her face, her wide smile beamed the moment she saw Todd and Roy. Dashing out from behind the counter she hugged them both. "It's so good to see you boys," she cried.

Hither, quickly walked toward them from the freezer carrying two Cherry Vanilla ice cream bars, and squeezed Roy's arm. "What brings you here?" she asked. "Just going to ask you the same thing Hither," Roy gushed, smiling. "Shopping of course," Hither answered as she held out her right hand with two bars of Chandrika Ayurverdi soap. "Roy, buy some of this soap for your Mom and yourself; it makes your body tingle all over!"

I don't need soap for that he almost said to Hither, but instead, he asked, "How about one of those ice cream bars?" Without answering, Hither looked at Todd, "How about you taking some of this soap to Jamie; she'll love it." "Okay Hither, I'm sold; I'll take two bars of your mysterious soap Susan," laughed Todd.

"I've got some minestrone soup all set for lunch and plenty of it," Susan chirped, "Please share it with me," as she began to ladle four mugs of hot soup, then sliced chunks from a seeded baguette.

"Damn good soup Susan," Roy said as Todd nodded with a mouthful.

They all ate slowly, savoring the taste and aroma of a very authentic Italian minestrone, dipping the crusty bread every now and then into it. The shop smelled sweet and pungent, the soft lights and classical music playing in the background adding to its special aura.

The ringing of Todd's cell phone interrupted the peaceful interlude.

"Hey Minx, what's up?" "We found a camouflage canteen, Todd, under a tree stump. I'll bet a month's salary on whom it belongs to and sure in hell there's got to be plenty of DNA cells on the mouth piece!" "Good work; damn good work CB, hold on a sec."

In the middle of explaining Minx's find to Roy, Hither flew into a coughing fit. Gasping for breath as Todd and Roy together yelled, "Look up at the birds," Susan tapped her on the back. "I'm okay, it was just some hard crust of the bread; got caught in my throat," Hither said huskily.

"You have to really dunk that Tuscan bread Hither," Susan reminded her young customer. "Sure you're alright?" Roy asked.

"I'm fine Roy, go ahead and finish your soup," Hither replied. Launching his puppy-catcher smile Roy chuckled and dug in.

Ending his conversation with Minx, Todd was keyed up. "Lt. Minx will have a lab report by tomorrow Roy. He and his guys bagged all the leaves around the stump. Looks to me that we'll nail this bastard by the end of the week what with DNA for sure! Doesn't get any better than that Sergeant!"

"You can say that again Lt."

A composed Hither had carried the mugs to the little sink in the back while Susan listened intently to the boys' conversation. When Todd inquired if she had seen any trucks pass her shop, Susan said she worked in the back until Hither arrived. "How about you Hither?" Todd asked, as she placed the clean, dry mugs on a shelf.

"I did see a blue pickup pull into Gone Fishing on my way here."

"How about the driver, Hither?" "Just saw the tail end of the truck."

"Thanks Hither and Susan thank you for the lunch. Roy here and I really enjoyed it. Sorry, but we have to roll." Let's move out Roy."

"Where to Lt., Gone Fishing?" asked Roy. "Gone Fishing it is sir."

Pulling in next to the main building, they spotted a blue pickup. Checking out the front seat and tail gate they found nothing. The tires revealed no sand particles.

Walking inside they met the owners', Tom and Maureen's, daughter Donna, working alongside Barbara. Looking up from her paperwork, Donna smiled, and greeted the officers, "Hi Todd, Hi Roy, you guys need a boat?" "Too late in the season for that," Todd replied. "Hey Donna, who owns that blue pick up outside?" asked Roy. Donna called over to the manager TJ and inquired. Immediately he yelled toward the back office, "Bob you've got visitors."

With a stack of marine supplies in his hands, Bob appeared, took a look at Todd and cried, "I'm innocent!" "Hey buddy," Todd said, got a question for you. When you got here today where were you coming from?" "Let's see... I took a run to Gin Beach, looked for any boats, saw three, checked out the water fowl and that's it." "See any other trucks?" Todd continued. "No Todd, you know it starts to get pretty isolated now with winter almost here."

"Thanks guys; catch you all later," Todd said as he and Roy hurried out, jumped back into the jeep, and headed for Jack's.

Settling back, Todd thoughts were of all those loveable DNA cells on the canteen's rim.

CHAPTER 53

An invisible blanket of fear and rage permeated the village of Montauk. When the residents learned of the brutal killing of the one officer, tension mounted. The townies had complete confidence in their law enforcement officials, understood how hard their police were working under such ominous circumstances, but they felt more and more vulnerable. Nonetheless, strong-willed and hearty, they by their heritage, carried on as usual, seemingly defying danger. Some how they would get through this 'winter of discontent' they told themselves.

No way can we allow the Bowman to continue Todd knew as he thought about the inconceivable horror that was infiltrating his sea side village.

Stepping back from the Bowman's chart while Roy re-examined pertinent documents, Todd looked at his chart like a junkyard dog with a grudge to settle. Indeed he relished the new evidence; the bowman's canteen containing DNA cells, one black eye lash, two 4" black head hairs (Minx had called earlier to inform Todd they were processing), and a total of eight Grim Reaper carbon arrows from Roland's rig and Travis' board.

Could this be enough to end these killing sprees at long last, Todd dared to think?

Re-filling his coffee cup, walking over to the front window and looking south over the vast grayish-green Atlantic, he stared out across the hypnotic, glistening swells mesmerized by the perpetual motion of the yellow slants of sunlight dancing across the windowpane. His mind drifted into a vortex of weightless, flickering clusters that appeared like the lights of heaven. Closing his eyes and sipping his coffee, he stood there thinking that nothing had really changed about this ghoulish investigation until yesterday's discoveries. Praying that the forensic team could deal the fatal blow to the sadistic psychopath by their findings and put a stop to these chilling November days of human suffering would at last put the murderer behind bars.

Suddenly the ringing of the telephone snapped Todd's attention. Roy listened intently to the voice at the other end and then replaced the receiver. "CB is on his way Lt." "Good Roy and always remember bud, psyche 101 says hard evidence are case breakers, soft evidence are teasers. You know Roy, this case has produced pretty ugly deafening silences that have clearly confused all of us but I have a good feeling about this new evidence."

"Jeeze, talk about oxymorons," Roy quipped, "you're right on this morning with your 'pretty ugly' Lt!" "Damn Roy," laughed Todd, "every so often you do come up with a winner.

Oxymoron, that's so cool little buddy." Smiling widely, Roy was proud of himself using the new word he learned last night watching Jeopardy.

Returning to the chart, Todd thought about how CB and his team had worked long into the night; forensics was tedious, painstaking, snail pacing work. Praying again for that nugget of evidential incite that would pay off in big dividends and link A to B and B to C, he was counting on these unsung heroes to bust the case.

Yelling, "Anybody home?" Lieutenant Minx, carrying evidence bags and a carton of fresh baked donuts from Brent's lumbered in limping stiffly, and placed them on the conference table.

"Looks like you guys had a late night, too," Minx said yawning. "Sometimes we have to huff and puff until we're ready to drop. On the other hand there are those occasions when we've time to kill, so we watch forensic video updates. I feel like I've been kicked by a mule from that cot I slept on in my office last night," he laughed.

Roy who hadn't taken his eyes off the donuts asked if anyone wanted some fresh brewed coffee. "I'll take it black," Minx announced; Todd waved a negative.

Minx rearranged his tired butt several times before settling down, then squeezed his tired eyes shut, lightly massaging them with his southpaw fingers. Finally he took a soft cloth from his pant's pocket and methodically cleaned the bits of pollution off his reading peepers and placed them over the bridge of his perfectly slender nose.

Trying to stay awake, he looked at Todd and Roy with sleepy amber eyes and said quietly but in a determined voice, "I know you guys are dying to pick my mind but please hold off your questions till I finish. I have good news and not so good news." "Minx, give it to me straight," Todd interrupted. "Do we have a case breaker or not?"

"Yes and no fellas. It all depends on how you look at it. Yes, we have a strong case of DNA evidence, but no, nobody connected to it. Shall I continue?" "Please do," Todd replied anxiously.

CHAPTER 54

Minx shifted into what he called his fifth gear and with typical crackerjack delivery, he began, "My techs bagged all the leaves under the stump and in the surrounding area, vacuumed for any fibers, spores, molds, etc. A video was taped of the entire scene and each frame checked to insure nothing was overlooked."

Clearing his throat and taking a sip of coffee he paused to explain, "Parsing this evidence was a Herculean task but we managed."

"Just out of curiosity CB, how does one analyze crunchy, fragile fall leaves?" Todd asked, putting on his best Manhattan College Jasper, inquisitive Sherlock Holmes face.

"In plain words Todd we laid out the leaves and the vacuumed material on butcher paper and examined each specimen using a boom stereo microscopic microscope which can enlarge items from a power of five to eighty times its size. The team went over every inch of the material dusting meticulously for prints."

"CB," chimed in Roy, "I didn't know you could dust leaves for prints." "Only dried out leaves Roy," Minx explained, "since fingerprints can adhere to them unlike new sprouting leaves which have a fresh coating of oil. Needless to say we know the Bowman wears gloves, hence no prints." "Damn CB, forensic work is a hard-assed grinding job," Roy said as his right hand swooshed down into the Brent's donut box once again.

Shrugging, Minx replied, "That's forensics Roy, we plug away until we find them golden nuggets." Taking a bite of his cinnamon donut and washing it down with more coffee, Minx continued like a patient professor, "You see Roy, it's a science that deals with the relation and application of facts and evidence to be presented in court to insure a successful conviction. Capice Roy?" "Capice CB."

"Let's take these hairs Roy," Minx said, holding up the evidence bags. "These hairs Roy contain mitochondrion which is a cellular material that is found outside the nucleus in the cell walls of hair. It qualifies as a very soft DNA sample. Now Roy, it's not as specific as the swab of DNA taken off the canteen. That cell material is hard evidence; it's a shoe-in, a prosecutor's dream. So now, follow me here guys, we matched all the DNA profiles against the FBI's-CODIS (which stands for combined DNA index system) and sorry to say and to every one's great disappointment, no hit. Our perp has no arrest record so we're in a 'hold mode' until we come up with a suspect. I'll put the profile into the Questionable DNA file and we'll have to wait.

Also there were no finger prints on the arrow or shoe prints at the scene."

Looking up from his yellow notepad, Todd's eyes narrowed and stared into Minx's amber eyes. Raising his left hand and holding his thumb and index finger two inches apart, Minx indicated how close they had come to catching the hinterland psychopath. "This close, fellas; the tide is changing in our favor," he said confidently.

"Taunting us and killing with impunity are coming to an end; we all know that, don't we?"

"Sure CB," Todd responded. "And just to assure you, let me tell you that this chameleon of ours is about to under-go a new color change that even he will find piercingly painful." "What color change?" Roy asked quickly. "Pin stripes Roy, good old fashioned pin stripes."

Unfolding his legs, Minx stood up, circled the command room slowly, like a caged lion, and stopped opposite Todd and Roy. "Guys I don't mean to lecture but this is important for you to understand. As much as forensic science has moved forward in the last hundred years, there is one axiom that never changes. And this comes from the renowned French criminologist Dr. Emile Locard."

Ring any bells boys?" "Not really," Roy replied, "the only doctors I know are Dr. Knott and Dr. Mapula from the Village Medical Center."

Preferring not to comment, Minx said, "Locard's theory simply put is one of the basic laws of forensic science. It states that the criminal always leaves something of himself at the scene of his crime, something perhaps even too infinitesimal to be seen by the naked eye, and always takes something from the crime scene away with him."

In silence Minx watched as Todd and Roy processed his words and when Todd said, "Okay CB, we know he left his canteen, but what did the creep take?" "That's easy Todd, his clothes carried away fiber, spores, mold, leaf dust, bits of dirt etc."

Minx sat down, resting his sorry butt again, lamenting his uncomfortable sleepless night. Roy suggested he purchase a Cabelas outdoor camper cot from the Amagansett Outdoor Store.

"Ask either Skye, Susan or Barry to order you one CB," urged Roy. "That old World War I army issue cot you are hanging on to will kill you; get with the times Lieutenant!"

As Minx prepared to leave Roy refilled his coffee cup, "You're good to go sir." Todd not wanting Minx to leave just yet said,

"This perp is ratcheting up his killing sprees, CB, in fact he could be out there right now - on the hunt; you know that."

"I sure do Todd; I can feel him but I sense his control slipping at the same time his rage is rising." Both officers looked perplexed.

"We have to also consider the issue of medication. Now we don't know if he's on any medication or drugs. Nevertheless, it has been determined that some psychotics can be extremely brutal if they stop taking whatever it is they've been on. But I don't know where to place this nut on a mental health scale." "Okay CB, let's have Roy check with his snitches, got that Roy, and see if anyone is using heavy drugs or any weird shit. In fact, Roy, assign two detectives to check out the local hospitals and rehab centers for recently released patients who have been on medication."

Edging toward the door, Minx said, "Well boys this is a rap. I'm going home to catch up on my sleep. So I will leave you with this: 'diem dulcem habes' guys." "What the hell does that mean?" Roy shouted. "It's Latin for have a nice day." "Hey, write it for me?"

Minx leaned over and scribbled the saying on Roy's pad.

Practicing aloud, Roy repeated 'diem dulcem habes' four times while Todd rolled his eyes and laughed.

CHAPTER 55

There were those surfcasters who could never get enough of fishing, and like the "metal man" who loved nothing more than fishing, Gary and Bill had hoped to join Mike for one more day of good old-fashioned camaraderie and a few keepers.

Gary kept trying to reach Mike and finally came to the conclusion that if he were still camped out at Camp Hero's lower lot, the cell signal wasn't working. As he waited for Bill at Montauk's west overlook, Gary thoughts locked back into his book that he was working on. In fact, he had been writing his book for years, and couldn't help but be amazed that his author buddy, Richie Prince, had banged out two mystery novels in two years and was working on a third. Talk about 'pride, pomp and circumstance' that guy's on a roll! How the hell does he do it?

Never figuring out the answer to his question, Gary was interrupted by the blast of a horn. "Vanstaal Bill" as the fishermen tagged him, pulled up alongside. "Good Morning bud," Gary's deep baritone voice called out, "ready to go and kill some fish?" "You betcha buddy; let's move our asses, 'time and tides wait for no man'."

Holding up his hand, Gary said, "Wait there a minute Bill, we have two hours till the last of the incoming so why don't we drop by Paulie's for some free coffee and I'll drop off Judy's homemade blueberry muffins, Paulie's favorites." "Mine, too, let's go!"

As Gary followed Bill he reminisced about all the fun times he and Bill and Mike and Richie had during the last several years. It's what fishing is all about; those moments shared with good friends on the same page.

Pulling into Paulie's Tackle Shop, Gary and Bill noticed several fishing buggies. "Must be a convention going on," Gary said. "Or a winter sale," guessed Bill. Whatever it was they knew it would be fun, especially with the group of characters that hung out there.

Why even some of their names were hilarious!

Entering the shop, they heard the loud singing of Happy Birthday Susan, Happy Birthday to You! Clapping, cheering and whistling followed as Susan, Paulie's faithful, pretty manager, opened the white sealed red ribbon tied envelope Jack handed to her which was stuffed with a bulging wad of birthday donations from her fans. Surprised and delighted, she thanked everyone warmly as she flicked away a few teardrops from her cheeks.

"Cut the cake, cut the cake," the gang cried. "Hold your bait," Susan sang out, as she took the knife from Paulie, closed her eyes, blew out the candles, and made the first slice into the huge strawberrry shortcake Paul had purchased at the Montauk Bake Shop. As Paul held out two paper plates, Susan laughed as she put a big piece on both while Paul announced, "Hey guys, I've got a wolf in my stomach!"

Doesn't get any better than this Gary thought as he looked around at the laughing, tough, no frills sportsmen; decent hardworking guys who were as generous with their hard earned money as they were with their knowledge of fishing and loyalty. He recognized them all; Pennsylvania Bob, Toad, Paul the Skisher, Bill the Cop, Jack the LegendaryYee, Florida Bob, Richie and Linda Prince, Ken the Orca, (Richie's brother), Coast Guard Charlie, Joe the Plumber, Smilin' Geoff, Ed and Jack, Craig the Laughing Man, Kathy the Charmer, Justin the Hunter, his girl Meaghan, Sean the Box Turtle, Marshall the Owl, Chicken Scratch Richie, Wood Carver George, Eugenia the Editor, Food Guru Ray, Jake the Handyman, The Michaelson, Ray Sherry, Lovebirds Tammy and Rick, Bob the Hack, Nick Lacross and chewing on biscuits, from Jack Yee's ever ready stash, was Austin, Vic's handsome dog.

No one had seen Mike for a few days. Although not unusual, for sometimes he got carried away, and stayed in his beat up old camper for almost a week, fishing his heart out, Gary and Bill decided to have a look.

Driving down to Camp Hero's lower lot, they parked, suited up and headed toward a major blitz.

Chapter 56

Reaching the water's edge they fired their plugs into the boiling fish. Voila! They both had bass on their lines. In the next moment Gary spotted a dead seal, pushed by the waves onto the beach. An arrow was sticking out of its neck.

Making a closer inspection, Bill asked, "Shit Gary, whada-ya think?" "It's probably some of the locals pissed that the seal was robbing their fish so they took matters in to their own hands."

"Yeah, can't blame them." Bill muttered, "It's hard enough to catch these striped beauties but then to have them stolen by this unremorseful stealthy opportunist, well….. serves him right!"

Satisfied that they had solved the riddle of the seal, they resumed their fishing. An hour later the birds and the fish were out into the deeper water. Bill ballyhooed, "Shit Gary it's over; they're too far out and the tide's carrying them out even further." A disappointed Gary agreed, "That's fishing Bill. Sometimes we win but most of the time they win. It's a game of quid pro quo."

Checking his watch Gary announced, "It's 11:40 pal, let's go and wake up our "metalman". They headed to the Sewer Pipe and took the path to the bluffs reaching Mike's newly painted old camper.

Knocking on the rear door Gary called out, "Hey Metalman, fish were in," to no response. "Mike, it's Bill and Gary, you awake buddy?" he called again. Weird, thought Gary, I know he's a deep sleeper but it's practically noon and with growing concern he pounded harder, his fist hammering away like a Swat Team's iron-ramming rod. Climbing up on the rear entrance platform, his head almost snapped back as he got a whiff of foulness that definitely smelled like rotting clams coming from the slightly opened window of the door. A jolt of cold shivers surged through his body as his hand closed apprehensively around the brass doorknob, slowly turning it and listening to the clicks of the tumbler.

All at once the door sprang half way open, almost knocking him off the platform. Poking his head around the doorframe he peered into the curtain drawn dark camper's living quarters. The smell of death rushed up, scorching his nostrils. Instinctively his right hand shot up covering his mouth and nose as he gagged on the stench jetting up at him, stinging his bulging eyes as he stared at Mike's twisted rigormortis ridden body with an arrow firmly embedded in his back.

Gary recoiled from the slaughter scene like a cornered cobra. His face, flushed with anger and bone numbing terror, his stomach taking on the heat and fury of an exploding volcano, he felt a large wave of larva like liquid spiraling up from the pit of his belly, ripping through his throat. It exited his mouth straight out like the flames of a sapphire-blue and crimson-orange fire from an enraged dragon. He doubled over; cold shivers were clawing at his spine. Desperately trying to regain control of this insane moment, he passed his hand through his curly gray hair, knocking his fishing cap to the ground. The only sounds were the seagulls circling overhead in the distance still working the bait. His heaving stopped; the inventory of his dinner and breakfast were splattered all over the ground, steaming up now in the cool Montauk air. Slamming the door shut he lowered himself to the ground.

His mouth felt like cotton. Digging into his backpack he retrieved his bright green embroidered towel his wife Judy had given him on his sixtieth birthday with the words 'Happy Birthday Honey'. Wiping the remains of the stinkin' hot vomit from his lips and face, he managed to choke out in profound bitterness, "Mike's dead Bill, he was shot with an arrow. It looks similar to the one in the seal."

Bill stood still. The news hit him like an incoming mortar round.

Seizing his water bottle Gary rinsed out his mouth, gulped down half of its contents, then sat with his head lowered on the camper's steps. Tears fell from his blue orbs as he shouted, "Oh my good Lord, son of a bitch, tell me this isn't happening!" Struggling to grasp the situation himself, Bill managed to say, "I know you and Mike were like brothers Gary but now isn't the time to mourn, we may be in danger here so let's get the hell away."

Fighting off hot and cold chills, his breath coming in short spurts while his heart hammered like a race horse crossing the finish line, Gary just sat without moving. Bill stared at Gary with sheer hopelessness, trying to comprehend what Gary had seen, for this was the first time in his life that Bill had been this close to someone that was dead; he was desperately fearful. The horror of the way Mike was killed made him feel as if he were swimming in quicksand. Stiff hairs sprouted on the back of his neck.

Somehow Gary, too, realized they could very well be the next target and got to his feet, snatched his rod, and said, "Let's get out of here." "I'm scared shitless, Bill admitted, "I feel like I want to run for my life." "Good," snapped Gary, "that's exactly what we're going to do; run for our lives!" Running as fast as they could down the pot-holed road to their trucks, some 150 yards from Mike's camper, they reached their vehicles puffing like two over-worked steam engines.

After jamming their poles into their front bumper rod holders, they hopped into their respective vehicles, turned on the ignitions, pounded the gas pedals, squealed and smoked along the hard, crusty trail surface creating a dust storm like two Nascar race drivers fighting for the checkered flag.

Arriving at the state concession stand, Gary pulled into the bus stop reserved for touring busses only. Bill pulled up fast to Gary's rear bumper, jumped quickly out of his truck, shouting, "Gary what the hell did you stop for?" Looking at Bill's still traumatized face, knowing how emotionally shocked his friend was he said, "Get a grip on yourself pal, we're safe here, I'm calling 911. You and I will wait here for the police and escort them to Mike's camper, okay?"

"Yeah, okay but Jesus Gary, I don't want to go back there." "Nor do I, Bill but we'll do it for Mike." Looking at the pavement, Bill nodded his head and said, "I guess it will be alright having police protection." "Hey buddy, I don't like this anymore than you do, however, it's the right thing to do," as his shaking finger punched in 911 on his cell. The responder asked, "What is your emergency?" Shit Gary thought, what a terrible way to end a perfectly good day of Montauk fishing.

CHAPTER 57

It is quite possible that the noontime sun-splashed rays from the cloudless turquoise sky shining brilliantly on this another cold, crisp November day, masked the dark foreboding aura in the community. At any rate, for Todd chewing on Jamie's Italian fried red peppers hero and Roy, chomping away at his mother's Chicken Popikosh and homemade dumplings, it was a rare but enjoyable break.

Turning to the cooking section in Dan's papers, Todd read a recipe for Montauk Potato Pancakes from Jack's Coffee Shop. His mouth started watering just picturing those golden brown scrumptious cakes. "Hey Roy, listen up. I know you're as crazy about potato pancakes as I am and guess what? Jack sent in his recipe to Dan's with a new wrinkle."

"I'm all ears, Lt. But how the hell can you enhance upon potato pancakes with a side dish of applesauce like my mother makes?"

"My very thought, too, but get this buddy," as he read directly from the paper. "Grate potatoes and onions into a bowl with a hand grater. Jeeze, I hate that job; Jamie won't grate so it's either me or no cakes."

"It's the same in Mom's kitchen Todd. I'm the grater; Mom claims she has 'senior citizen hands'. Why not use a blender or a food processor Todd?" "Because you get a thinner dough Roy, that's what the city folk do. Anyway, here's the new twist, add lemon juice to keep the potatoes white and put the mixture into a strainer. Squeeze out as much liquid as possible. Hold the liquid for about ten minutes and let it settle thus enriching the flavor of the potatoes. Then simply add starch back to the potato mixture. So that's Jack's secret - aha."

"That's very interesting Lt., I've helped Mom hundreds of times and she never did that. Make me a copy; I'll surprise her with this new take on the recipe." "Sure Roy, and do you know what, I like Tabasco sauce on mine; gives them a New Orleans kicker."

Looking at Roy's dumplings Todd remarked, "Those Haluskami are the perfect size. "What's a Hakus….?" "It's a Hungarian term for dumpling." "Oh, I'll have to tell Mom, she likes to be up on her cooking terminology."

Abruptly, their conversation was disrupted by the ear-piercing ring of the hot line phone. Here we go again, Roy's frown announced, more human slaughter. This ulcer-producing case was weighing heavily on him; his nerves became more brittle with each red phone siren. Picking up the phone on the third ring with Todd on the extension, they listened in silence for five minutes.

"Are we rolling Lt.?" Roy stood up and asked.

"Wait one, Roy, I'm trying to piece this puzzle together. Let's see now, male victim found in camper parked in lower Camp Hero lot. Shot in back with arrow, seal found close by, killed by arrow. Ask yourself Roy, why kill a seal?"

Before Roy could reply, Todd said, "Because Roy, he set up an ambush." "An ambush, Lt?" "It's logical Roy; the guy was out fishing; he sees the seal get shot. What do you think he's going to do?" "Run for his life." "There you go Roy, he runs back to his safe haven - except the killer is already there."

"I'm with you Lt. every step of the way."

"Okay Roy, now the poor guy starts to enter his camper and the killer takes him out. Now from the odor of the camper it probably happened a few days ago. This is a job for Minx and his team, Roy. So, call CB, have him conduct the interviews of the two witnesses. As soon as you get CB rolling, we'll go up and inform the chief."

"Roger Lt. Am on it."

CHAPTER 58

Today's Woman's Big Bucks Shoot-Off Tournament, an event held quarterly at the lodge, was well attended with the usual prevailing excitement; just what the townies needed to take their minds off the critical current catastrophes.

Money exchanged hands; the betting to win, place and show was fierce. Scheduled to begin at 9:00am sharp, the competitors were still practicing as the spectators took their seats. The hot and heavy bets were placed on Hither, Meaghan, Jamie Miller, Lisette Jacobs of Reese's Pro Shop, Cathy the Charmer and Susan from Paulie's Tackle along with Kathy of Johnny's Tackle Shop and Corrine, the Bucktail.

Justin Winchester's voice roared over the intercom asking the twenty bow women contestants to take their positions while last minute bets were placed. A simple sheet of rules had been given to member and guests. The tournament consisted of six rounds, five shots for each round within a three minute time limit for each round. Points would be added up and winner declared. The bull's eye was worth ten points; the next five rings decreased by one point - 9,8,7,6,5 accordingly. Three hundred was the perfect field point score. First place prize was a whopping $5,000, second place $2,000, third place $1,000 and the last five runner-up spots $500 each.

The range officer set the official rule levels. Field point scoring was determined as follows: 298-300 put a shooter into the triple AAA class level, 295-297 was the double AA level, 290-295, the single A level, 280-290, the B level, 270-280, the C level. The X in the middle of the bull's eye had no point value unless there was a tie. If there was a tie, the X'S were counted to determine the winner. However, if a tie still resulted the dreaded water shot would determine the winner. If there was a water shot tie there would be two winners. The likelihood of that occurring would be like trying to catch the wind in a net; totally inconceivable bow-wise speaking.

Shooting order was established by the luck of the draw. Two competitors would shoot simultaneously at two different targets sixty feet apart. Two range officers would accompany the shooters to the targets throughout all six rounds, recording their scores, which would be posted immediately on the large lighted digital score board for all to chew on.

As the official tournament clock struck 11:30am Lisette and Jamie had just completed their rounds. Both field scores placed them in the double AA level. Reese and Todd shook hands, proud of their wives' performances, also patting themselves on their backs for doing such a good job of coaching them. Susan wound up in the single A level and both Cathy and Kathy the B level.

Tension rose as the last two shooters stood at their firing marks. You could almost hear a bird's feather touch the ground. Everyone sat at the edge of their seats, their eyes glued to the cliff hanger of a finish that unfolded as Hither's and Meaghan's arrows whistled to the targets. The scene was right up there with a Kentucky Derby breathtaking finish.

Hither, by shooting quickly in rapid succession as Roy taught her, helped to avoid muscle fatigue and the shakes. She shot with a cool head, target smarts, good trigger release and with considerable accuracy. On the other hand Meaghan's approach was thoughtful, patient and uncompromising. Her routine was slow but calculating. Both girls were hitting their bull's eyes dead center. Roy and Justin kept an ongoing score in their heads and concluded at the end of the fifth round it was going to be damn close. In fact it would take a sixth round to determine the winner. The score board reflected their first five rounds:

MEAGHAN
Round 1 - 10/10/10/9/10
Round 2 - 10/10/9/10/10
Round 3 - 10/10/10/10/10
Round 4 - 10/10/10/10/10
Round 5 - 10/10/10/10/10

HITHER
Round 1 - 9/10/10/10/10
Round 2 - 10/10/9/10/10
Round 3 - 10/10/10/10/10
Round 4 - 10/10/10/10/10
Round 5 - 10/10/10/10/10

Hither completed round six first. Sixty seconds later Meaghan completed her sixth round. Elie called out the scores: Meaghan

10/10/10/10/10, Hither 10/10/10/10/10. Both had shot thirty five X'S. "So ladies and gentlemen we have a tie," bellowed Elie.

"Both shooters shot 298 field points plus 35 X'S. This folks is a tie in the Triple AAA class level and you know what that means boys and girls," he yelled as loud as he could and handed the mike over to Justin.

Justin's shock matched that of the wagering audience. No one could believe that Hither and Meaghan were tied. Talk about failure of expectations, this was a bitter pill to swallow. Oh well, this is Montauk and all one could do is to go along with the drum beat, Justin thought.

Clearing his throat and preparing an upbeat tone, Justin called out, "Okay folks, settle down now…. settle down. This is the first time, the very first time in the history of our lodge, that we have had a tie between two competitors in the Triple AAA class level. As a result of this situation we must adhere to the rules book."

Turning to page seventeen, he read, "*A tie is defined as two competitors having the same field point and number of X'S hits. The shooters must resolve the tie utilizing the water shot if and only if they are in the Triple AAA level. All other ties may be resolved by shooting another six rounds; five shots with a three minute limit.*"

Justin paused, looked up from the rules book and asked, "Are there any questions?" No one spoke. From the look on their faces all were in a subdued, dreamlike state, absorbed by the turn of events. The thought of a water shoot out was mind-whirling and perhaps a bookmaker's jackpot to boot. Justin, too, realized the gravity of rule #130. Suddenly, he turned to the range officer and asked him to arrange for the water shot.

Several members began to ask Roy his opinion. Shit, he thought, even a master marksman had difficulty with this kind of shot. It took years of practice under my belt, he well remembered, when he performed this feat. These girls didn't have the mastery of bowmanship even though they had achieved the triple AAA level.

Almost ready to protest, Hither took the wind out of his sails, as she sidled up to him, "Roy, this'll be a tough shot but I can handle it!" "Oh, pardon me Robinhood, I didn't know you were the "best of the best. Have you any idea how formidable that shot it? Jesus, get real." "You taught me it's all in the timing, right?" "Right." "So it's just another shot that has to be executed with extreme precision Roy; draw, set, aim, fire. That's what you drummed into my head."

An angry Roy retorted loudly, "Just listen to yourself; you're a Triple AAA level, that shot is on Houdini's level. Who do you think you are?" "Raising his voice a notch higher, "And it's a neon green moving target the size of a quarter twenty yards out! That's sixty long feet and every foot the arrow travels has to be pure perfection with exact timing. Damn it Hither, it's one of the toughest shots in archerydome! There is no, and I mean no, room for error. I know; I've done it."

"If Meaghan's game, then I'm game."

Overhearing their discussion, Meaghan and Justin approached and Justin started to explain, "Hey guys, this is the only fair way to determine a winner. You all heard the rules. Meaghan's willing, how 'bout you Hither?"

"This is bullshit," stormed Roy, "and you know it Justin. Neither one of them are ready for this shot." Before Justin could answer, Meaghan responded in high spirits, relaxed and confident, "I'm more than willing to play by the rules; it's the water shot for me. You in or out Hither?"

"I am in; let's get it on!"

CHAPTER 59

Like a dog with a bone, Roy shook his head back and forth, thinking in compound bow disgust how wrong the situation was.

With the odds heavily in Meaghan's favor because of her years of experience, Hither was doomed. Sure Hither could get lucky but luck didn't figure in on the water shot. His eyes bore into Justin's as he said to him, without looking at Hither, "Okay, if that's what Hither wants she's in." "I am in Roy and that's that." "I still say this is bullshit Justin but it's Hither's call."

"Let the competition begin," Justin announced uneasily and then to Roy, "when the shooting commences you and I can view the results with the super slow video camera. Both girls will be allowed a half hour target practice; fifteen arrows for each of them." Taking a coin out of his pocket, "Okay Roy call it," as he flipped it into the air. "Heads," predicted Roy. "Heads it is pal."

Fifteen minutes later Hither and Roy were standing on the firing line staring down at the mechanical water shot device. The tank was 3' wide, 2' deep and 4' high. The 6' tube in the shape of an inverted J protruded from the top of the tank. Every twenty seconds a bright green neon drop of water dripped from the tube and splashed to the floor. The white walls of the indoor range were a good contrast for the tiny neon droplet.

Concentration replaced Roy's pissed mood. "We're in good position Hither," and answered her querying glance, "you're up first both times; that puts the pressure on her and the best part is you'll get more arm and body rest. Nodding, Hither wide-eyed listened attentively as Roy continued. "Now study the drops coming out of the tube and count to yourself the number of seconds it takes to reach the parallel line where you want your arrow to intercept it. Okay? Now Hither, when you're satisfied you have the correct count, then start shooting. But remember Hither, you must become one with the arrow and the target."

Patting her butt affectionately and smiling, Roy whispered, "You're the best of the best Hither; you can do this. My money's on you!" Hither's astonishing dark eyes swept into his and in a soft voice she murmured, "Thanks teach, I'll take it from here."

She's got nerves of steel thought Roy, amazed at her utter calmness. "I'll be watching the camera replays of your shots Hither, so any adjustments you need to make I'll call them out to you."

Confident and determined, Hither intensified her focus. She sliced through the neon green drop twice during her practice period. Meaghan, not faring well at all, missed the target with all fifteen arrows.

"Hither take your mark, fire at will," Justin announced. Her first shot hit the drop on the left front of the arrow. The second shot splashed off the right middle. Her third shot was premature; the water splashed off the arrow's feathers.

Joining Roy at the camera, Hither showed no emotion, as they watched Meaghan's first shot. The bubble dropped to the floor before her arrow connected. Aiming her second shot, she squeezed the release trigger on the moving target slicing it dead center. With exhilarating satisfaction, she waited for confirmation.

Moments later Justin shouted, "Meaghan is the winner!" An explosion of applause, shouts and whistles ricocheted through the indoor range while an euphoric Meaghan watched the replay of her stupendous shot. Standing beside her, Justin's beaming face confirmed how proud he felt, and the sweetheart of a kiss he planted fully on her lips, thrilled the crowd once again. "That was one hell of a shot," Justin said, "pure perfection Meaghan. This will go down in women's tournament history. We'll call it "the Meaghan split!" Turning toward Elie, he asked, "Can you make blow ups of this shooting frame?" "Sure thing Justin, not a problem." "Good; make up six Elie and have them framed. I want to hang them up in my office, in Meaghan's office, the trophy room and in the bar and dining room."

What a day for a daydream to come true Meaghan thought, not to mention a check for $5,000! And what exquisite pleasure to have beaten Hither. Why it was like taking a bite out of the forbidden fruit!

When Hither and Roy congratulated her, Meaghan returned their words with a smug grin that resembled a wolfish curl ready to snarl. Justin's announcement interrupted the testy atmosphere as he said "Drinks and lunch on us guys," and grabbing Meaghan's hand left quickly. "Thanks Justin," Roy called out, "meet you at the bar."

After the crowd had dispersed Hither and Roy sat on the empty gallery bleacher seats. "Roy, you're a good teacher," Hither uttered earnestly but unemotionally. "This has no reflection on you; I blew it. After all someone had to lose. Next time I'll win."

Wrapping his arms around her and leaning his head on her shoulder, he heard her whisper, "That bitch is a winner today; tomorrow has yet to come."

Lifting his head, Roy looked fondly at her face, "I never met anyone like you in all my life. You have a true bowman's composure and spirit." Gently he kissed her on the forehead, "Let's go; they'll be waiting."

"Let's go Mr. Best of the Best, I'm starving!"

CHAPTER 60

An early morning with overcast skies was a perfect condition for duck migration. Parked up on the highest hill in Montauk, the site of the old but now covered dump, east of the recycling center, and over looking Fort Pond, the view reaching to the Connecticut shoreline was a site the Bowman often enjoyed. The fact that there were no people to disturb this beautiful backdrop was an extra bonus.

Dressed in heavy dark winter clothing on this 32 degree morning, the Bowman with much delight spotted a flock of mallards consisting of green headed males, brown females and their chocolate colored young brood. As they drew closer to Montauk they began to descend in a tight formation and banked sharply. The Bowman envied how the ducks effortlessly glided. Studying their wing beats confirmed a brace of greenheads were mostly likely flying to Montauk's rich farm fields still laden with quack nourishment.

More than any other kind of wildlife, birds and water fowl had an almost magical hold on the Bowman's imagination. Montauk was obviously the place to see these vibrantly alive, beautifully plumaged creatures, especially at the bird and duck sanctuary along East Lake Drive. The "old gray lady" was a magnet for water fowl. In fact, thought the hunter, the entire East End provided one of nature's largest bird habitats, nesting sits and food stores.

Who could not help but be charmed with the birds' myriad of songs, their unique calls, their brilliant colors and their wondrous gift of flight? The Bowman was also fond of birds of prey and identified with the warlords of the air such as the owls, hawks, eagles and falcons. Like the Bowman they were swift, fearless and superbly equipped.

However, water fowl was the hunter's real passion. From majestic swans to multicolored ducks, seagoing puffins, and to saltwater king eiders, the Bowman thought of them as kings and queens of bird - dome; unsurpassed in their unique appearance, life style and behavior. Now the flock was cupped and committed to their landing fifty feet off the bay's cool water, right over old Navy Pier where the locals fished.

Suddenly shotgun fire exploded, ripping into the tight group of ducks; feathers showered down and a number of ducks fell into the chilled gray November waters ending their quacking lives. What was left of them wisely surged easterly away from the bay. A trembling raging fury welled up within the Bowman watching a family of ducks fall from the sky like hail stones. With closed eyes, the images of the creatures splashing into the bay, served to increase the agony. The killer's body tightened like a parker compound bow, thoughts smoked like a pit bull's anger.

No longer able to stomach the scene, the Bowman snapped on the ignition. A furious left turn on Navy Road and speeding to the edge of the woods, another turn to the right to an old forgotten dirt trail where the truck stopped was completed in record time. Grabbing the bow from under the blue tarpon and racing along the trail to the tall grass at the water's edge, the psycho weaved through the five foot high grass, catching sight of an armada of rubber duck decoys floating on the water roughly 150 yards out.

Surmising this was the area of slaughter, (the hellish butcher's pit) AKA a duck blind had to be opposite the decoys.

Gulping deep lungfuls of cool air, the hunter was determined to stop the duck murdering bastards. Stealthily cutting through the underbrush, chest heaving as a thin sheen of cold sweat formed on the creep's forehead, the focus to save the next duck family and their tender hatchlings was paramount. One of the hazards of being a duck is man for he poses a far more insidious threat than all the animals in the wild who wish to make a snake of them. Not to worry my little quacking friends, birds of nobility and majestic beauty, I am the tiger of the woods. Absolute power is mine. I am your guardian spirit. In duck speak terms I am the most intelligentsia of justice against evil duck killers. Let's see how they like getting shot. Dark, tormented thoughts reverberated in the hunter's mind as he snaked through the grass.

CHAPTER 61

Listening to their quacks as well as their stiff wing beats whistling in the distance high above the entrance to the bay, the Bowman knew that soon, too soon, the flock would be over the grizzly decoy deception.

Abruptly stopping ninety five yards out from the cursed pit, the Bowman's sharp eyes caught sight of the approaching brace starting to descend to their rubber decoy kin. Swelled with excitement, with the thoughts of saving the quackers as they began back winging to prepare for their final maneuver of cup and commitment, made the rescue extra sweet.

Just then the hunters pushed opened their blind camouflage hatches and took deadly aim at the feathery angels of the air. Deciding on a lightning quick assault, the Bowman released an arrow. It flew at maximum force plowing through Curt's back, immediately thrusting him forward and knocking out his life force. His duck killing finger froze hard on the trigger, discharging three automatic shots into the water; his body came to rest atop of his shooting hatch.

Rick's heavily muscled body quivered with rage and fear as he gasped and stared at his buddy's lifeless corpse. An instinctive reflex allowed him to duck back into his hatch not a second too late as a second arrow zinged over his head.

Like a large dark shadow the ducks, too, moved swiftly and veered away in tight unison, pushing their wings downward with all their strength; then pulling them upward, surging higher and higher. Their strong wing feathers gathered in the air currents and whistled through their secondary feathers as they rose to safety. Whooshing madly over Fort Pond Bay, they quacked hysterically at their close brush with death. In duck talk it meant "we're not going to die today".

Rick screamed in a terrified high pitched voice, "Oh my God," from his pit hatch. Curt's painful wails as he fell dead echoed in Rick's ears. Thinking, oh Lord what to do, Lord what to do, then putting those thoughts aside, he stood up, pumped his shot gun and shot three bird shots at the brown target who was knotting a new arrow. The object recoiled backwards as some of the #2 steel shot made contact. Kneeling to safety, Rick reloaded, shooting six shots and watched as the target retreated back in the grass. Still he continued firing but knew it was an unlikely hit since there was at least one hundred yards between them.

With fingers shaking he jabbed 911 on his cell. The operator said, "If you would like to make a call............" "Oh shit, I hit 11."

Steadying his hand as best he could he redialed and explained the bone chilling situation and his location.

Back in his pit, Rick reloaded his shotgun just in case, patted Noel his golden retriever who lay placidly at his feet. Tearfully Rick said, "I peppered the bastard Noel. If only he was ten yards closer, shit I would have taken him out." Noel's head snapped up, his ears perked up. "Hey boy, what is it?" Noel barked softly three times.

Rick heard it, too. In the distance sirens whined their message.

Todd and Roy walked directly to Rick's blind. Minx and his forensic team unload their gear. "Are you alright buddy?" Todd asked as he put his hand on Rick's shoulder. "No Todd, Christ, no way am I alright. My best friend is lying there dead. What the hell is going on Todd?"

Taking his cue from his master, Noel barked several times as though putting in his two cents. Looking down at the handsome retriever, Todd decided it was best to let Rick calm down; Minx could get his statement later. Todd asked softly, "Buddy did you happen to get a look at the prick?" Wiping his face on his sleeve, Rick retorted, "Yeah, he was dressed in dark brown, wore a tan bandana, about 5'10" to 6', Caucasian, out 100 yards in the grass. Couldn't really see anything, it happened so quick. But I shot the motherless bastard."

"You shot him?" Roy snapped. "Well not really shot him Roy, let's just say I tagged him; peppered him with #2 steel shot. I saw him jerk back. It's possible that some of the pellets may have pierced his skin." As if to say that's how he saw it, too, Noel barked again.

269

"Once last thing Rick," Todd said, "show Minx exactly where he was standing." "Sure thing, Todd."

"Okay Roy, have someone check out the ER's and the medical centers. Hopefully, some of the buck shot hit his face; wouldn't that be a nice break, huh? But then #2 shot only has the penetrating ability up to eighty yards, right Roy?" Roy nodded. "Oh well, it's up to Minx and his boys. Best we get back; the chief will want to be brought up to speed."

"Roger Lt."

CHAPTER 62

"Good evening! How are you all on this cold night?" "We're good, thank you," Justin replied, smiling at one of his favorite wait staff. "Can I get you a table or would you all like to sit at the bar?" Roy answered quickly, "The bar will be just fine, thanks."

"Oh by the way, great job on your fine shooting Meaghan, you really smacked down the competition," said the waitress. "Thanks hon," smiled Meaghan.

Walking through to the crowded bar where luckily just four stools were available, Meaghan suggested, "Hey guys, I think we should all start off with a shot of tequila. How 'bout it Hither?"

I hate that shit, figures that bitch knows I don't like tequila. She better not spoil my night off. "Oh sure Meaghan," she replied with a smirk, "I think the boys can handle that." "We

271

sure as hell can," Justin laughed. "And while we're at it, let's wash those down with some cold Guinesses." Roy jumped in, "Hey you know what? Let's make that two rounds of tequila, it's freezin' out!" Smiling flirtatiously and grabbing his arm, Meaghan gushed, "I couldn't agree more Roy! I love it when a man takes charge."

Discussing the best game plan for the next morning's hunt between drinks, they agreed to split up and hunt in pairs. Deciding the safest and best location to score a trophy buck was a more difficult task.

"So Hither and I are going to set up on the south side of Oyster Pond. I heard from a few beach rats that are still plugging bass, they've been seeing a huge buck cross the marsh right after day break for the past five days. And since there's been a northeast wind for almost a week now, I'm sure he'll be traveling the same route tomorrow morning."

Purposefully budding in to take control of the conversation to show Meaghan that she, too, could take charge, Hither announced, "Since the buck is going to be moving downwind of the northerly breeze, I figure Roy will set up on the south side corner of Oyster Marsh. Hopefully he will get a shot as the buck funnels through the cattails."

"That a girl Hither," Roy smiled, "You sure know how to ambush a deer!"

Slightly tipsy, Meaghan laughed an obnoxious laugh, "Well, what about you Miss Hunter Shot? Where you gonna set yourself, hmmm?" Pissed off and staring straight into Meaghan's blurry blue eyes, Hither retorted, "Well, Miss Robin Hood I plan on setting up at the east corner about 150 yards from Roy; he doesn't want me too far away from him as everyone knows, right Meaghan?"

Slow on the uptake, Meaghan's stammering retort was ignored as Hither continued, "That old buck I'm sure is prone to be very sneaky and smart. He'll slip by Roy, for sure, and when he comes my way, his days of roaming will be no longer 'cause I plan to finish his day and put him down for the count! Nothing gets passed me when I'm in the zone!"

"Guess you weren't in the zone when I kicked your ass in the competition, huh!" Meaghan managed to say. "Even the losers get lucky sometimes, bitch. Be sure of this, I WILL be in the zone tomorrow morning."

"Easy girls," urged Justin the two cougars. "We're all friends here, aren't we?"

"Anyways Justin," Roy asked, "What's your plan for the am?" "Meaghan and I are gonna head for this place I call the Dead Woods. It's the lowest, most secluded spot in the area, just south of Rocky Point and north of the overlook. It looks like an old beat up scary painting; not much life down there. Really guys, even the trees don't move and the old mossy oaks and rotten stumps cover the dead looking ground. When the wind blows the leafless trees, the branches clink together, making you think something is prowling around and watching your every move. Let me tell you, every horror movie or monster or any scary thought that you can think of enters your mind when you're in this desolate spot. Even the spooked animals walk around on their highest alert."

"Sounds like a place you don't want to be," Roy remarked. I never knew that area was down there. So what would make you even want to go there, Justin?"

"Just happened to be near the area last summer and I put a trail camera up to see if anything was cruising around." Interrupting, Hither asked excitedly, "Did you get any pictures of any big deer?" "Sure did; two small eight pointers and then on the very last picture, there he stood, only a few feet from the camera. I named him Ol' Drop Tine. He's a main framed ten point, with two-drop tines about a foot long on each side. It's got to be every bit of twenty two to twenty four inches wide. Guys, he's a monster! Got it all; lots of mass, eye guards like daggers, super long lines, stocky and stout like a mule; has to be 300 pounds on the hoof. Grayish ghost like color with a long patch of white that runs down his whole neck, man he is something; every hunter's dream come true!"

Mesmerized by Justin's description, Roy was tongue-tied. But an eager Hither asked, "So do you have your spots picked out where you two will set up?" Not wanting to reveal the secret spots Justin had chosen, Meaghan answered, "Don't worry about where we'll be, maybe we'll tell you after one of us gets Ol' Drop Tine.

"Hey Meaghan, stop it," Justin laughed, "I'm not worried about these two jumping in our spot. In fact, I have to tell you where you're going, don't want you getting lost." "Fine," Meaghan said.

"I hung two stands just two weeks ago. You'll be on the very bottom of the ravine. So you take the north trail from the overlook parking lot for about three hundred yards, then you'll come to a sharp bend. You'll see the two reflective tacks

I put into a pine tree and from there you just follow the tacks another hundred yards or so to the bottom. I marked the stand with a pair of tacks. Everything is ready to go, just climb the pegs, and your stand will be about twenty feet up"

Meaghan thanked Justin very sweetly but asked one question, "Do I need to bring a rope to hoist my bow?" "Already there, Meaghan, it's tied to the bottom peg." "You're the best honey," Meaghan cooed.

"What about you Justin, where's yours?" Roy asked. "Well, where the trail bends I'll keep following around the topside until I reach the northern corner. I'm probably ummm… let's think, probably about seventy or eighty yards from Meaghan, something like that. Sounds like us four have some good spots, right Roy?"

"Yup, one of us has to get some action. And on that note we all should get going; 4:30am comes around very fast." "Sure does," agreed Justin, "Good Luck, you two, I'll get in touch with you after the hunt."

While driving home with Roy, all of a sudden Hither slapped her hand against the dashboard, "Shit, tomorrow is Saturday, Roy. I didn't realize I have a nature walk planned with the Montauk Environmental Group to go seal watching at 7:30am. I can't miss it. Oh Roy, what am I going to do?" "That's okay Hither. Hey, you already made plans so you should go. We'll have time to go hunting again, don't worry about it." "Thanks Roy and maybe we can go out later in the afternoon." "Yeah maybe, we'll have to see how the morning turns out."

CHAPTER 63

It was just about 4:30am as Justin and Meaghen loaded their gear and headed to the woods. The dense cold air filled the silent forest with a thin glassy layer of frost. Twinkling stars fluttered like thousands of candles on their last breath of air. Not even a trace of the slightest breeze could move the steam away from their faces as their bodies released oxygen into the frigid air. It was the kind of weather that gives hunters butterflies in their stomachs; they both knew the climate was ideal; purposely made for a bow hunter.

"Oh crap!" Meaghan whispered, "I forgot my headlight in your truck, got to go back and get it." "Do you want me to go with you?" Justin asked quietly. "No it's okay; you go and get settled into your spot. I remember your directions. I'll be fine. Give me a kiss for good luck honey." After he kissed her, he whispered, "God I love those soft lips of yours; good luck baby."

Meaghan grabbed her flashlight, turned on the blue light, strapped it over her head and made her way back down the path. At the bend in the trail she spotted the two tacks in the black pine tree and cautiously followed the trail down the hill.

He was awakened by the crackling sounds of twigs crunching beneath her boots. The sounds of the broken dead branches reflected off its surroundings into the distance. Not realizing it, he must have dozed off shortly before the quiet woods were startled by the foreign sounds of footsteps that echoed through the trees. Scanning the area for the noise that had awakened him, he saw a dim bluish light slightly illuminating the landscape as it made its way closer and closer. He took the stance of a statue.

As Meaghan got closer and closer she could just about see the two tacks in the distance. A mere ten yards now to her spot, yet she had a funny feeling that she was being watched. Her sixth sense told her something was wrong. Hairs on the back of her neck stood erect, her heart beat quickened and pounded, her legs trembled and buckled. Resting in her tracks, she paused, held her breath and listened.

He thought to himself, now's my time, must make my move. Slowly he stood up, ready to let loose at any given moment. As he straightened his legs, a twig snapped and resounded through the woods like a faint gunshot in the distance.

Meaghan whirled around, her light illuminating the area like a fire on a dark night. As she focused her eyes into the blue-lit tunnel, a ghost-like image appeared before her not even fifteen yards away.

She froze, he froze. They stared each other down not knowing who would make the first move. His breath flowed from his nostrils like a raging bull. Every exhale made a dense foggy cloud, shielding him from her light. Should she run, should she drop to the ground, should she scream? Instinct took over; she grabbed an arrow from her quiver and tried to knock it onto her string, her hands shaking so, it took forever, it seemed, to lock it in. He took one step closer, preparing to release his rage. She came to full draw, trying to find him in her sights. She couldn't pinpoint a clear shot. The steam from both their heavy breathing filled the air, creating a wall. Suddenly like a blessing from the sky, a slight gust of air swooped through, lifting the shield of fog. She could see his eyes glowing like phosphorous floating on the ocean on a full moon night. It's him she knew even as she was almost blinded by the reflection of his massive horns. It's Ol' Drop Tine!

Taking a deep breath, trying not to shake out of control, she accidentally hit the release trigger and shot right over his back. At once he launched like a drag car from the starting line, crashing and smashing through everything in his path and disappeared into the thick darkness. Meaghan listening to the sounds of the fading woodland chaos tried not to burst into tears and wondered if she would see him again after the sun rose from its late night bed.

Drained and tired she turned around, her light shone on the black pine standing like an old southern column. As she approached her spot she noticed the bow rope was untied and dangled loosely beside her tree. Curious she walked her light beam up the tall pine, her eyes focusing into the tree's canopy, searching for her stand. Something is not right, she thought. A dark camouflaged silhouette appeared to be on her stand.

"Oh my God!" she screamed, its reverberations resonating through the bleak frost-bound thicket. Her siren was cut short the second the arrow sliced through her throat, coming to a halt deep into her chest cavity. She landed with a crashing thump on the frozen forest floor. Her blank blue eyes looked as if they were staring at the bright, shimmering stars. Her body began to tremble as she took her last gurgle of a breath in this cruel world known as the Dead Woods.

CHAPTER 64

Just as he was sipping hot coffee from his thermos and entertaining thoughts of how he planned for Ol' Drop Tine to meet his waterloo, a piercing scream knifed through the woods. Cocking his head to the right the sound of the ominous shriek came from Meaghan's location. Grabbing his cell phone and punching in her number which went directly to voice mail accelerated his concern. No, he was not leaving a message.

With his bow in hand he climbed down from his tree stand thinking she may have fallen from hers. After all it does happen.

He ran as fast as he could and stopped abruptly when he saw Meaghan at the foot of her tree lying lifeless on the ground with an arrow stuck in her neck. The image of his girl sprawled dead among the stumps of Dead Woods caused shock and disbelief and attempts to feel a pulse only resulted in rage and terror. In an instant he realized he, too, could be a target and quickly crouched between two stumps knotting an arrow. Listening with the keen sensitivity of an edgy buck in danger, his fine honed hunting skills steeled.

If the Bowman is lurking out there, I've gotta bag that monster, he thought. Scanning as far as he could see in the dawn's early light, he detected no movement in the still forest.

A roosting turkey broke the silence as it flapped its wings leaving its perch high up in one of the nearby trees. When it landed the hush of death returned. An agonizing number of minutes passed before Justin felt satisfied he was alone and could make the call.

He hit Todd's number.

Startled by the ring at 5:20am, Todd bolted straight up in bed, still half asleep, and fumbled for his cell phone, unlike Jamie who only stirred at the intruding musical ring; the sandman having added a liberal amount of sand-dust to her shut-eye.

Todd took a quick inventory and assured himself his family was safely asleep in their beds and wondered who the hell was calling at this darkened hour. Feeling a bit pissed off from being torn away from his dream, (and, yes it was a good dream, too) he picked up his cell and saw Justin's name on the screen. Some what relieved, yet thinking if he woke me to tell me that he and Meaghan took out some big buck, I'll brain him! Speaking angrily he said, "This better be important buddy or your ass is going to be raw hamburger meat from my twelve inch boot."

"Todd, Meaghan is dead," Justin said. "She was shot in her neck with an arrow." Listening to Justin's words in stunned silence, Todd felt as if his head had just blown off. "Son of a bitch Todd; the friggin' Bowman took her out!" Shit Todd knew, Justin's gotta be in danger.

Both phones were intensely quiet. Choosing his words very carefully Todd asked in a calm even tone, "Justin are you on thin ice?" 'I'm okay Todd; he's gone. That much I'm pretty sure of. I know my woods." "Yes buddy, you do. What's your location?"

"Dead Woods, off of Rocky Point; Roy knows exactly where we are." "We'll be there ASAP.; say ten to fifteen minutes tops." "This sucks big time Todd, I can't believe she's dead." "Don't torture your self, keep alert, hang in there buddy."

Closing his phone, Todd jumped out of bed, dressed as fast as a fireman going to an early morning burn. Jamie now aware of the odd early noise lifted her head frowning, "What's going on Todd?

Where you going?" Holding his phone to his ear, Todd raised his left hand motioning Jamie to be quiet.

A half awake, half asleep voice came over the air waves, "What? Who the hell is this? It's not even dawn." "It's me Roy." Oh shit Roy thought, here we go again; the case taking another turn for the big weird. "Brace your self Roy. Meaghan's dead; another Bowman killing."

Roy was quiet for a moment while Todd watched sadly as Jamie's hands shot up to her face, shaking her head back and forth. "Meet me in the I.G.A. parking lot, pronto Roy."

"Roger Lt."

Roy leaped out of a warm bed into the frosty cold of his open window bedroom, threw on warm clothes and ran out of the house to his cold black truck. What a blood-curdling nightmare this had to have been for Justin, he thought. Damn the diabolical bastard never gets enough, does he? Crushing the gas peddle to the floor, Roy's tires screamed and smoked mimicking his pent-up anxiety.

Holding Jamie close, Todd whispered, "I'm so sorry you had to hear this, Jamie." Kissing the top of her head, "Got to go honey, Justin could be in danger." "Todd, please take care," Jamie said softly.

As Todd sped to town he placed two more official calls then pulled up next to Roy's parked truck in the empty store lot. In a flash Roy hopped in. "Take the old dump trail around Rocky Point, Todd. It'll bring us right to the edge of Dead Woods."

Within ten minutes they arrived at the scrubland grove and a few minutes later spotted Justin sitting on a rotten log and lowered their shot guns. "You guys made good time. Meaghan's fifty yards up the trail. This was a set up guys; someone overheard us at the lodge." "That's exactly our thinking Justin," agreed Todd, "we'll take a DNA sample tomorrow from each member. Whoever doesn't show up will be a target of suspicion and receive our full attention. Keep it on the QT." "Sure thing buddy and thank you guys; thanks for getting here so fast." "Why don't you go sit in Todd's truck Justin," said Roy, "we'll take care of things here." "Right Roy," replied their good but obviously distraught pal.

In the distance the wailing of the forensic truck sirens followed by the K-nine dog teams resounded in the cold early first light of day.

"Can't believe they're here so soon Lt." "When I called HQ's they told me Minx was already at the lab working on something. Can you beat that Roy?" "When the hell does he sleep Todd?" "Good question Sergeant but it's his crime scene now so let's go and keep Justin company. You know how CB hates anyone contaminating his crime scene."

"Roger Lt."

CHAPTER 65

On his way to HQ's Sunday morning, Roy stopped at Brent's for coffee and a bacon and egg sandwich, adding a box of fresh donuts for good measure and placed his order with Corrine.

Dave, the manager, was arranging the lunch displays as Roy walked over to him. "Top of the morning bub." "Hey Roy, good to see you buddy!" "Ditto pal. By the way did you get into that big boil of fish and bunker yesterday?" Roy asked one of his favorite fishing buddies. "Don't tell me they hit up front at the IGA." "Yep, the whole town was there catching silver striper beauties, my friend." "No shit," Dave said, "damn it Roy, my brother Jim and I drove on the Gansett beaches to Hither Hills; never went as far as Montauk." "Not to worry pal, there are more on their way down from Massachusetts."

"Your order's ready Roy," shouted Corrine. "Thanks, be right there. By the way Dave how did your seal walk go Saturday morning?" "What walk Roy? The seals left Montauk last week; heading north for the big herring." "Really, gee I guess it's that time. Catch you later Dave, keep tight lines and smooth drags."

"You got it Roy; same to you."

Roy picked up his order, jumped in his truck and drove to Indian Wells Beach to eat his breakfast, with a nagging thought that kept popping up in his mind. No seals, no walk; that's odd. Why did Hither tell me she was going on that tour and couldn't go hunting with Justin and Meaghan and me? Was it the policeman inside his head or was it the green eyed monstrous boyfriend?

Shit, is Hither seeing someone else, he wondered? Is she blowing me off? Now don't get your Irish up he scolded himself. There's probably a simple explanation. But the policeman side grew more suspicious as he crunched away at his sandwich. The paradox he created was becoming more and more uncomfortable.

Set your mind at ease boy, he said to himself, go over to Hither's and confront her. Be macho. On the other hand, there was no way he wanted to lose this beautiful girl. What the hell am I doing? Overreacting? But the policeman voice told him to uncover the truth.

The closer he got to her cottage in Culloden Shores, the more anxious he became. Hey I'm a good catch with a good salary and benefits and I'll get a good pension. And damn I'm even considered a hunk by most females so what's the catch here, Hither? Are we a team or not? Besides I'm looking forward to Christmas and putting a sparkler on her finger....... or maybe cuffs.

Why does my policeman side keep cropping up? Relax, don't get yourself all worked up but why did she lie to me?

This is getting ridiculous man. I bet she went shopping since my birthday is tomorrow. That's got to be it! What the hell have I been thinking? So screw you two guys; you've been driving me crazy. Get the hell out of my head!

Making a sharp right, Roy pulled into her small sea shell crushed driveway.

CHAPTER 66

Pulling alongside her Jeep, Roy grabbed the donuts as an excuse as to why he was here so early in the morning, hoping she was not still in bed. As he walked passed her truck hood, the cool metal told him the vehicle had not been recently used. Knocking firmly on her door and hearing no answer, he opened it and called her name; no response. He went into the kitchen, glancing off to the left into her open bedroom door. The bed was made.

Okay, he figured, must be taking one of her nature walks since the cottage was only 75 yards off the beach. I'll surprise her and make coffee and set out the donuts. As he puttered about the kitchen, he was startled by a small gray mouse staring up at him from the middle of the kitchen floor. Quickly opening a cabinet door, he snatched a 29 ounce tin of San Marsano tomatoes to clobber the little beast. The furry little creature took one look at the huge tin and dashed off into the bedroom. Watching the mouse come to a screeching halt in the bedroom, looking for an escape route, gave Roy a chance to take deadly aim. Just about to hurl the can, he saw the clever rodent dart off, taking refuge in the half opened closet.

Running after him, holding the lethal weapon in a threatening manner, he opened the closet door wide and stepped in with one foot. Roy's looked back and forth and under determined to find the mouse.

Suddenly his eyes spied a black Vengeance compound bow. Shit, I didn't realize Hither had another bow he immediately remarked to himself. In its quiver he saw arrows with brown and white turkey feathers. Damn, he thought, very familiar, in fact they look like the arrows the Bowman uses. Reaching with his free hand to slide up an arrow, he read the manufacturer's name - GRIM REAPER CARBON ARROW.

He released the arrow as if it were a hot poker back into the quiver and began backing slowly out of the closet with rushing thoughts of disbelief and shock; the name of the arrow spinning in his mind.

Roy never heard or felt her presence as she raised her hunting knife high above her head, watching him retreat inch by inch from the closet. In a matter of seconds she plunged the knife down on his head. Excruciating pain exploded in his brain, he collapsed to his knees, his upper body surged forward hitting the floor with a thud as warm blood trickled down the sides of his face. The last thing he recalled was a burst of white lightning ripping through his head.

Trying to move his arms, then his legs, he couldn't. He tried to shout but his lips were sealed. It was if he were in some kind of enclosed tank; no sound, no light, no nothing. Shit, if I'm dead why can I think? Maybe deductive reasoning is the last to vanish.

Just then he felt a frigid sensation at the top of his head. He could feel it move to his forehead and down his cheeks stopping at his neck. It seemed to go on for five minutes until an icy black towel was removed from his head.

Roy's eyes opened quickly and shut as fast since the light blurred his pupils which sought the safe darkness. He opened his eyes again and caught sight of a dark figure looming above him. Trying to lunge, he was trapped by restraints.

Gazing down at him, Hither said, "You're alright Roy, don't worry, I'm not going to hurt you."

What the hell does she think she's done so far? Not going kill me?

That's a relief but this is one crazy situation here and this girl is beyond what I call insane.

"If you promise not to make a fool of yourself Roy, I'll remove the tape from your mouth."

What should I do but nod yes? There are no options. Was she good for her word or not? What a joke; "You'll be alright Roy," after she knocked me out with the butt of her knife, tied me to her bed and froze my face with a cold towel? Here I am hog-tied listening to a deranged killer whom I know as Hither.

In one fast swoosh she ripped the tape off Roy's lips. "Sorry Roy, I know that hurt." You betcha it hurt but said nothing. Macho, huh? Trying to reason with her he said, I've got an

idea Hither, why don't you untie me and let's work this out."
"Oh yeah Roy, and you promise to be there when they inject
me with that syringe? No way Roy, what do you take me for,
a fool?" "No, I take you very seriously Hither."

Sitting down next to him and placing an ice pack on his
head, she tilted his chin up, giving him a sip of water for which
he thanked her thinking why would I even do that. Still in
shock from discovering the compound bow and the brutal
smash to his head, her behavior teetering like a see saw, cau-
tioned him to play the game.

"I'm sorry I hurt you, I'm very sorry for you are the only
person in this dark twisted world who was ever truly kind to
me. I'm a freak of nature Roy, you gave me hope. Trust me
Roy, I have it all worked out."

"Okay I trust you. Now what's your plan?" Her black eyes
narrowed, looking directly into his, and without saying a word
she stood and walked over to the dresser. She unscrewed the
cap of a medicine container, emptied a few of the pills into her
hand, turned to him and with her outstretched hand of pills,
cried angrily, "They turned me into this monster Roy."

"Who are they Hither?

CHAPTER 67

The tone of Hither's voice was peculiarly flat. Void of any emotion she said, "My father, Night Raven and my brother, Golden Eagle were barbarians, possessed with the most depraved brutality imaginable. No longer do these two savages walk the sacred grounds of my homeland.

Roy detected a sudden hint of anger in her dark eyes as he listened and watched in astonishment as she continued. "They taught me how to shoot a compound bow at the age of ten and soon I was an expert hunter. Years later they became my first victims; my revenge was sweet. To watch as they quivered and struggled as my arrows in their backs sucked out their evil life force was the best gift I would ever receive. I dumped their asses into a hole, a hole I gladly dug myself, instead of the noble Indian burial where a body is burned high up on a stack of wood, allowing the spirit to rise into the Promise Land. Five gallons of gasoline and a match later, they were toast. Their half burned corpses are rotting in a welcoming hell. That's my story Roy; everything goes up in smoke."

Roy's feelings of sympathy for Hither, he knew, could not cross the line into the world of depravity where she evidently had dwelt, yet it appeared that her black world made perfect sense to her and the unforgivable, loathsome pain lessened degree by degree each time her aim and contact snuffed out another life. Looking into her eyes he could also almost see and feel and fathom her crippled soul.

As if to talk was a catharsis, she moved on, "I live each day with the thoughts of my father breaking down the bedroom door, killing my mother's lover with an arrow shot from his long bow and my brother slicing my mother's throat with his hunting knife. I was stirring a pot of stew when my father and brother came home early that day. It is all so real to this day in my mind - even the smell of the stew meat. After they dragged the bodies outside and tied them to one of the mules, my brother rode off into the dessert where he fed them to the wolves.

"My father took a bottle of whiskey off the kitchen counter, sat down and drank some while he watched me still stirring the stew.

I don't remember what he said but he mumbled something before he pushed me to the floor and raped me. My brother returned and did the same to me. Never was I the same again."

Roy's face twisted into a palate of anguished, ugly contortions. Not under any conditions had he ever felt such an intense perception of disgust and abuse. To also learn that she remained imprisoned by those savages and subjugated to their every demand for so many years until she escaped not long ago was horrifying. For Hither to have been afflicted and affected by such physical and emotional wretchedness it was no wonder her retaliation took a determined, dangerous and vile route.

"Here Roy," she said quietly opening her fist," take these, they're valium," wedging them between his lips with the rim of the cup of water. "I will say good-bye now Roy. Please know I love you." She leaned down, kissed his lips softly and walked quickly to the front door.

He knew, too, he would never be the same again.

CHAPTER 68

After trying to get a hold of Roy without any luck, Todd called Brent's as a last resort, figuring he probably stopped there for breakfast. "Hey Dave, it's Todd." "Yeah Todd, what's up?" "Did Roy stop in this morning, buddy?" "Sure did; picked up his usual, even donuts." "He seem preoccupied?" "Not really, but he was a little annoyed when I told him the seals left Montauk last week." "Really, sounds crazy to me." "From what I gathered Todd, Hither was supposed to go on a seal walk with the group, at least that's what she told Roy." Oh, okay Dave, catch you later."

Strange, Todd thought, but at least it gave him a good idea of where Roy might be. As soon as he spotted Roy's truck in her driveway he was relieved and pulled in beside him. He must be waiting for Hither to return since her jeep isn't here he assumed or maybe they're out on a ride

Todd knocked twice, opened the door, calling out "Anybody here?" "In the bedroom," Roy replied dejectedly. Something's not right here crossed Todd's mind, and as he waked into the bedroom and saw his partner hog-tied to the bed, his hair crusted with blood, he was stunned. "You okay buddy?" Todd asked as he took out his pocked knife, bent down, and began to cut the rope.

"Hither's the Bowman." "Hither? Oh my God............!" Where is she?" "Gone, Todd; long gone; popped some valium in my mouth and left. I woke up a little while ago."

Listening intently as Roy quietly and very slowly explained what had occurred, Todd's slack-jawed expression reflected utter astonishment. By the tone of Roy's voice and the look on his face, Todd realized that Roy had experienced a terrible life changing ordeal.

No longer physically restrained, he stood up, did a few stretches and walked over to the front window, staring out across the bay, contemplating the carnage of Hither's life. "May the Lord have pity on her, "he whispered, with his head bowed.

"Are you sure you're okay?" Todd asked breaking into the silence.

Turning around, Roy responded, "You know that saying "what you don't know won't hurt you'? "Yeah, buddy I know it and now you're living it, only in reverse."

"When I was looking out the window Todd, I was thinking about what the doctor said at Jack's that day about the "mask of sanity".

It's damn hard for me to know she was.... I mean, she is two different people. Talk about camouflage; her mask is the real deal. You know I haven't even thought of what she did; I just keep thinking of what she went through," Roy explained, paused and thought about what she did and said to him before she left.

Seeing the reflection of sadness and anxiety in Roy's eyes not to mention the transformation from his happy go lucky, mischievous twinkling eyes persona to one of gaunt misery, compelled Todd to suggest, "When we get back to HQ's Roy, how about talking to Dr. Bridegewater our trauma doctor?" "Sure thing buddy, I need that and maybe I'll have a look at your bible Todd."

"You're quite a guy Sergeant Thompson," Todd declared, "quite a guy."

"How about we stop at Jack's on the way? I could use a good cup of coffee or two." "Me, too Roy. Let's roll"

CHAPTER 69

After driving for three days, Hither arrived a little after midnight, back at the place of her birth. She hurriedly packed all that was there even the cash hidden under the floor of her mother's bedroom. Checking her watch at 1:15am and totally exhausted, she decided to spend the night. After all, no one knows I'm here, and it will be the last night I'll ever be in this cabin.

Lying in her bed, she thought how much she hated to be there. Tomorrow I will torch this loathsome place. Yet, it was oddly comforting to know that the misery of her existence wasn't wholly self-inflicted.

Her eyes strained opened at early dawn, still in need of more sleep.

Knowing that it was time to leave, she arose, opened the heavy cabin door and looked out on to the beautiful rolling hills of bitter sweet, evergreens, bayberry, silver-tipped junipers and huckleberry. The brown winter grasses bending northward in the light November breeze were offset against a backdrop of unending breathtaking snow capped mountains. The intoxicating beauty of all she so well remembered allowed for a sudden change in plans as she decided to take one last short walk through the magnificent wilderness. Hither's dark eyes soaking in the dramatic landscape reminded her again of what is was to feel in harmony with nature.

As she hiked up the first hill, a golden brown pheasant took off from behind a clump of junipers. Reaching the meadow, a flock of turkeys flew into a group of holly bushes. To her left she saw a large buck and his mate run into a grove of evergreens. It was easier to thrust aside the scrambled thoughts rattling in her mind amidst the glories of nature and it almost gave her a balanced perception of who she was and a flash of peace.

Hawkeye Gray Wolf Hightower watched her every move. Dressed in traditional Indian rawhide clothing, her braids swinging from side to side as her soft footwear carried her quietly through the wilderness, she was startled when like a wolf he sprang up behind her.

"Hither stop, don't move," he commanded in the Indian tongue.

Halting, she recognized the voice of her uncle, an Indian of great height and character. "I so misjudged your spirit Hither. You never showed any sign of being a killer." At hearing the word killer her lips twisted into a deranged grin as she cried, "I am motivated by cruelty brought on by man! Do not judge me Hawkeye; listen to my words."

In loud anger she said, "My father, Night Raven, and his puppet of a son, my brother Golden Eagle, wiped away any emotions rooted within me. They vandalized my adolescence; I survived on hatred." In a lower more chilling tone she continued, "They're responsible for their bloodshed. May their wicked souls rot in hell for all eternity, Gray Wolf. Listen to me very carefully, Uncle. I, Hither Yellow Tail Hightower, cast their spirits below to learn an eternal lesson in righteousness. I am pure of crime and free of guilt."

Overhead a tight formation of blue-winged teal ducks passed heading north to the lakes and ponds far up in the tundra. Hither watched them soar, envying their freedom, as Gray Wolf's steely stare bore down upon her.

"You are quite right Gray Wolf if you are thinking I'm a psychopath. Do you also know that I am devoid of morality and ethics, that I have no compassion and that I find it satisfying to kill?" Slowly enunciating his words, Gray Wolf asked, "So Yellow Tail, do you have delusions of grandeur, does it not matter how many you must murder?"

"YES!" Hither whispered; her face taut and red.

In a firm, stern manner Gray Wolf observed, "Aha, that's it then, you killed to improve the behavior of mankind. You're a self appointed apostle from the dark side? This is a load of elk dung Hither. You killed my brother and his son to improve their twisted behavior? Yellow Tail, what say you?"

"They were animals," she snarled, "both of them. "They got what they deserved and now I have to do it again and again because of what they did to me," she screamed and bent over wrapping her arms around her chest in wrenching pain. He watched until she gradually regained her posture and heard her say, "Why are you here Uncle?"

"I have been reading about your exploits in Montauk, New York, and when I read that you wounded a police officer and vanished, it wasn't hard to figure you would be heading back here. All Indians return to their homeland so I waited each day until you showed up."

"Why didn't you turn me in to the authorities?" "It's not our way; we are a proud and honorable people. You Hither are the soul of mud; a child of darkness. By killing your father and brother you committed two diabolic scarlet sins. Our forefathers taught us how to right wrongfulness; justice must prevail. You Hither are an abomination to our people."

Narrowing his bulging deep dark brown eyes, his high cheek bones stiffening, his face tight with emotion, he said in a resentful, demanding, and powerful voice, "It is you Yellow Tail who has dishonored the name of Hightower." Gripping his long bow ever so tightly, it was as though there was a symbiotic relationship between him, her and his long bow. "Do you know the history behind the name Hightower?"

Standing quietly, contemplating how she could kill him, he said, "Ah niece, I know your thoughts but you have already let your guard down. We people survive because of our inherited sixth sense. Hightower is the spirit of strength, adaptability and resolve. Hightower is the eagle that soars high above all the other noble beasts. Now you are no longer a Hightower Hither; you have undermined the realities of our faith, bringing shame to us. We are mighty warriors; you are a coward."

"I am no coward!" she screamed. "Who are you to judge; you betrayed the nation of our people. You cannot be pardoned and must be held responsible for your family and those strangers in Montauk."

"No," she cried, "I killed them because it was necessary." "No Hither, you were wrong. We of the high council have condemned you for your murderous behavior and it is I, Hawkeye Gray Wolf Hightower, who has been appointed to put down a sick animal."

"So you and the elders have decided my fate? Well, to hell with you all!" "Turn around Hither," Gray Wolf commanded. Face to face now, Hither noticed the tomahawk hanging from his side and a full quiver of arrows on his back. His full rawhide dress included his war bonnet, a mixture of colorful eagle feathers (fashioned from the tail feathers of young golden eagles), denoting his rank as High Council Chief. A long train of feathers hung down his back to the ground brushing against the tall brown grasses swaying in the breeze.

Pulled at full draw, his long bow with its traditional wooden arrow aimed at her chest, depicted the utmost danger. Standing erect and catching the spilt second of a steeled flint stone arrow head aiming at her, Hither's heart pounded, her breath in gasps. Staring death directly, she smiled a twisted sneer, and cried out, "You're going to kill me in cold blood, Uncle?" "Stop right there Yellow Tail," he demanded as she made a move backwards. "You don't like being at the other end of an arrow?" "No, I don't and you Gray Wolf don't seem to understand that they turned me into the monster that I am."

"Yellow Tail, you made a mistake. You should have come to me or to the council for help. But you chose not to and you stayed." Raising his voice Gray Wolf asked the question that baffled him, "Why Hither, why did you stay?"

As if she were posing an answer she titled her head, looked up at the large gray cumulus cloud almost ready to cover the golden sun, and after a minute or so she replied, "Because I had no choice; they kept me tied like a dog." Repulsed by her answer, Gray Wolf recoiled back a foot.

"Because I had no way out, it made me strong," she said proudly, strong enough to kill both of them!" "No Hither, you are not strong, you are insane. No Indian would ever commit such madness. We are warriors and a great people. We would never sink to your cold-hearted level."

Knowing her next statement would be her last on earth Hither spoke with pride, "At least I'll go down in Indian folk lore as one of the greatest warriors ever to have walked this earth. Our people will sit around their campfires telling stories of my bravery. I Hither Yellow Tail Hightower had the courage to stand up for my convictions. What say you, Gray Wolf?"

He spat on the ground, an Indian insult, rubbing his saliva into the soil with his right moccasin, to let Hither know without a doubt that never would her spirit soar or find peace. Steadfast in his resolve and as he pulled his long bow string back another notch, an enormous prince of all predators, a bald eagle, swooped down in majestic splendor, wings spread wide in golden fire, its piercing shriek deafening. Swift, fearless and powerful, he was superbly equipped for life in the wild. No other winged-warrior, not even the elegant golden eagle was as much at home aloft.

Gray Wolf interpreted his presence as a symbol of the justified soon to be demise of his traitorous niece. When the bird pitched forward its massive wings propelled it over the cool air and like a screaming projectile it sailed again through the sky. As it closed the distance to them, Gray Wolf's sharp eyes gazed upon the creatures golden brown wing beat while its white fan tail spread fully to gain speed. With its golden beak held wide open, the eagle released a high-pitched *Keee-Yrrr, Keee-Yrrr, Keee-Yrrr.*

With its screams of its fighting song echoing off the mountain peaks, Grey Wolf thanked his ancestors for what the Council assigned to him to do. As Yellow Tail, with her head still arched, watched the soaring prince fly high over the rolling meadows of flowing grasses, Gray Wolf released the arrow. Silently it ripped into her chest. She clutched the arrow as if to pull it out just before she fell to her knees. Her body slumped into the tall grasses with a dull thud and rolled over.

Shouting to the heavens, "holchko, holchko, holchko" Grey Wolf communicated that Hither was now "the sleeping one" and the family honor restored.

The tiger in the sky circled overhead once more in the November currents, fanning the air like a great spirit, screeching an answer,

Keee-Yrrr, Keee-Yrrr, Keee-Yrrr, Keee-Yrrrrrrrrrrrrrrrrrrr, justice triumphed.

EPILOGUE I

Michelle who worked in the mailroom entered the Command Center clutching a 3X3 foot brown package. Always cheerful, she smiled and greeted Todd and Roy with a "Hiya guys! Hey Roy, what did you order from Anchorage, Alaska, hmmm-mmm?" Hope its king crab legs!"

From behind his desk, Roy looked puzzled, "Michelle, I didn't order anything from Alaska and besides I don't like crab legs. I'm a meat and potato kind a guy." "Whatever Roy," Michelle laughed as she placed the package on the conference table. "It's addressed to you Roy." "What's the return address?" Todd asked. "Funny; there is none," Michelle chirped.

For some reason Todd was reminded that it had been ten days since Hither had vanished. Reading the address written to Sergeant Roy Thompson, c/o EHPD, EH, NY 11937 set off red flags. "Don't open this package Roy, it may be... ...."Interrupting Michelle said, "It's not a bomb Todd, I ran it through the scanner; no explosive material detected." "Who else touched it besides you and the carrier?" Todd pressed. "No one Todd and the delivery guy wore brown gloves."

"CB," Todd said into his cell, "we have a suspicious package addressed to Roy, been through the scanner, it's negative, but my gut feeling is that it has something to do with the Bowman case." "I'm on my way; make sure no one touches it."

"Do you think it could possibly be sent by Hither?" Roy asked Todd. "We'll soon see; CB is on his way." "Thanks Michelle for alerting us," Todd said as he dismissed her. "Oh no you don't Lieutenant! Now that you've tweaked my curiosity you're not getting rid of me. Besides I'm a policewoman, Private Michelle Killings." "So you are private, so you are. Why don't you go upstairs and invite the chief down here pronto."

EPILOGUE II

Rushing into the Command Center, followed by his forensic team, Minx carrying an evidence kit, went directly to the conference table and read the address label. Chief Becker and Michelle joined the group shortly as CB placed a recorder next to the brown bundle. His gloved hands slowly and carefully cut through the thick brown wrapping. The packing fell away revealing a black elongated corrugated box which he described into the recorder. As he lifted the box, one of the forensic techs placed the wrapping into an evidence bag while thirteen pairs of eyes fixated on the carton.

Minx resumed speaking like a medical examiner performing an autopsy. "Black box one contains two items; one is a narrow white box, two is a brown manila envelope. I am taking the white box out and opening it."

Opening the lid carefully and placing it on the table, Minx then reached inside and retrieved the contents. "The box contains a wooden arrow with brown and white turkey feathers," he said, "and the arrow has what appear to be dried blood stains on it. The broadhead is also stained and most likely is made of flint stone." The tech placed the arrow and its box into plastic evidence bags. "I am now opening the manila envelope," Minx continued.

"There are three 12X12 colored photos and a small white envelope. Picture one depicts a female body with an arrow embedded in her center chest; arrow appears to match arrow in evidence bag." Showing the photo to the group, all concurred matter of factly that it was Hither Hightower but Roy experienced a sudden stab of sadness.

The second photo showed Hither's body lying on the roof of a cabin. The third photo exhibited the entire cabin engulfed in flames. Minx placed the three photos in another evidence bag. Taking out a card from the white envelope he read, "Sorry for your loss. Hither Yellow Tail Hightower paid with her life for the carnage she brought to your people. May the Great Spirit in the sky take pity on her soul. It is signed Gray Wolf."

Minx turned off the recorder. "Case closed everybody," he announced.

Roy walked over to the water cooler, took a long sip, and just stood there for a moment until Todd came up to him asking, "How are you doing buddy?"

"I'm okay. Hey what goes around comes around; she paid the piper, end of story." Chief Becker echoed Roy when he said to the group, "Well lads, that's that," and as he glanced over at the Grim Reaper charts asked, "Do you think she came from a tribe up in Alaska?" "No chief," replied Todd, "Minx indicated to us that she belonged to a mid-west tribe. The package postmarked Alaska was a ruse to throw us off." "It was a most revealing morning lads but now time to move on with our lives, like our heavenly father wants us to do," Chief Becker said and smiled that matchless smile which illuminated his broad Irish face with radiance and dignity. "The value of life lies in our will to endure lads; trust me. And we shall endure to the 'last syllable of recorded time' or more specifically our natural God-given life span. Well, that's enough philosophizing for one morning! Let's go celebrate in my office, my dear wife just so happened to send Irish soda bread; you guys in?"

"Yes sir," they all said in unison.

EPILOGUE III

The Christmas season arrived bringing a renewal of spirit to the villagers of Montauk. It was again a time to reflect on one's grace, faith joy and love. For generations the people of Montauk played with the cards they were dealt, no matter the deal.